The Amulet

CHARDY WALKER LIEB

CRIMSON
ROMANCE

F+W Media, Inc.

This edition published by
Crimson Romance
an imprint of F+W Media, Inc.
10151 Carver Road, Suite 200
Blue Ash, Ohio 45242
www.crimsonromance.com

I would like to dedicate this book to Martha Ferris, Nancy Hall, and Judy Harvey—the best writers' group any author could ever have. Not only are they the most talented writers I have read, but their continued support, boundless encouragement, and unconditional friendship mean the world to me. They are, and always will be, my inspiration! I also have to thank a few of my non-writer friends who have been there with me every step of the way—Nancee Brown, Rita Pond, and Cathy Rhoades. Your continued support makes every single word I write mean more to me. Thank you all.

Chapter One

Jack Hawthorne dangled the necklace between his thumb and middle finger and held it up to his office window for a better look. "What the hell am I supposed to do with this, Max?"

Twenty-three stories above downtown Boston, the sky was blue and clear. Typical for October. He eyed the interesting gem in the daylight then turned to face Maxine Spencer, his one and only secretary for the past ten years of his law practice.

"My e-calendar slated it for today, so I pulled it from the vault.' Maxine slapped both hands on her hips and shrugged. "I log every task, and my schedules don't lie."

"I wasn't questioning your—"

"It says to locate the client named in file number 1692 today and bequeath this necklace."

"Yes, Ma'am." Jack grinned out of respect. The woman was fifty-ish, or so he guessed, and had never been married. Tall and thin, she wore tailored suits; sensible heels; and galoshes, when it rained. Maxine prided herself on taking care of business, specifically Jack's law firm, in the most straightforward, efficient manner possible. "Who's the recipient?"

"My records indicate a Miss Abigail Corey."

"Abigail," he repeated. As Jack spoke the suspended stone seemed to respond, twirling counterclockwise between his fingers. He dropped the chain. "Son of a—"

"Beg pardon?"

Jack scooped the necklace off the floor. "Did you see that?" he asked, but the blank look on Maxine's face answered before she did.

"Well, I saw you drop the bequest, if that's what you're asking." She shook her head. "You'd better put it away, or you'll break it before we ever find the owner."

He slipped the amulet back into the small pine box and met her stern expression. "Okay, let's do it, Max." He leaned back in his chair and shrugged. "Locate this Corey woman."

Before Maxine could close the door behind her, a striking, dark-haired beauty sidestepped her with the grace of an NBA point guard. "Excuse me, *Nadine*," the woman breezed.

"Maxine," the secretary corrected in her no nonsense, drill sergeant tone. Standing her ground, she added, "Mr. Hawthorne is busy, you'll—"

"It's okay, Max," Jack assured her, considering Bridget had practically done a pick and roll to slip into his office. A feat that no doubt would have been impossible had she not caught Maxine in a revolving door of sorts.

When Max slammed his office door—hard, Jack gestured to the seat opposite his. As Bridget sat, her crimson cape parted, exposing a black knit dress with a neckline cut just low enough. "Why the hell do you do that?" Jack's lip twitched which should have told her to tread lightly—had she known the first thing about him.

Bridget crossed her legs and arched one dark brow. "Why do I do what?"

Another slight twitch.

"The woman is your secretary, Darling, not your wife." She offered an unapologetic grin.

"And neither are you, *Darling*." Jack didn't smile. As beautiful as Bridget was, and she was damned beautiful, something about her, besides her obvious edge, had really started to rub him the wrong way. He met her pale blue gaze. His voice was low and even—another warning sign Bridget should have recognized if she knew him at all. "Don't ever speak to her like that again. Got it?"

She arched one brow. "Loud and clear, but—"

"Good." He checked his watch. "Why *are* you here?"

She crossed her legs and frowned. "I'm beginning to wonder the same thing."

Impatience focused his attention. "Exactly what can I do for you?" His words were clipped, and he meant them to be. "Look, Bridget, I'm busy." He watched her pale blue eyes narrow. Unimpressed, he told her, "I'm in the middle of executing an inheritance."

She toyed with the jangle of silver bracelets cuffing her wrist. "Doesn't exactly sound like brain surgery."

Jack allowed her frosty comment to slide, this time, but only because he remembered her jewelry expertise and decided to exploit it. "Well, since you're here, take a look at this necklace for me, will you?"

She continued to fiddle with her bangles. "Well, I don't know, Darling. You're awfully busy. Maybe I should just go."

"Okay." Jack shrugged. "Forget it then."

The first to break the uncomfortable silence between them, she sighed. "Oh, alright. Let me see your precious bauble."

He heard her tone soften as she slanted her striking gaze his way. Unaffected, he pulled Abigail Corey's amulet from the box. "What do you make of this?"

Bridget jumped up so fast she tipped over the chair.

"Are you okay?" Jack stood, but she held up one hand to stop him.

"Just a cramp in my foot," Bridget said, quickly righting the seat and standing behind it rather than sitting back down.

Jack stared. The woman looked like she was using the damn chair as a shield. Why the white-knuckled grip? And why did she sound so breathless—and not in a sexy way?

"Where did you get that?" she demanded without letting go of the chair.

"This is the inheritance I'm working on." He dangled the necklace for her to see again. When she visibly flinched, he took one step forward. "So, what do you think? Ever seen a stone like this before?"

"Never." Bridget shook her head and took a step back. "Looks like junk to me."

"Junk?" Moving two paces closer to her, he twirled the chain between his fingers and watched it catch the light. "Really?"

Still facing Jack she backed up and fumbled for the doorknob. "Probably old costume jewelry."

He watched Bridget grope for the door. She never took her eyes off the stone. "Are you sure?" he pressed, closing the distance between them.

"Positive." She backed into the wall.

Jack shook his head. "No, I don't think so." Extending his hand, he offered her the necklace. "Here, take a closer look."

"No!" She slapped his hand away.

Her vehement refusal made no sense. He stared at her—plastered against the door, both palms flush against the smooth oak, cheeks flushed. "What the hell's wrong with you?"

"Nothing," she insisted. "I have to go."

"You never said why you're here."

"I thought we'd, um, have coffee." Her hand fumbled behind her back and finally found the knob. "But I remembered something I have to do," she insisted, blue eyes still fixed on the necklace.

"Immediately." It wasn't a question.

"Yes. This can't wait."

It wasn't until Jack slipped the amulet into the pocket of his sports jacket that Bridget met his gaze. "Suit yourself," he told her and meant it. Beautiful or not, he was done with her. Maybe next time he'd switch it up and try something new. Like dating a woman with a little more character and a little less cup size.

When the door slammed for the second time this morning, Jack barely noticed.

Chapter Two

Salem, Massachusetts
15 September
Year of our Lord 1690

With each careful step, Bridget Bishop's candle flickered, less from nerves than the deep seeded thrill of anticipation. She steadied the trembling light and prepared for the first time to perform the passion sleeping ritual. Her mother had coaxed her father into a moonlit walk, so her daughter could cast her spell as she had instructed her to do. Bridget's breath quickened as she carefully set down the candle and searched through the kitchen knives. Selecting the very sharpest, she picked up the blade and watched the metal gleam in the candlelight as she ran her thumb down its length. She was careful not to cut herself—not just yet.

Relishing the sensation—the overwhelming feeling of power and freedom—Bridget's black lashes fluttered shut. She enjoyed the sharp, cold metal's feel against her skin. She loved the way her breath quickened and her pulse pounded at both wrists and temples. Slowly and deliberately she opened her eyes then in one fast, deliberate gouge, she pricked the ring finger of her left hand. She found the pain exciting. Just as her mother had promised, the blood that spurted, staining her pale skin, made her feel more alive than anything she had ever experienced before.

Bridget pinched the wound hard and smiled as her blood dripped into the cup of water she had drawn from the well at sunset. Dipping a robin's feather into the mixture, she painted a piece of parchment, turning the paper a rosy shade of pink. She placed the damp sheet before the crackling fireplace to dry while she gathered together the remaining ingredients that were need.

A pinch of cinnamon. Some sandalwood. Several dried patchouli leaves. Bridget sprinkled the triad into a stone mortar and used a pestle to grind the mix into a powder. She transferred the mélange onto a large, flat rock at the foot of her bed and used the candle flame to burn the fragrant blend into ashes.

Bridget wrote the name Jackson Hathorne on the now-dried, pink paper and slipped it beneath her pillow. She scattered rose petals on the floor around her bed before pulling back the cover and getting in. Bridget realized she was a novice at her craft, but she also knew she had followed her mother's instructions perfectly and would repeat the same ritual for the next six nights. By the full moon, Bridget was certain her spell would be successful, and she would get exactly what she wanted. Not only would have a passionate, sensuous dream of Jackson Hathorne, but she would be one step closer to making her fantasy a reality.

• • •

Patience had never been Bridget Bishop's strong suit. Tapping the toe of her black Jimmy Choo stiletto against the industrial-strength tile floor, she raked her blood-red fingernails through her hair. This should have been impossible. After all these years, how the hell had this happened? Not only was the damned amulet here in Boston, but Jack Hawthorne had it. And that could only mean one thing. *She* would follow. Unless, of course, someone stopped her. Bridget licked her lips at the thought of taking care of that bitch once and for all. Knowing the timing was not right for that, at least not now, she had to make other arrangements.

After leaving Jack's office, Bridget had made the appropriate phone call and set up the meeting. She checked her watch—11:00 A.M. exactly. This guy had better be on time. The last thing Bridget needed was to be seen talking to him, but under the circumstances, she had no choice.

Seated on the two-sided bench that faced the south entrance to the mall, she waited. As the crisp October breeze scattered dried leaves across the sidewalk, their skittering sound reminded Bridget of her cat running across a hardwood floor. The sun felt comfortably warm through her lightweight cape. And then the air chilled.

She sensed the muscular man's presence before he slipped onto the seat directly behind her. Settling his broad shoulders against the slatted wooden back that separated them, she knew before he spoke that this was the man she had contacted.

Without turning, she angled her head in his direction and asked their prearranged question. "Excuse me, do you have the time?"

"Midnight," Zeke answered.

"As I told you on the phone, the timetable has changed," Bridget whispered. She pulled a slip of paper from her cape pocket. Passing it behind her back, she handed it to him. His large hand was every bit as rough as his reputation, and nothing could have pleased her more. "This is where she lives."

Chapter Three

With Bridget gone, Jack pulled the necklace from his jacket pocket. This time he palmed the stone and noticed it actually felt warm. As if it drew heat from his skin. He had held it in the sunlight earlier; maybe the unusual stone absorbed or conducted heat.

The mental image of a woman flashed in his head so quickly, he didn't have time to blink before the sensation passed. Strawberry blonde or auburn hair—not dark. Brown or green eyes, he wasn't sure which. Definitely not blue. The details weren't clear, but the recognition practically crystallized. The impact of the vision or hallucination or whatever the hell it was punched him hard in the gut. And just as quickly, she was gone.

Momentarily blindsided, Jack rationalized. He'd been working way too hard lately. Too many cases. Too much court. Too few earthly pleasures. But then that was easy enough to remedy. It always had been.

And that's when he heard it. A soft, sweet laugh that was as exquisitely feminine as it was familiar. Laughter so identifiable that he actually looked around. So unmistakable that he would swear the woman was standing next to him.

Either this was nuts, or he was. Jack Hawthorne did not believe in hocus pocus bullshit. That said, why did he know that the laugh he'd just heard belonged to the mysterious woman who had flashed through his mind? He couldn't explain how he knew. He just knew.

One thing for sure—whatever was going on, somehow the necklace had triggered it. So, he took a closer look. The chain was plain, nothing fancy. Appeared to be gold, but that wasn't a given. The length was pretty average—maybe eighteen or twenty inches.

Nothing special. But the stone…now that was a different story. In comparison, it was about the size of a nickel, and the rich color reminded him of honey. Except for the tear-shaped design in its center, the gem was flawless. For all he knew that marking might make it more valuable.

Other than the necklace, there hadn't been anything else in the old wooden box except the yellowed, handwritten note scrawled:

Deliver to Miss Abigail Corey—Springfield, Illinois—by October 31

Unwilling to ride this bizarre little sci-fi merry-go-round one more minute, Jack took a leap of faith and jumped off. He put the amulet back in the box and checked his calendar. Maxine had scheduled a one-week time frame to find the Corey woman. He buzzed her.

"Yes."

"Just curious," he began. "When did we receive Miss Corey's heirloom?" He heard her fingers clicking computer keys faster than seemed humanly possible.

Silence.

"Maxine"

"Yes."

"Got a receipt date?"

"Well, hmmm, this says October 31, 1692." She cleared her throat then quickly made a connection. "I obviously logged the file number as the year. I'm very sorry about that."

A dark cloud momentarily obscured the sun, casting a shadow across Jack's desk. "Forget it." Maxine never made a mistake like that. Never. When it came to work, the woman was a machine. In fact, he couldn't remember her ever making any significant kind of clerical error. So, what gives with the date? The last time he had a hinky feeling this strong, one guy got his eye poked out, two went to prison for life, and a monkey lost his tail. "On second thought," Jack added, "do some more digging, will you? Maybe you can track—"

"Wait a minute," Maxine said. "That date *is* correct."

"It can't be." As he listened to her computer keys tap dance, a larger, darker cloud replaced the first in the late morning sky.

"It is," she insisted and left it at that.

Her I'm-right-and-you're-wrong silence always amused Jack. "Okay, Max, then you tell me exactly how—"

"Because, this is an account you acquired—"

"What do you mean?" Now it was his turn to interrupt. Jack watched the dark clouds pass and blue sky reappear. He propped the phone between his left ear and shoulder and listened to her explanation.

"You acquired it," she repeated, "when you bought out Parris, Goody, and Lynch."

"And you're not kidding?" Jack asked without thinking. When he heard her mutter about *having bigger fish to fry*, he remembered Maxine Spencer did not joke. "So, this time-dated execution, for lack of a better term, has actually been passed down from law firm to law firm for more than three hundred years?"

"According to my records, that is correct."

"Can't be." His tone was definitive. "Springfield, Illinois, did not exist in 1692."

"I know it didn't, but—"

"No buts." He tapped his pencil on the desktop. "Not possible."

"But," she insisted, unwilling to be stopped, "I just called up the entire account history, and we have the paperwork to back this up.

Jack stopped the pencil mid-tap and thought a moment. "Not only was there not a Springfield," he spoke as much to himself as to Maxine, "but no one could have known this Abigail Corey would exist."

"Doesn't matter," Maxine stated.

"Seriously?" Jack snorted. "I'd say an inheritance passed down over three hundred years naming and locating some yet-to-be born woman in some yet-to-be established city is pretty damned—"

"Doesn't matter," she repeated. "We have the necklace. We have the paperwork," she told him as if there was nothing more to be said. "It's our job to find her."

Jack noted Maxine had said "find her," not try to find her. He had heard that matter-of-fact tone way too many times in the past decade to do anything but step back and stay out of her way. The woman had a sense of duty that took no prisoners, and this little execution was no exception.

"Well then, get cracking, Maxine. I'd say waiting three centuries to search for someone is long enough." When she didn't even chuckle, he cleared his throat. This had to be the wildest God damned goose chase he'd ever been on. His only reply was the woman's haunting laughter as it echoed through his mind again. He shook his head. "Check it out and see what you come up with in Springfield."

Chapter Four

The rental car Zeke Taylor had chosen to drive tonight was, in a word, nondescript. The black Toyota Camry was a popular model, not too flashy but nice enough not to raise suspicion in a decent, law-abiding part of town. It would blend in, and that's exactly what he needed. He drove by the first time to locate the address Bridget Bishop had given him.

Halfway up the street and just as it had been described, the ornate, cast iron lettering spelled out Aromatiques, the name of the Corey woman's shop. After driving around the adjacent streets for ten minutes or so, he pulled to the curb about a half a block from the two-story, brick building he targeted. He killed the headlights and took a long, careful look. Satisfied he had a clear view, he put the car in park and turned off the ignition.

Zeke unhooked his seatbelt and lit a Marlboro. For some reason, waiting had never been a problem for him. It actually felt like an exercise in restraint. And if there was one thing Zeke liked, it was the feeling of control. Whether that was behind the wheel of a car, on top of a woman, or holding a gun to someone's head.

Positive or negative, as long as he held the reins, nothing else mattered. He would go to any lengths. In that respect he always thought he'd have made a great Navy seal. As part of their training he'd heard they had to stand motionless in a pond filled with snakes for hours. That kind of discipline trained them to focus. To put the mission above all else. To rise above their fears. Without a doubt, Zeke bet he could do that without blinking. Especially if it meant killing all the snakes on command when the exercise was completed. *That* he would like.

Checking his watch, Zeke realized he had not only made damn good time flying from Boston to Springfield, Illinois, but he couldn't have planned his arrival better. The surrounding businesses had been closed for several hours, so foot traffic in this part of town was practically nonexistent. The streetlights lined the sidewalk opposite the building, so they didn't illuminate the particular entrance that interested him. Not that it really mattered.

Somehow, despite his six foot, six inch height and powerful frame, Zeke could pick a lock in broad daylight without being noticed—and he had. He was really that good. He took a long drag off his cigarette and blew a string of concentric smoke rings. One perfect circle followed the next until he smiled and broke their form. From where he sat, this job would be the easiest ten grand he'd ever made.

At least what he was doing tonight wouldn't be as messy as last week. Not that he couldn't do wet work, because he sure as hell could. In fact, from time to time he liked blood. Really enjoyed it. And if there was one thing he liked best about contracting out his services, Zeke decided it would be variety. Always something new and different. He sure as shit never got bored. Not many people could say that. Zeke opened his window and started to flip out his cigarette. Instead, he ground it out on the side of the rental car and slipped the butt into his jacket pocket. No sense leaving DNA on the sidewalk where some Barney Fife might accidentally stumble upon it.

As a cab pulled up in front of Aromatiques, Zeke grabbed his small binoculars and slouched in his seat. He watched as a young woman got out and paid the driver. Shoulder length hair. A thank you wave at the curb. A confident walk toward the front door. Bag and purse in hand, she hurried up the sidewalk and let herself in the building. He smiled and lit another cigarette. Now there was a bonus he hadn't counted on. He didn't think the Corey woman was supposed to be home tonight. Oh, well. That was her problem, not his.

A few minutes later he saw the second floor lights go on. He sat ever patient and gave the Corey woman plenty of time to settle in.

Eat. Bathe. Get ready for bed. It was the least he could do, Zeke thought. Hell, everyone deserved a *Last Supper.*

Since her surprise arrival was not a part of his plan, Zeke thought long and hard about what to do with her. He got off on power of any kind. The power of victory. The power of deception. But this particular power—the power of deciding whether someone lives or dies—was by far the most intoxicating aphrodisiac he ever experienced. Like God, he could choose to save her. One phone call could have her out of that apartment. Or he could proceed as planned and kill her as an unexpected casualty—a bonus, of sorts. Or he could have a little fun with her first and decide what to do with her later.

Like that job in Las Vegas a year ago, a traveling companion might be nice for a week or two. He could use her until he got tired. Or bored. And then, well, she might end up like that sweet kindergarten teacher he'd snatched at the mall. What was her name? Emily? No. Natalie…something or other…Ah, Vegas. something about the irony of a cold desert night made disposing of a body so much easier. It felt like nature was out of whack, so why not the rest of the world—which Zeke happened to believe was a fact. He might be fucked up, but the universe had him beat fifty ways for Sunday.

One hour later, Zeke had made his decision. He stepped out of the car and ground out his cigarette butt with the heel of one shoe before closing the door. Walking to the back bumper, he carefully scanned the street. Satisfied there was no one around, he opened the trunk. He removed the red, plastic container and crossed the street like a regular guy who had simply bought some gas for his lawnmower.

As for the woman, Zeke knew the end would be the same— whether it was tonight or two weeks from now. The time in between, he decided, was his for the taking, if he wanted it. And he'd always had a thing for a longhaired, city girl with smooth, soft skin and legs up to her ass.

Grinning, he whispered, "Hi, honey, I'm home."

He paused a beat at the building's entrance and set down the container, still careful to assess his surroundings. Pulling a leather envelope from his jacket pocket, he retrieved the slender lock picks and within ten seconds he heard the familiar click. One turn of the knob and he was inside. No fuss. No muss. No problem.

• • •

Wangling her Save-The-Earth shopping bag, her fabulous new Dooney and Burke purse, and her keys, she managed to unlock the ornate front door before the cool September breeze chilled her entirely to the bone. Funny, she thought, it hadn't felt nearly that chilly when she'd hailed the cab less than half an hour ago. Once inside, she paused before going upstairs.

As always the appealing, satisfying scent of Aromatiques greeted her. As many times as she had crossed that threshold, she never tired of the inviting aroma, because it hung in the air like an invisible safety net. That spicy, homey fragrance met her at the door and shadowed her every step throughout the shop. So, why—tonight of all nights—did something feel different? Just the dark and the chill of autumn, she decided as she flipped the lock behind her.

Looking around, the mission style, Tiffany nightlights placed throughout the store not only cast a comforting, warm glow, but they even made turning on the overheads unnecessary. Besides, she loved this place, knew it backwards and forwards, and could make her way through every aisle blindfolded. She frowned at how quickly she had lapsed back into victim mode. One skittish moment and she had faltered. That was just not acceptable. Shaking her head, she tossed her keys into her purse and shifted it to one shoulder. She straightened her spine and reminded herself of the mantra she had selected shortly after vowing to change her life. Always a Poe fan, she had chosen the one word that summed up her decision like no other could. "Nevermore," she whispered.

Before Aromatiques, her life had been drastically different. Frightening. Tumultuous. Violent. Her hand touched one cheek as she remembered the first night she had spent in this building. Battered and confused, she had been broken and alone with nowhere to go. All she had known for sure was that escape was her only way out, and this shop had proven to be a much-needed soft place to land. This place, these brick walls had not only given her shelter, but they had provided her with exactly what she'd needed—a fighting chance. Since that fateful night, she had known that being involved in Aromatiques had been the single smartest thing she'd done in her entire life. And tonight she knew for a fact she'd been right. As bitter as those memories were, they made her news tonight all the more sweet.

She smiled, made her way through the store and took the stairs in the back room to the second floor. Stepping inside the apartment, she flipped on the light and headed for the kitchen where she ceremoniously removed the chilled bottle of Dom Perignon—her biggest splurge ever—from her bag. Filling an ice bucket from a nearby cupboard, she snuggled the champagne between the cubes and smiled. She pulled the envelope she'd received in the mail today from her coat pocket and carefully laid her good news on granite counter. Hardly able to contain herself, she rifled through the drawer next to the sink, found the corkscrew and set it next to the bottle. This is what she'd been waiting for and working towards for what seemed like forever. And, finally, it was right there in front of her…literally within her grasp. She touched the envelope one last time to make sure it was real. And it was.

Over the moon with excitement, she hurried to the bathroom to shower—her feet barely touching the floor. Frothy with suds, she was determined to wash away her past, for so many reasons, but especially so her good news could soak in. Wanting to secure it deep inside her, she dried and slathered rich, creamy lotion all over her body. She needed her future sealed once and for all and buried so deep that nothing or no one could ever take it away from her again. Slipping into her PJ's, she couldn't stop smiling as she headed for the kitchen.

And that's when she saw him.

• • •

Maxine Spencer stepped into Jack's office before leaving for the day. "Don't forget tonight. Seven o'clock at Giovanni's."

"You can't even say her name, can you?" When Maxine didn't reply, Jack looked up and shut his laptop. "Hell, I don't blame you. *Bridget* can be a real bitch."

Maxine almost smiled as she buttoned her raincoat.

"Didn't think there was a need. I always assume you know who you are meeting."

Jack shrugged "Sometimes it takes a while to *really* know who you're meeting." Lightening split the sky outside his window.

"Whatever you say."

There was that "almost" smile again.

Somewhere in the distance thunder rumbled, and Jack thought back to Maxine's instant dislike of Bridget. He had to admit that when it came to business or people, Max had the instincts of a bloodhound. And she hadn't been wrong yet. He stood and checked his watch. At this rate, he'd be lucky to beat the downpour. Where the hell had this weather come from anyway? And why was Maxine always so damned prepared? The forecast had been sunshine for Christ's sake.

Jack slipped the necklace back into the box. "Reservations?"

"Made," Maxine grunted.

He watched her check the *Go Green* canvas tote for her galoshes. "Thanks."

"That's my job." She turned on her heels and left.

Used to the prim huff Maxine called goodbye, Jack sat a moment after the door closed. He should probably hurry before the storm broke, but he wanted to take one last look at the amulet's wooden container. Three hundred years old and not a single hint, he thought. Plain wood—probably pine. About six inches long and four inches wide. No markings. No date. No clues.

As Jack slipped the box into the lap drawer of his desk, thunder rumbled, closer now. Suddenly thoughts of dinner with Bridget just pissed him off. The bottom line—he was sick of her. The social climbing. The attitude. The disrespect. She may be beautiful, but in her case, it really was only skin deep. Screw her, Jack decided. When he was done with someone that was it. He was finished. And Bridget Bishop had shit her nest today. Let her eat alone, he thought without regret. Take out sounded just fine to him tonight.

Chapter Five

Salem, Massachusetts
14 September
Year of our Lord, 1690

The loud knock rattled the log cabin's rough-hewn door.

Abigail's broom stopped mid sweep. Her heart thudded against her ribs. Her mouth felt like cotton. Yet, she stood as though both feet had been nailed to the floor.

Sarah Corey didn't miss Abigail's motionless posture or the wide-eyed look as her daughter anxiously glanced up and chewed her bottom lip. Hoping the girl would at least take a breath, Sarah wiped both hands on her apron and hurried to see who was outside.

When the ax-wielding, dark-haired young man dipped his head respectfully, then just stood there grinning like the town fool, Sarah prompted, "And what can I do for you, Jackson Hathorne?"

"Nothing, Ma'am." His grin widened. "I just wondered if Mr. Corey could use some help chopping wood?"

Sarah leaned against the doorway and noted the three neat stacks young Hathorne had split for her husband just five days ago. Not that Ethan had questioned the lad's ambition, because he hadn't. Nor had she. The Hathornes were a long line of respectable, hard-working people, most of whom were lawyers and judges.

No, it wasn't Jackson Hathorne's pedigree that had the two of them whispering in bed long after the candles had sputtered into darkness. They had, however, both seen right through Jackson's motives. Twenty years old and head-over-heels smitten, that's exactly what Hathorne was. Anyone would have to be blind, deaf and dumb not to see it, much less a lovely young girl's mother and father. And their one and only Abigail was exactly that—beautiful and just about to turn sixteen.

Sarah sighed, knowing all-too-soon this young man would be asking for so much more than to help chop the firewood. But for now, there he stood in the crisp October afternoon, his grin fading as he waited on pins and needles for her answer. Unwilling to prolong his pathetic agony, she gave in. "Suit yourself."

A smile nearly connected Jackson's ears before he nodded politely and headed through the red and gold fallen leaves that covered the path to the woodpile.

Sarah turned to face her daughter, who still had yet to move. "Helpful lad that Hathorne boy," was all she said.

Abigail shrugged, then began sweeping the already spotless planks, conveniently looking at the floor and not her mother. "He seems nice enough."

Desperate to understand the sudden sense of dread she felt, Sarah stood perfectly still and focused her attention. Certain the bad feeling was coming from outside, she parted the muslin curtain and watched the Hathorne boy carefully.

Nothing.

Whatever Sarah was feeling, it wasn't coming from him. But it was out there. Of that she was sure. Despite her uneasiness, Sarah turned away from the window and went back to her bread making. Kneading the flour. Feeling the dough, like her daughter's life, changing form beneath her very fingertips.

• • •

Bridget Bishop hid behind a giant oak, peeking through its branches to watch the same man who had haunted her dreams. Last night her spell had been a success. Today, she had discretely followed Jackson Hathorne to the Corey's cabin and was content, for the moment, to watch him chop wood from afar. His dark hair gleamed in the warm, autumn sunshine. His handsome brow furrowed as he concentrated on each deliberate cut. His strong, broad shoulders brought down the ax time and again with rhythm and precision.

When Bridget heard the log cabin door open and saw Abigail Corey hurry to the well, her stomach twitched. Her eyes narrowed as she watched Abigail give Jackson a long-handled ladle filled with water. With one boot resting on a nearby stump, he accepted the drink and grinned. Abigail, in turn, reached into the pocket of her skirt and offered him a hanky. Swiping his brow with the delicate square of white cotton, he nodded his thanks.

Bridget couldn't hear what they were saying, but between that Corey girl's bashful looks and Jackson's polite smiles, Bridget's stomach clenched. No one, especially not some mousy, red-haired fool like Abigail Corey, would stand in her way when it came to getting exactly what she wanted.

When she saw Jackson lower his mouth to Abigail's, Bridget's nails gouged the tree bark so hard they snapped. Oblivious to the pain, Bridget's icy blue eyes narrowed and her jaw clenched.

"You've crossed the line, Abigail," she swore through gritted teeth. "But you will not take what is mine. Not now. Not ever."

Wasn't it just last week that Goodwife Glover had been tried and hanged as a witch, Bridget mused? She glanced at Abigail and arched one brow. So, she would simply begin by planting the seed of doubt about Abigail with…a couple of high strung girls she knew in Salem…next she would mix the ergot in the rye dough… so the bread she baked would cause hallucinations…if she gave the loaves to Elizabeth and Rebecca…the rest, she decided with a sneer, would be history. Abigail Corey would be out of her life forever.

"Make no mistake," she hissed, "Jackson Hathorne will notice me." A smiled curved Bridget's blood red lips as she pulled a snow-white ribbon from her pocket and twirled it around one splintered fingernail. "Because I know exactly how to make that happen."

Chapter Six

10:38 P.M.
September 30, present day
Springfield, Illinois

Fire snapped and popped in the night wind like laundry on the Devil's clothesline. Sirens wailed. Staccato blue and red lights on top of police cars blinked frantic Morris code. Black smoke hovered over the scene like a gigantic billboard from Hell.

Abby Corey dashed toward the blaze. Her heart hammered. Her three-inch heels pounded the sidewalk. Her lungs burned with each gulp of cold air.

She saw the officer's arm dart out. His long reach stopped her just shy of the yellow perimeter tape. Unlike a runner at the end of the race, Abby would not break the ribbon and claim victory tonight. One glance and she knew there was nothing left to win.

"It's my—" Abby struggled to breath and talk, so she pointed toward the raging fire. "My shop." Through a blur of tears she could still make out the elegant wrought iron sign—*Aromatiques.*

"I'm sorry, Ma'am, but you'll have to stay back." He hesitated then added, "There's really no point."

His words dwindled, but his message may as well have been delivered through a megaphone. "No point?" Stripped of hope, her voice was small, like a silent leak from a broken heart.

He offered a sympathetic shake of his head.

On her drive home, Abby had spotted the bottleneck of fire trucks and police cars. Since the chaos looked dangerously close to the location of her shop and traffic had come to a complete standstill, she parked in the first available spot. She left her coat and purse in the car and started out on foot. The closer she got the faster she walked, running the last two blocks and praying every step of the way.

Abby's chest tightened. *Dear God, anything but fire.* Selling candles had even been hard for her, and now she watched her lifelong fear manifest before her eyes. She stood by helplessly at the scene as red-hot flames licked the walls and floor of her shop, devouring them like a starving dog. Despite the blast from each giant hose, the blaze raged.

"Abby."

Swaying, coils of fire struck back at the spewing water like giant, crimson cobras. Cracking and popping, the inferno hissed its defiance. Mesmerized by the horror, she didn't turn at the sound of his voice. She didn't speak a word until strong hands took her by the shoulders.

"Abby."

She blinked. "Jacques? What are you doing here?"

"I saw it on the news."

Abby allowed him to wrap both arms around her, but it wasn't any surprise Jacques had shown up tonight. After all, when a man's true love is in danger…

"Abby?"

Abby lifted her head from Jacques's chest and took a step back. "J.T.?"

"I came as soon as I heard."

She watched the two men square off without a word and waited a beat. Satisfied there *might not* be a scene, she turned her attention back to the blaze. "How could this happen?" Her words were small. Unlike her heartbreak.

"My guess," J.T. began, "a design problem."

"If anything it was probably shoddy construction," Jacques said.

"Like hell," J.T. shot back. "Why are you even here, Asshole? You got what you wanted out of Abby ten years ago."

"What's that supposed to mean?"

"Just what I said." J.T. jabbed his finger in Jacques's direction. "You wanted to be featured in *Architecture's Digest* and that's why you designed *Aromatiques*. Not for Abby. She was just a means to an end for you. And don't get your hopes up. I don't suppose they'll revisit the ashes in a follow up piece."

"You ought to talk." Jacque took one step in J.T.'s direction. "Do you think I was blind? I saw how you looked at her the entire time you were working on that building."

J.T. matched Jacques's step forward.

Abby moved between the two. "Stop it."

J.T. shoved both hands in his jeans' pockets. "Sorry, Babe."

Abby glared at Jacques.

"My apologies *to you*, Abby." Jacques cleared his throat.

J.T. took one step back. "It's about time *Jock* apologized to you."

"Jacques," Abby corrected automatically. In the beginning she'd known Jacques was ambitious. In the end, she'd realized just how ambitious he truly was. Somewhere in the middle, however, she'd learned a helluva lot about herself. All her life, Abby had been searching for something. She'd been engaged to Jacques and J.T. hoping to find it. Jacques hadn't had it, and J.T. hadn't been it.

"*We* may be over, but you know I built that building just for you." J.T. wiped a tear from her cheek. "I'm so sorry about the fire."

"As am I, Abby," Jacques added. "Is there anything I can do?"

Shivering, she shook her head. For first time since leaving her car, Abby realized her little black dress was no competition for the crisp night air.

J.T. shrugged out of his black leather jacket and wrapped it around her shoulders. "You can stay at my place."

"Or mine," Jacques offered.

Abby shook her head again.

"You always were as independent as a hog on ice," J.T. said. "But you realize this won't be a quick fix. Looks like the shop's gone, but your apartment may just be smoke damage."

"Right now, I don't know what I want to do." Abby prided herself on being self-sufficient, and she already knew dealing with this particular setback would be no different. She thought about the phone call she'd received from the lawyer's office earlier today. Suddenly and without warning, she made her decision. "I'm planning a trip out east as soon as I can make arrangements. I'll take some time to think about all this while I'm gone."

"Miss?"

Abby turned to face a man with a badge in his hand. No uniform. Plain clothes. Solemn face. "Yes."

"Detective Stevens." He flipped the badge shut and slipped it into the inside pocket of his suit jacket.

Abby nodded.

"A neighbor pointed you out. Said this was your shop."

"Yes, it's mine." She fought back the tears. "Well, it was mine."

"I'd like to ask you a few questions."

Abby said nothing as she watched him take out a small pad and pencil.

"Just routine," he said.

"All right."

"Your name?"

"Abby Corey."

"Phone?"

The night wind gusted and Abby felt the heat from the fire on her face as she recited her cell number.

"Have you had problems with anyone lately?"

"No." Abby considered his question as she fanned away the smoke. "Nothing comes to mind."

"Upset customer? Competitor?"

"No one." She watched him eye Jacques and J.T.

"Old boyfriend? New boyfriend?"

"No." Feeling two pairs of eyes zero in on her, she clarified to Stevens, "They're harmless. Just ex-fiancés." He didn't blink.

Stevens pointed first to Jacques and then to J.T. and logged their information.

Turning to Abby, he told her, "I'll also need the name of your landlord."

"I don't rent, I own."

"Just the store? Or the building?"

"The building." As she answered, he jotted down her response.

"Where were you tonight?"

"Me?" Abby met his gaze. "I was…wait a minute. This was just an accident, right?"

He didn't blink. "Just answer the question."

"I attended a PETA fund raiser at the Hilton."

"Can you give me a couple of names of people who were there? Just to verify."

"I sat next to the mayor and his wife. Ask them." Abby's gaze narrowed. "Are you kidding me? You think I had something to do with this? Are you crazy? I worked day and night for eight long years to establish my shop." She paused to take a breath.

"The firemen called me in because they suspect arson."

There it was. The look. She saw it in his eyes. This man was the bearer of bad news. And not just bad news, but really bad news. Suddenly she didn't want to hear more. Instead, she saw more. She watched a dark van pull up next to the ambulance.

Not just any van, *the* van. Black. White letters. *Coroner.*

Abby's chest tightened. Slowly, she directed her eyes toward Stevens. Desperate to look away, to run away, she did neither. Instead, she focused on his mouth. Words were about to come out. Mean, horrible words. Words she did not want to hear. As his lips parted, she noticed how straight and white his teeth were. Too bad they couldn't fence in what he was about to tell her.

Abby struggled to listen.

Something about an eyewitness seeing a bald man.

The front window shattering.

A dark sedan screeching away from the scene.

Abby's attention strayed to the ambulance's warning lights. As they continued flashing their S.O.S., one of the paramedics leaned against the side of the vehicle. Relaxed. Arms crossed over his burly chest. The other P-med smoked a cigarette. The fact that they had nothing to do must be a good sign, right? Besides, emergency vehicles always showed up at fires, didn't they? Didn't necessarily mean anyone had been hurt.

But what about the van?

Through the smoke and flames, Abby saw a third paramedic unload the gurney.

Okay. Minor injuries were not uncommon at a fire scene. Still not so bad—maybe.

But what about the van?

All three men entered the building. Two led the way, and the one pushing the gurney followed. But why? She hadn't been home. But, the firemen…Time, like suspended smoke, hung in the air above the blackened hole that, just a few hours ago, had been the store's entrance. Abby held her breath. Waited. Watched. Willed away the inevitable.

When the three emerged, Abby did not see an injured party. There was no poor fireman wearing an oxygen mask and suffering from smoke inhalation or minor burns. No stranger who lay neatly tucked in with a pristine sheet and a dangling IV. Instead, there was only a black body bag. Zipped up. All the way.

The now-hideous, spider-legged mattress for one wasn't being loaded into the ambulance, no siree. It was being loaded into the wicked, wicked van.

And that was what the van was all about. Why it was here. Why it made her want to scream.

The fireman, the stranger, the fatality was being carted off to the morgue. No quick trip to the hospital for this guy. No taxi ride home after a visit to the ER. No tomorrow. Ever.

"Ms. Corey?"

Abby didn't remember shutting her eyes, but she must have, because at the sound of Stevens' voice they flew open. "I'm sorry. What?"

"Are you all right?"

"No, Detective, I'm not," she shot back. "What else do you need to know?"

"The firemen said there was an apartment upstairs," Stevens said. "Who lived there?"

Abby coughed and turned her back to so much more than just the smoke-filled breeze. "I do—did."

"Anyone live with you?"

"No." Abby pulled J.T.'s jacket tighter. "Dammit. That reminds me that I need to call Kat. Excuse me just a minute." She turned to Jacques and J.T. "Can I use one of your cell phones?"

Both men nodded, but J.T. pointed, "Jacket pocket."

"Who's Kat?" Stevens asked.

"Kat Richards," Abby continued, pulling out the phone and punching in the familiar number. She's a friend of mine who has worked in the shop for—" When a nearby phone echoed the ringing in her ear, Abby froze. Listening, she turned and followed the sound. Expecting to see Kat approach with her long auburn hair swinging in the cool night breeze, what Abby saw instead made her legs buckle.

She did not see Kat's infectious smile and her enthusiastic phone-in-hand wave. She did not even see some stranger who, by some freakish coincidence, was simultaneously receiving a call. What Abby saw was Kat's purse. The classic black Dooney and Burke bag her friend had lusted over for weeks. Knowing Kat would never break down and buy herself an expensive purse like that, Abby had purchased it for her last week.

But tonight Kat's handbag was not draped over her slender shoulder or clutched in her hand. Instead, the purse hung from a metal hook at the foot of the gurney. As the paramedics loaded the body bag into the van, that eerie ghost of Christmas past dangled and jerked from the horrible, hateful hook as if suspended from a hangman's noose.

If Jacques and J.T. hadn't grabbed Abby under each arm, she would have puddled to the ground.

"Head between her knees," Stevens ordered.

Jacques helped J.T. bend her over.

"Breathe, Babe." J.T.'s voice was firm but calm. "Atta girl, take nice deep breaths."

Abby instinctively followed the instructions. Unsteady at first, she regained her sea legs and stood up. With shaky fingers, she was finally able to slap shut J.T.'s cell phone and silence the unbearable ring of her best friend's phone—forever.

"Kat." The name escaped Abby's lips like a prayer. "Her apartment was painted today. I had a voice message earlier." Tears scalded both cheeks. She shook her head so hard J.T.'s leather jacket dropped to the ground. Trembling, she pointed to the Coroner's van and sank to her knees on the wet concrete. "She was going to spend the night."

• • •

Maxine peeked into Jack's office and announced matter-of-factly, "Miss Corey has been located and notified."

"Nice job." Jack shelved his disbelief; certain only Max could zero in on someone three hundred years after the request was made. "Has the package been" the haunting laughter of the beautiful woman played in his head like an impossible memory, stopping him mid-sentence.

He tapped his pencil to refocus then asked, "Have you mailed the necklace yet?"

"I was on my way now."

"Well don't," Jack heard himself say. "I've changed my mind. I would like her to pick this up in person."

He saw Maxine's eyebrows shoot up in perfect unison, but she said nothing. No interrogation? No argument? No Way. Maxine never accepted anything at face value. Not even from him. "Under the circumstances, I don't feel comfortable mailing it," he explained, certain she must have forgotten to ask.

"I'll call her back."

When she left to use the phone at her desk, Jack sat speechless— for so many reasons. Nothing about this inheritance added up. The time line was insane. Hell, the city was nonexistent at the time of the bequest. Not to mention that the benefactor named would not be born for more than three hundred years. And if that weren't crazy enough, the damned amulet itself was like nothing he'd ever seen. It twirled counter clockwise. Changed temperature. Made him hallucinate? Made him hear voices? Made Maxine sooo not herself. Made Bridget sooo much herself.

All Jack could do was stare at the door and wait. Somehow he knew this Abigail Corey would come. The necklace was important. *She* might even be important. Why, he wasn't sure. Not yet anyway. A knock interrupted his thoughts.

Maxine popped her head in. "Ms. Corey will be picking up the necklace in person."

"That was fast."

"Not my doing. She was the one who called. Said she was coming."

"She called you first—just now?" Curious, he tapped his pencil. "And she suggested coming half way across the country?"

"It seems she needs some time away and asked to come pick it up."

"I'll be damned." His pencil stopped mid-tap. "Okay then. Thanks." Before Jack could ask Maxine about her, she ducked out. But then, with a prissy name like Miss Abigail Corey and given the facts in this case, the mystery woman would probably be a three hundred-year-old librarian. Unfortunately, for just one more unexplainable reason, Jack sure as hell knew better.

Chapter Seven

Salem, Massachusetts
31 October
In the year of our Lord, 1687

The blindfold forced her eyes shut, but Abigail Corey didn't move a muscle. Didn't struggle. Didn't breathe. Waiting, she planted both feet on the floor and held tight to the carved pine bedpost. She heard the night wind moan as it gusted, stirring dried, fallen leaves and slapping them against the windowpane. Nimbly knotting the clean handkerchief at the back of Abigail's head, Sarah Corey was careful not to tangle her daughter's waist-length, auburn curls. "We have been chosen," her mother began.

"For what?" Abigail asked, unable to stand still a moment longer.

"Patience, Child," Sarah coaxed. "That's the first lesson you must learn. Be patient, and I will tell you." Satisfied that Abigail could not see, Sarah straightened the square, white collar of her daughter's dress, then turned her around. Flames from the fireplace cast ominous silhouettes on the log walls of their one room cabin. "Tonight is very special—"

"Because it is my thirteenth birthday?" Abigail splayed her fingers as she inched her way across the room.

Sarah shook her head and smiled as she steered Abigail in the right direction. Her sweet daughter had much to learn indeed. "Well, yes, your birthday is very special, but there is something else I want to share with you. Something very important about today—"

"What? What is so important?"

"You were born on the day we call Harvest Festival. It is an ancient sabbat called Mabon."

"What's a sabbat?"

"It's like a holiday," Sarah explained.

"What do we celebrate?"

"We give thanks for the harvest."

Abigail thought a moment. "Is that why we made the cornucopia this morning?"

"Exactly. This day is also very special because it represents the date that night and day are of equal length. The earth is in perfect balance." She guided Abigail to the table, seating her in front of the crackling hearth. Returning across the small room, she pulled a loaf-sized wooden chest from beneath the bed and placed it in front of her daughter.

The promise in her mother's voice excited Abigail. "So do I get something special for this holiday?" she asked, unable to wait for a response. "A gift?"

"Of sorts," her mother told her, lifting the lid.

"But you and father already gave me my birthday present this morning." Abigail's new kitten rubbed against her ankles, making her smile. All she really wanted to do right now was play with him. To hurry this game along—for it was surely nothing more than blind man's bluff—she picked at the white cuffs of her sleeves and declared impatiently, "Nothing could be as precious to me as Shadow."

"I would not be too sure." Her mother could hear the black cat purr as he wove himself between the chair legs that were curtained by the hem of Abigail's dress. "Besides, you'll be happy to know that Shadow and your new gift go hand-in-hand," she assured her.

"Really?" Maybe it would be worth playing silly games after all, Abigail thought.

"Yes, really," her mother repeated, pulling a small candle from the pocket of her long, dark skirt. She plucked a piece from the broom that leaned against the hearth and ignited the willowy straw in the fireplace. Lighting the candle's wick, she told her, "Listen now and don't say a word."

Abigail reluctantly obeyed her mother's serious tone. Smelling the beeswax warm, she wanted desperately to ask…something, anything, everything. Why must I listen? Why can't I see? What does my present have to do with Shadow? But the moment her mother began speaking softly, Abigail did listen—carefully—and without question.

"Eyes be blind. Touch be keen. Let Abigail choose this stone unseen. Hold its fate close to her heart. Let the two be one—never to part. So mote it be."

She took Abigail's hand and stirred the box of stones with her fingers. "You must use your soul to pick one—not your sight, so don't peek," she cautioned. "Be slow, girl. Take your time. Search for the one that truly feels right."

"Right?" Abigail repeated, sensing but not understanding the importance of what she was about to do.

Sarah searched the pocket of her skirt, found her own stone and held it. Soothing and comforting, it warmed her fingers, the palm of her hand, and her heart. "You'll know which one is yours when you find it, Child. Trust me."

• • •

Abigail Corey eyed her exquisite amber stone in the light of the full moon. She felt silly standing atop Hangman's Hill all alone on all Hallows' Eve, but her mother had insisted that she go there by herself say and do exactly as they had practiced, then wait. For what, Abigail wasn't entirely sure. Something wonderful, her mother had promised. Something special. And very, very secret.

So tonight, in honor of Samhain, the Witches' New Year, Abigail placed her stone in cupped hands and extended both arms toward the midnight sky. Her mother had told her that this special night had been set aside to honor the dead. And so she would. It was believed that the veils between the world of the living and those who had passed were at their thinnest.

The cool October breeze nipped at the hem of her long, black cape, but she did not shiver. Dried leaves skittered across the ground, disappearing into the darkness without a trace. The circle of trees surrounding the clearing creaked and moaned like unsettled spirits of the dead. Yet Abigail could not be swayed from her purpose. She trusted her mother like no other. She believed in her. And she would do exactly as her mother had asked.

"This stone I offer with purpose clear, to encircle the magick within its sphere. Let it survive and bind it long. Release the magick—make it strong. As I have spoken, so mote it be."

There. Her first spell was cast and carried by the crisp, autumn wind for the night to hear. Abigail struggled to harness the temperamental impatience that cursed all girls her age. She took a deep, slow breath, and consciously released it. Then and only then, the stone warmed slightly in the palms of her hands. As the sensations increased, she saw the cracks between her fingers glow as radiant as a sunset against the indigo sky.

How could that be? Dare she look? How could she not? In one swift movement, Abigail switched the stone to one hand and lowered both arms. Her breath caught. Her beautiful amber stone turned blood red. Hot—but it did not burn. Pulsing—but it did not crack. Breathing? Impossible—it was not alive. But something was.

Abigail blinked. Were her eyes playing tricks? Maybe it was the moonlight. She rubbed both lids with the heel of her free hand, looked back at the stone and blinked again. She was not imagining things. The warm gem looked like liquid fire. Suddenly, she wanted to drop it and run away. Then just as suddenly, her fear dissolved into something different—something much more powerful than anything she had ever felt before. There, just an arm's length in front of her, she saw…what? Something? Someone?

The gossamer form materialized in front of her like smoke captured in a life-sized jar. The spirit was so impossibly familiar that without thinking, Abigail reached out, but her hand felt nothing. Her heart, however, felt everything.

"Grandma?" Abigail whispered, blinking again as the elusive image took form. Kind face. Loving eyes. Tender smile. Her favorite dark bonnet rested just above the graying bun she always secured at the nape of her neck. Her customary long black dress trimmed in white dissipated into the darkness as the gently spirit hovered in front of her.

"Yes, Child."

Abigail's breath caught. "It can't be. You're…"

"Dead," the spirit finished gently.

Unable to repeat the word, Abigail nodded.

"Yes, My Dear, it's true. I have passed from this life to the next."

Cradled by the soothing, familiar voice, Abigail felt no fear. She had adored her Grandmother and whatever veil was lifted tonight, it didn't matter. Just one more chance to talk to her filled Abigail with such joy. "Oh, Grandma, I miss you so much."

"Abigail, you must know that I am always with you."

"But there are so many things I want to ask—"

"Ask your Mother, Child. Mind what she tells you. I passed 'the ways' onto her just as she will pass them on to you."

"But—"

"Hush now and listen to me. I haven't much time."

Abigail pressed her lips together. Willing away the thought of losing her Grandmother again, she waited with baited breath, afraid to take her eyes off the beloved apparition for even a second.

"Ours is a very special gift, but with it comes a great responsibility."

Abigail nodded.

"Pay careful attention to your mother's instructions and, above all else, always use your power for good."

"I will."

"Only for good," she repeated. "Promise me."

"I promise."

"No matter what happens, you must trust your instincts. Know that your gift will show you the way."

"I will trust my instincts and my gift to show me the way," she repeated carefully.

"Understand that the answers you seek may not always appear in this lifetime—" At Abigail's intake of breath, she added, "But don't be afraid, Child."

Abigail swallowed hard. "I won't be. I swear."

"You must also know that others will use their power for evil. But you must believe what I am about to say. I have seen you in another time and place. I am telling you to remember three things. Remember to seek what is yours. Remember a place called Springfield, Illinois. Remember the year."

Confused, but trusting Abigail repeated, "Seek what is mine. Springfield, Illinois. Twenty-first century…I'll remember."

"I warn you, Child. Don't forget."

As the image began to fade, tears scalded Abigail's cheeks. "Don't go, Grandma. Please don't leave me again."

"Hold close your special stone, and I will always be with you."

Curling her fingers around glowing amber gem, Abigail felt the cool night breeze dry her tears. Her grandmother was gone, but so were Abigail's fears. Rather than feeling heartbroken and alone, joy filled her soul. She turned on both heels and raced as fast as her legs would carry her. Home. To tell her mother. And no one else. Not ever. Those were the rules.

Chapter Eight

Abby Corey checked her watch and tapped the toe of her sleek black pump. Arriving at Mr. Hawthorne's office ten minutes early simply gave her more time to consider the bizarre circumstances. How often do you fly clear across the country to receive a three hundred-year-old inheritance from an anonymous benefactor? As anxious as she was to see the necklace and get this ordeal over with, keeping her skepticism at bay the past couple of days had been a far greater challenge. Still leery, she looked around the upscale law office.

On the surface, at least, this Hawthorne guy appeared to be successful. Soothing blue walls. Plush, navy carpet. Rich antique furnishings. Her racing pulse calmed a couple of beats. Besides, she had checked out the firm before agreeing to meet with him in person, and according to her lawyer, Hawthorne's practice was well respected.

"Lovely office," Abby commented.

Maxine nodded. "Mr. Hawthorne's having it refurbished in a couple of days, but for the life of me I don't know why," she huffed. "I told him it was just a waste of good money—"

When the intercom buzzed interrupting Maxine's well-intentioned observations, Abby couldn't help but think of Kat. She had been outspoken in that same way. And right now, Kat would be the first one to tell Abby to straighten up, ditch the survivor's guilt, and get on with her life.

"Miss Corey?" Maxine smiled. "Mr. Hawthorne will see you now."

According to the brass nameplate on the desk in the outer office, Abby was following Maxine Spencer, the secretary who had telephoned her. As prim and business-like as Ms. Spencer appeared to be, Abby had taken an instant liking to her, both over the phone and in person. With Kat gone, connecting with another female even on a superficial level offered an achingly familiar feeling that she missed. She waited while the older woman gave a courtesy knock before opening the door, then accompanied her into his office.

"Mr. Hawthorne, Miss Corey is here to see you," Maxine announced before stepping back into the hall and closing the door behind her.

Jack looked up from a note he was writing. When dark eyes locked with green, his pencil point snapped like a dry twig. He tossed it down without a glance and gestured in the direction of the plush, leather chair opposite his desk.

"Please, sit down, Miss Corey."

"Abby," she corrected, unable to move or take her eyes off his face. *That face.*

That's the face I saw the day I held the amulet. He smiled. "Call me Jack."

Unsure if her legs would carry her, Abby nodded. Who wouldn't be shaky after losing her friend, her home and her business just weeks ago? This may have been her first personal meeting since the fire, but she was determined to keep her poise. So Abby focused on the obvious and sized Hawthorne up as she crossed the large, spacious room. Probably six foot four in his bare feet. Dark hair. Dark eyes. Resurrecting her most business-like smile, she sat down.

"Coffee?" he asked.

"I'd love a cup." *She didn't even drink coffee.*

"Cream or sugar?"

"Black." *She loved cream and sugar in her tea.*

Brimming cups in hand, Jack turned and passed one to Abby.

"Thanks." The beautiful piece of antique furniture centered on the expansive wall behind his desk caught Abby's attention. "I love your sideboard. Someone has an extremely discerning eye."

"Family heirloom," he clarified.

Abby liked the way he had put the handsome piece to good use. Coffee pot. Pewter weathervane. Exquisite bouquet of burgundy-colored mums. Her breath caught at the sight of them.

"It's gorgeous." She noted the heavily carved human figures, dragons and griffins.

Jack leaned back. "You like antiques." It wasn't a question.

"As a matter of fact, I do." She studied the sideboard more carefully, then met his gaze. "Tell me that's not an R.J. Horner."

"You're familiar with his work?"

"Absolutely. He was New York City's premier furniture maker in the late nineteenth century."

He steepled both hands. "One and the same."

"My guess," she took in every carved detail, just for the beauty of it, "circa 1890."

"Right again."

A price tag of over thirty thousand came to mind. "I guess I don't have to tell you that piece was quite a find."

"Just one more reason I'm glad I didn't have to pay for it. That sideboard has been in the Hawthorne family for over one hundred years."

"Lucky you." Her attention switched to his massive bookcase and matching desk. She reached out and touched the leather top. "These, too?"

"No, I found this set at an estate sale in Boston."

"About the same time period, though, late 1800's." She noted the beautifully inscribed legs as well as the intricate carvings that detailed the bookcase. "Walnut?" Without waiting for his response, she added, "I'd guess…French Henry II."

"You'd be right."

Abby's mental cash register cha-chinged a ballpark twenty thousand for the pair.

Jack took a drink of coffee. "I'd say your interest in antiques goes a little beyond a hobby."

"Not really." She shook her head. "I just love history in any form."

"Me, too."

"Speaking of unusual finds, I guess that's why the necklace I inherited intrigues me so."

"It's a strange one alright." He took a drink of coffee. "Odds are this particular scenario will never happen again. But I am surprised you flew clear across the country just to pick it up."

Abby studied his dark gaze and set her cup on the corner of the immaculately polished desk. She thought about the fire and decided not to discuss it. "I wasn't comfortable trusting the mail or any other delivery service with an heirloom."

"I see."

Abby wondered why he was still staring at her. Not that other men hadn't—didn't—but this was different. Jack Hawthorne's eyes didn't just look, they searched. The scary thing was that something deep inside her responded—big time. And as unnerving as her intuitive reaction to him was, she didn't falter.

"If you don't mind, I'd love to see the necklace."

He shoved the wooden box across the expanse of his desk, his eyes never leaving hers. "Of course."

So, it had been there all the time. She removed the lid and carefully picked up the gold chain.

"Exquisite," slipped from her lips as the large amber stone emerged. Dangling the gem, she glanced at Jack. "And there is no way to trace who gave this to me? Or why?"

Jack shrugged. "According to our records, the originating law firm received the necklace on October 31, 1692."

"All Hallows Eve." Her voice was almost a whisper as she dangled the necklace in the sunlight.

"Throughout the years, it was passed down from one law firm to the next. When I purchased the law practice of Parris, Goody and Lynch, I ended up with it," he explained. "Obviously my firm was the last in line before the transaction deadline of October 31, this year."

She momentarily turned her attention to Jack. "Do you know anything about gems?"

"I don't know a diamond from an ice cube, but when I saw that stone, I have to admit that I was tempted to ask around."

"But you didn't."

"Nope." Jack tossed down his pencil. "But if it were mine, I would."

"I'll have a jeweler look at it, but only because I can't place it," she told him. "It's just so…interesting, don't you agree?" Abby smiled.

Jack returned her grin. "I'd say interesting is an understatement."

"It's not that it's beautiful like a diamond or a sapphire. Not nearly as refined," she noted, settling the gold chain back into the box. "It's just unique."

"I never thought to ask, but would you like help putting it on?"

"No thanks. I'd rather not." Abby shifted in her seat. "I've just never liked necklaces—on me, that is," she told him.

"Not jewelry in general," he pointed out.

"Nope." She fiddled with the large onyx ring she wore. "In fact, I don't own a necklace."

"Talk about Murphy's Law."

"Oh, it's okay." Thoughtful, Abby turned the stone in her fingers. "Don't get me wrong. I like the look of necklaces, and this is by far the most beautiful one I've ever seen," she qualified. "I think they look great on other woman."

She couldn't help but notice his amused expression. "Smirk, if you like, but I don't even like turtlenecks. They just feel too tight, or something."

"Neck phobic? Now that's a new one." Jack eased back in his chair and studied her face. The angle of her jaw. The tilt of her chin. The curve of her lips. "Or maybe you were attacked by a vampire in a past life."

"I don't think so." For some reason, she found it easy to play along with him. "I believe if that were true, I'd have turned into a vampire myself."

"Not necessarily," he pointed out. "You wouldn't change if you were only bitten once or twice. If you check your basic vampire lore, I'm pretty sure it takes three bites to transform the victim."

"Third time's the charm?"

Jack shrugged. "Only if you find that whole eternal life thing appealing."

"And you don't?" Abby slipped the lid onto the box.

Willing his gaze away from the box, Jack took a breath. "Not if I had to go through eternity alone."

"Now that's romantic." She grinned.

"Ya think?"

"Um hmm. What good would flitting through the ages do without your true love? That would make living forever—"

"One helluva long time." Jack cleared his throat. "I realize it's late, but if you haven't eaten lunch, I know a great place nearby."

"I'd like that. I came here straight from the airport." When Abby's mouth opened, the words had simply tumbled out. Had she based her decision on the haunting sense of familiarity that had settled around her since she met Jack Hawthorne? Or was it simply hunger? Regardless, how much harm could one meal do?

"Lunch it is." As Jack stood, the phone rang. He checked his watch. "This might be the call I was expecting," he explained. "Excuse me just a minute."

"Hello."

Hawthorne shook his head in Abby's direction, confirming the change she'd heard in his voice. This phone call was personal, not business.

"I'm on my way out." Jack snagged a piece of paper from his desk, crumpled it and tossed it in the waste can. "I'll call you back."

Abby rose, purse and pine box in hand.

"We can discuss that tonight." He held up one finger. "I told them we'd be there at seven."

The moment Jack put down the phone, Abby insisted, "I can see you're busy, so, I think I'll just pass on lunch. That obviously wasn't the call you've been waiting for, and I really should be going anyway."

Jack nodded an apology. "Thanks for coming. I'm sure Maxine already had you sign all the appropriate forms."

"Yes, she's really quite amazing," Abby commented, moving toward the door.

"Maxine?"

"Efficient and friendly. In my experience that's rare." She faced him. "You look shocked."

"Let's just say, it normally takes people a while to warm up to Maxine."

"That's funny. We clicked right away." Abby shrugged. "Thanks for everything, Mr. Hawthorne."

"It's been a pleasure."

"Yes, it has." Abby reached for the door.

"Do you want to get a hotel room?"

Her hand missed the knob. "Excuse me?" She held her breath.

"Reservations," he clarified. "If you're not leaving tonight, I just wondered if you made your reservations yet? If not, you can call from here."

She exhaled. "Yes, I made those arrangements before I came." This time her fingers found their mark. "I'm staying in Salem."

"Ah, the witch city."

His comment sent a shiver down Abby's spine. "Uh huh."

Jack rounded his desk as she opened the door. "Sounds like you'll be doing some sightseeing."

"Well, I did come a long way." All she had to do was just thank the man and go. So, why didn't she? Instead, she stood in the doorway, trying to spit out the simple word *good-bye* to a total stranger. "Things back home are kind of up in the air right now, so I'm staying a few days."

Trying to keep his mind off the amulet, he closed the gap between them. "Then let me show you around while you're here."

Abby liked his relaxed grin. His easy way. And something else she couldn't quite put her finger on. "Thanks. I'd like that. I guess there's no better guide than a local, right?"

"Absolutely. Let's start with breakfast tomorrow morning," he suggested. "What time?" He leaned against the doorframe.

Abby shrugged. "How about ten o'clock?"

"Ten it is."

"I'm staying at Hannah's Inn. I think it's on…Esther…No, Lennox"

"Essex Street," he corrected.

"That's it." Pine box in her grasp, Abby hiked up the shoulder strap of her purse and extended her free hand. "Thanks again for finding me."

"You're welcome."

When the phone rang, Jack released his grip. "That might be your call." She flexed her tingling fingers.

He rubbed his palm. "See you tomorrow."

Chapter Nine

Exhausted and probably a little jet lagged, Abby propped up her pillows before settling into them. The devastating past few weeks had ripped Abby Corey's heart to shreds and literally destroyed her world. Her business had been torched. Her home had been gutted. And her dear, sweet friend had perished in the fire.

Since that fateful night, Abby had battled the agonizing pain and put up a damned good fight. But as the hours had turned into days and the days turned into weeks. Abby realized she might have won the battle, but she was definitely losing the war. An ache had settled deep in her chest like a powerful magnet that was drawing every ounce of life from her blood. Regardless of how hard she had tried, Abby could not come to terms with all she had lost. Her memories had rolled and ebbed like the tide, until she suddenly felt them stagnate in the bottomless pool of dread that had replaced her soul. Should she die tomorrow, Abby wasn't sure that would be the worst that could happen to her. She pulled the fluffy down comforter under her chin.

Despite all that, or maybe because if it, right now, more than anything, Abby needed to feel connected to something…someone. Although she shouldn't have, for some reason Abby trusted the way the lawyer distracted her from the empty grave she recently called her life. Realistically, of course, she knew that she didn't know Jack Hawthorn from Jack the Ripper. Besides, a five-year-old wouldn't believe the story he'd told her about the necklace she inherited. Not to mention the fact that her judgment had been clouded by sorrow so deep it made her bones bleed. Now, she decided, was not the time to make decisions about distractions in general, men in particular and that elusive void she was beginning to call her existence.

And that's when Abby smelled it. *Impossible.* She closed her eyes and inhaled. That was the fragrance Kat had created. *No way.* Abby shook her head and willed away the all-too-familiar scent. But the recognizable bouquet refused to budge. Instead, it lingered around her. Teasing. Taunting. Maybe it was something that just smelled like Kat's cologne. Opening her eyes, she felt like a fool. After all, Boston had to be full of fresh, innovative scents. Surely there could be at least one that smelled similar. Besides, how could Abby even trust her own judgment right now? The stress she'd suffered since the fire had been unbearable. She'd lost her home and her business, but most of all she'd lost her best friend.

Abby inhaled again very slowly this time. No, dammit, that was Kat's scent. Abby would know it anywhere. Who could forget the delicate blend of flower essences, exotic grasses, rare wine resins and essential oils from France, Italy, and Egypt?

Kat had had such a talent for combining fragrances. The scent her friend created had been in a league of its own, and that's exactly why Abby had convinced her to name it *Extraordinary*. Because, just like Kat, nothing could compare.

Abby refused the tears welling up in her eyes as she willed away the past. For now, she had to exorcise the good memories along with the bad. Maybe someday it wouldn't have to be that way, but for now they all had to go.

Abby smelled it again. *This is simply not possible.* You're halfway across the country. She sniffed. *It was not only possible, her mind conceded, it was, in fact, Extraordinary.* Abby gasped, then held her breath. At least, if she didn't breathe, she couldn't be affected by it. Didn't have to think or feel or hurt. Her lungs began to burn, but she refused to take a breath.

When she could stand it no longer, Abby let out a huge exhale. "Dammit, Kat, is that you?"

Abby felt foolish. Smelling Kat's cologne was bad enough. But talking out loud to her dead friend—Jesus H. Christ, she had finally lost it—big time. And then the fragrance grew stronger. Abby's gut twisted. "Okay. Let's just say you're here," she said. A pressure built up in her chest, mimicking what it felt like when they piled stones on people to kill them. And that's when the tears began to fall, scalding both her cheeks.

"I'm so sorry, Kat," she whispered, tossing off the covers and coming to her knees in the middle of the bed. "I am so very sorry you were in my apartment. If I could have changed places with you that night I would have." She clasped her hands together as if in prayer and closed her eyes. "If I could change places with you right now, I would. I swear I would. It should have been me who died, not you."

As the fragrance faded, Abby gradually regained her composure and her eyes fluttered open. Flipping out, she reasoned, probably wasn't that unreasonable. In fact, it was a freakin' miracle she had held it together as long as she had. She took a calming breath and sat down, bracing herself with both arms. Regardless, falling apart wasn't Abby's style, and she knew it. She was a pulled-together woman, who could weather even the harshest tragedy, which obviously this had been, and she wasn't about to lose it now. Besides, Kat would have kicked her butt fifty ways for Sunday for not bucking up. Abby swiped both cheeks and rolled her shoulders. Maybe a good night's sleep was all she needed. Well, that and one helluva stiff drink. And, since there was no liquor in her hotel room, she'd have to settle for sleep…when all she wanted was answers.

What really happened that night? Why did some son-of-a-bitch break into her apartment and brutalize Kat? Why did the bastard torch her shop and her home afterwards? Too exhausted to bear the weight of these questions, much less their answers, she turned out the light. Pulling the soft comforter under her chin, Abby closed her eyes. She'd had enough unanswered questions for one night. Hell, she'd had more than enough for a lifetime.

Chapter Ten

"She's the one!"

The dark-haired beauty pointed a finger at the woman seated across the room and remained quiet while chaos broke out around her.

"Are you absolutely certain?" The deep voice of the man behind the podium could barely be heard above the crowd, but his penetrating stare commanded the woman's attention.

Her face flushed, matching the red bodice of her otherwise unadorned black dress. Long dark curls bobbed up and down, escaping the confines of her loosely-tied bonnet as she nodded. Slowly standing, her pale blue eyes pinned the accused and everyone in the room grew deathly still. Her cheeks hollowed as she hissed her accusation, "She's a witch!"

The meeting room went wild. All eyes focused on the beautiful red-haired woman being held in her seat by a grim looking guard. Despite his efforts, the accused jumped to her feet in horror.

The candles reflected the panic in her emerald eyes and highlighted the deep copper colored hair cascading around her shoulders like a shawl.

"I'm not a witch," Abby shouted, trying desperately to be heard above the din. "What are you saying? Are you crazy?"

The guard's firm grip on her arm brought her soundly back into the chair.

Wooden floor planks vibrated beneath her feet as the mob stamped in unison. The people shouted, and the dank musty air hung heavy with intensity. Men cursed, raising balled fists in anger, while women fainted.

"Stop this," Abby cried. "There's been a mistake. I've never seen that woman before in my life…"

She heard her words dwindle away in the madness. Licking her lips, she tried desperately to wash away the fear and keep her wits.

Huge wooden shutters blocked the windows, making the room so dark she could barely see. Where was the door? She couldn't remember. There had to be a way out! Her eyes darted frantically. Tears scalded her cheeks, but she refused to lose control. She knew if she did, all was lost.

"Witch! Witch! Witch!" The chant surrounded her.

Abby heard what sounded like the pounding of a gavel trying to restore order. Or, was it the pounding of her heart?

"Hang her by the neck," one man shouted. A cheer rose from the mob.

"Burn her at the stake," her accuser screeched in a shrill voice filled with insanity. "The flames will match the fiery crown of hair Satan has already bestowed on her and prepare her for an eternity in hell!"

Reaching a fevered pitch, they cried, "Send Satan his queen!"

Shadowy figures cloaked in black moved closer. Their white collars floated around her like ghostly apparitions. Hands reached for her as the candlelight shimmered on their distorted faces. Fighting the terror rising within her, she wiped her clammy palms on her skirt. They were coming after her and Abby knew if she gave in to the urge to panic, it would be fatal.

Someone on the floor grabbed the hem of her skirt. "Get her!" the faceless woman shrieked.

They were too close. Abby's mind reeled when she felt their hot breath. All she could do was back away.

"What do you want from me?" she pleaded.

Everything was happening so fast. "Don't touch me!" she implored. Her only hope was escape.

From somewhere in the darkness, steel-like fingers wrapped around her wrist like a shackle. Her arm felt nearly broken by the iron grip claiming her like a possession.

She turned to face the tall man whose muscular body was clothed all in black. Leather boots encased his legs up to his thighs. His face was hidden in the shadows, but she could tell his hair was as dark as the cape hanging wildly about his broad shoulders.

Was it the devil himself? Before Abby knew what was happening, he snatched her from the greedy mob as if it were child's play. Somehow he found the door.

Once they were safely outside, the moonlight at his back again made it impossible to see the face of this man who had just saved her life.

He reached out and gently lifted her hand to his lips. She had never experienced such a sensation of relief as his mouth reassuringly touched her palm. His lips were soft and moist against her skin. She wanted to stay forever within this haven of safety.

Then, like the crisp October breeze enveloping the shadows and chilling her to the bone, he was gone. She was alone.

Chapter Eleven

Abby sat straight up in bed, gulping back the scream that threatened in her throat. Frantic and disoriented, her eyes searched for a point of recognition. Something, anything familiar that would cast out her nightmare. And that's when she saw it.

The soft glow from atop the chest of drawers grounded her back in the present. The soothing night-light reminded her she was at Hannah's Inn in Salem. Its gentle radiance reminded that she'd just had a bad dream, nothing more. Her breathing slowed as she brushed the tears from her cheeks and snuggled back under the covers.

She'd had nightmares all her life, and some had been unsettling, almost precognitive, but they had never been this realistic. She stretched both arms overhead and yawned. Suddenly, very relaxed and very sleepy, she watched the comforting light and thought only of the tall, dark stranger in her dream.

. . .

Abby's lashes fluttered as her eyes adjusted to the brilliant sunshine. Even though she remembered her dream and knew it had been vivid, to say the least, it seemed more like a vague memory this morning. Funny what a little sleep and broad daylight could do for the psyche. Besides, who wouldn't fantasize about an angry mob? For crying out loud, she was in Salem, Massachusetts.

Anxious to see the New England countryside, she hopped out of bed and opened the window to invite in the crisp, fall breeze. The view was nothing short of magnificent. As far as she could see, the trees weren't just red; they were crimson. Yellows were rich shades of gold and bursts of orange ranged from pumpkin to rust.

A frosty gust sent Abby diving back under the cozy, down comforter. Snuggling beneath the bedclothes, she surrendered to the inn's nostalgic aura and the majesty of the huge brick fireplace opposite her canopy bed. Daylight enabled her to distinguish the intricate birds and hearts carved in low relief along the mantel. Taking it all in, Abby sighed in appreciation. If it hadn't been for Jack's promise of breakfast and his offer to show her around Salem, she would have spent a very uncharacteristic morning right where she was.

Instead, she shut the window, showered, then slipped into jeans and a comfy, cotton sweater the color of freshly ground cinnamon. As she rechecked her makeup and brushed her naturally curly, auburn hair, uninvited thoughts of Jack came to mind totally without Abby's permission. Her hand stopped mid-stroke. Hawthorne was a stranger. Nothing more, nothing less. So, why on Earth did he feel so damned familiar?

Abby banished the tall, dark image of the man she had dreamt about, swearing he did not resemble Jack Hawthorne. Besides, the man's name was Jack for God's sake. Remembering J.T. and Jacques, Abby realized she had *done Jack* twice before in her life, and both relationships had ended with less than stellar results. And even if the dream guy did remind her of Hawthorne, common sense insisted he was the only man she had met since arriving in Salem. It wasn't any wonder a man fitting his description appeared in her dream.

Refusing to fuss, Abby set down her brush and decided there was nothing to do but wait. Well there was that…and to listen to the clock tick. The steady beat challenged the silence and made it impossible for her to sit still. Recalling bits and pieces of Salem's modern day folklore, she went to the window and looked out on the peaceful town below. Could what she'd heard be true? Did Salem really have a large group who still practiced witchcraft?

Drawn to the small pine box, Abby stood in front of the chest of drawers and realized she had left the necklace out last night. But had she? She could have sworn she put it back in the box before getting into bed. That's when she remembered the soothing night light that had comforted her back to sleep after her dream. So, where the hell was it?

Except for her amulet and the box it came in, the dresser top was uncluttered. There was no light of any kind. No lamp. No bulb. No lantern. Not even an electrical outlet. Fortunately for Abby, broad daylight didn't lie. That much she knew. However, nightmares, especially the vivid ones, could seem pretty darn real—even the next morning. That much she also understood. The only explanation was that the strange nightlight must have been part of her dream, too.

Abby lifted the chain as though it were made of spun glass and dangled the stone. She had the same thought every time she looked at it. Exquisite. Moving to the mirror above the dresser, Abby held the amulet above the V-neck of her sweater. Against her smooth, tanned skin, the amber stone seemed to warm. Fascinated she watched as it pulse in the sunshine. Slow and steady. Like a heartbeat.

Her brow wrinkled.

Impossible. The sun wasn't shining directly on the necklace. So, how on earth could the pendant catch the light? Well, she reasoned, that was a no brainer—it couldn't. The odd glow must have been glinting off something inside or maybe a shiny object outside. She looked around the room—nothing. The same when she went to the window. Not one reflection as far as the eye could see. Again the soothing, pulsating stone drew her gaze. Confused, but not quite frightened, Abby shook her head.

"Witches, nonexistent nightlights and phantom strangers be damned." About mid-rant Abby's stomach reminded her that she'd been jet lagged and exhausted last night and had forgotten to eat dinner. Suddenly famished, she checked the time again. Ten o'clock.

Tag-teamed by relentless intuition and a niggling, unexplainable disappointment, Abby placed the necklace back in the box and started to put it in her suitcase, but before she could a gust of cold air stopped her mid step. The curtains fluttered. She blinked.

"What the hell?"

She checked the window. It was still shut and locked. But the curtains had moved. She had seen them. Hadn't she? Of course she had. There must be a draft coming in from somewhere—that was the only logical explanation. And at least for now, that was good enough for her.

Suddenly as anxious to get the hell out as she was unwilling to leave the necklace behind, Abby slipped the pine container into her purse. Shaking off the strange events of the morning, not to mention her dream, she shut the door behind her. Hawthorne or no Hawthorne, she was out of there.

"My breakfast. His loss," she muttered.

A brisk walk to a quaint, sun porch cafe combined with coffee and a warm cinnamon roll did wonders for her disposition. No more unexplainable chills. No compulsions to pull out the amulet and look at it. No bizarre pulsing lights as far as the eye could see. Satisfied that she was surrounded by nature's beauty—nothing more, nothing less—Abby relaxed.

Funny, she thought, how impossibly familiar the surroundings seemed. Gold and rust colored mums lined garden paths separating the tables, while the last roses of summer dignified an old, brick privacy wall nearby. Just like that wonderful autumn picnic on her sixteenth birthday.

The day had been beautiful, she recalled. So much like today. Turning leaves, an unseasonably warm breeze. Glorious sunshine. She would never forget receiving the riotous bouquet of burgundy mums—much like the ones in Hawthorne's office.

Abby stopped. Wait a minute. That wasn't right. She'd spent her sixteenth birthday in the hospital. Not only had it stormed like something out of a horror movie, but she'd had an appendectomy. The picnic memory, she decided, must have been some other birthday. Although, try as she might, she still couldn't remember which one.

Turning her attention, Abby breathed in the sweet, soft scent of a nearby bed of petunias and understood why even the locals preferred to travel Salem on foot. Her eyelashes fluttered closed as she imagined the early Americans traipsing these same streets in their black and white pilgrimesque outfits.

Abby could almost see Benjamin Hooper building the Hathaway House in 1682. Hadn't that structure housed the first public bakery? And there was the Witch House. Hadn't the magistrates held preliminary examinations of witnesses in the 1692 witch trials there? Yes, she remembered, because Magistrate Jonathan Corwin had been one of them.

Her eyes widened, and she glanced around. What the hell? Why did she feel like she had just taken an unexplainable trip down memory lane?

Historic surroundings. That had to explain it. Well, that and one too many travel brochures. Refocusing on the scent of freshly baked bread wafting through the outdoor restaurant, Abby shook off her cryptic, not to mention ridiculous, thoughts and finished eating. After breakfast, she walked to the foot of Turner Street and entered Hawthorne's House of the Seven Gables.

Chapter Twelve

Umbrellaed in shadow, Zeke leaned against the trunk of a giant oak tree and observed Abigail Corey through the veil of crimson leaves that weighed down its branches. As imposing as he was, he somehow managed to blend in—a talent his line of work had demanded. As he studied the Corey woman finishing her coffee on the sunny café patio, his thoughts returned to the night that he torched Aromatiques.

As feisty as her friend had been, and she had put up one amazing fight, in comparison, Zeke wished Abigail Corey had been the one he had found upstairs. Not just because that Bishop woman flipped when she found out it had been Abigail's friend, Kat Richards, who had perished in the fire. But from the looks of the illustrious Miss Corey, he had missed out on one hell of an opportunity.

After seeing her this morning, he definitely planned to make up for losing out the first time around. From her shiny auburn hair to the curve of her ass in those jeans, the woman was hot. And even from his vantage point across the street, he sure as hell didn't mind looking. Of course, touching would be better, much better, but he would save that for later. Zeke's gaze narrowed as he interlaced his fingers and straightened both arms. As his knuckles cracked his resolve strengthened.

• • •

Abby started out with a gregarious group of tourists, but quickly struck out on her own. For some reason, the congenial group grated on her nerves. But, more than that, she was aggravated with herself for not having a better time. And why was that? She couldn't put her finger on it, but the strange uneasiness she'd experienced earlier had returned. And not just come back, but it had grown into a foreboding restlessness, much more than anxiety, and she simply could not shake the feeling. Probably just the events of the past few weeks, she reasoned. The fire. Kat. Her heart sighed. She had to use this time to regroup and take hold of her life again.

If nothing else, Abby had needed distance. A true, physical separation. September thirtieth had changed her entire world. She would never, ever be the same again. Right now, however, what Abby needed most was time enough to contemplate her future. Or, at the very least, the uncertainty of her future and what that meant.

Lagging behind the others, Abby heard their irritating chatter fade as they moved on. Finally, peace and quiet. Able to browse at her own pace, she coaxed herself to relax and enjoy. After all, she had always wanted to visit Salem. Not only was the town steeped in legends, but its history had fascinated her for as long as she could remember. So why was she still so on edge?

A cloud veiled the sun, casting a disturbing gloominess over the room. She shivered. Anticipating, what? Abby noticed a tall man, probably a good six feet six step around the corner at the far end of the hall and face her. Muted by the shadows his bald head and pale skin accentuated dark, penetrating eyes. He stood momentarily and stared. The hair on the nape of Abby's neck stood on end. Behind Abby a door slammed.

"Did you know the wood-closet next to the fireplace contains a secret passage?"

Abby gasped. It took a split second for the sound of Jack's voice to register. She turned to face him. "No, Mr. Hawthorne, I can honestly say I did not know any such passage existed—secret or not." When she turned back the tall, menacing man was gone.

"About this morning—"

"Forget it." She shrugged.

"I'm sorry about being late."

The sincerity she sensed in his tone touched her. "Really, forget it."

"Okay." He looked around. "How's the tour going?"

"It's just getting started, but it's great." Who was she kidding? She was not enjoying the tour. And she hadn't just taken this trip out east to pick up the amulet. She had come to Boston to make some major decisions about her life. As much as she would have given to change the events of the past few weeks, she couldn't. No one could.

"So, why don't I believe you?"

"Beats me. I guess lawyers are just the suspicious type." As the sun came back out and chased the shadows away, Abby knew going forward, whatever path life presented, the one had always been her only option. Presently, however, she was not in any way prepared to face the devilishly handsome man asking the questions. If possible, she decided, Jack was even more attractive than she remembered. Dark, windblown hair. Sexy grin. Sunglasses.

Abby fought the obvious resemblance between Jack and the man in her dream, trying her best to ignore his black cotton sweater and well-worn black jeans—a modern day version of the phantom's attire. She shook off the nightmare and folded her arms, not sure exactly what it was she wanted to hear. "Well, what happened?"

Jack pulled off his Ray-Ban Aviator sunglasses and slid one bow down the front of his sweater. "Maxine called at the crack of dawn. Major computer problems among other things. I had to go to the office." He moved in Abby's direction.

She took a step back. "Ms. Spencer works on Saturday?"

"Maxine works whenever she damn well pleases. Always has," he explained. "As it turned out, it's a damn good thing she went in today."

Abby couldn't argue with his explanation. "So, everything's fine now."

"Yes." Jack shoved both hands into his jeans' pockets. "When I found out I wasn't going to make it by ten o'clock, I tried to call, but you had already gone."

She listened. Wishing he wasn't so close. Wishing he was closer. Wishing she could figure out why this stranger simply did not feel strange to her.

"You know," he added, "you could have cut me some slack and at least waited a few minutes."

"When you didn't show up, I decided your offer might have been tentative." She arched one brow. "You know a proper offer to placate the client."

Jack stepped directly in front of her. "Legal or otherwise, I don't offer my services lightly."

The sincerity in his eyes echoed the honesty in his voice. "That's good to know," she managed, considering how close he stood.

Jack glanced around. "Don't look now, but I think you've lost your tour guide."

Deliberately putting a little distance between them, she walked to the doorway and peaked around the corner. "I guess I did."

"My offer still stands."

"Oh, I don't know." She shrugged her shoulders but returned his smile. "Maybe I should find a real guide. You don't even live in Salem, do you?"

He raised both palms. "No, but my ancestors did. Does that count?"

"Really?" She thought a moment, then snapped her fingers. "Did your Hawthornes used to be Hathornes—until they added the 'w'?"

"Guilty as charged."

"So, you're related to John Hathorne, the magistrate that conducted the preliminary examinations prior to the witch trials of 1692." It wasn't a question.

"My great, great, great Grandfather, or however many greats it takes to go back over three hundred years."

"And Nathaniel Hawthorne?"

"Culpable again." Lowering his hands, Jack slipped one arm around Abby's waist. "Since I've got the Hawthorne, or should I say the Hathorne clout, looks like you're coming with me after all." In the professional monotone of a guide, he continued, "Now, as I was saying, this wood-closet hides a secret stairway to the master bedroom. It was used as a means of escape from possible Indian attacks."

Abby couldn't help but relax. Neither could she ignore the warmth of Jack's hand on the small of her back, nor the comfortable, ridiculously familiar feeling she got from the gentle pressure of his fingertips.

"Just Indian?" she asked. "Or any type of unwanted attack?"

Jack's laugh was low and suggestive as his fingers tightened against her skin.

"You misunderstood." He enunciated clearly, "I said the passage led to the master bedroom."

"Oh, I understood all right," Abby assured him. "Apparently you haven't talked to some of the same women I have."

"Touché. But that's simple enough to explain," he said.

"Really?"

"Those women just haven't met the right man."

"Talk about over simplification." Her eyes narrowed. "And you believe that's all there is to it? Finding your true love solves everything?"

"That's it in a nutshell," Jack concluded. "The operative word being *right*, of course. Well that, and the concept of one man and one woman who are meant to be together."

Abby rolled her eyes. "Surely not soul mates." She turned away from the certainty in Jack's stare.

Without answering, he led her through the doorway and continued through the rest of the house.

Abby bent down. "Look how low the doorknobs are."

"That's because in 1668 people weren't as tall as we are now. See, even the furniture is smaller."

Her eyes narrowed. "Are you sure you don't do this for a living?"

"Positive."

"Maybe just on the weekends?" she prodded.

"Nope."

"But, you're so good at it."

Jack looked her straight in the eye. "There are a lot of things I'm good at that have nothing to do with my job."

"Then, what you're saying," Abby arched one brow, "is you're just not good enough at these other things to earn a paycheck."

Jack pressed both hands across his chest. "You're killin' me here."

"And to think I never believed lawyers had a heart." Abby didn't wait for a reply. Instead, she opened the door and stepped outside into the bright, autumn sunlight. Back into the twenty-first century.

As she expected, Halloween week in Salem was notoriously popular. Camera toting tourists flocked to Massachusetts to experience All Hallows Eve in the Witch City. *October thirty-first in Salem.* The thought snaked through her mind, desperate to unearth something that felt as though it had been buried a long time ago. Something ominous. Maybe even dangerous. But just out of reach. Whatever it was, Abby felt confident her psyche would exhume it eventually. Until then, her unease would just have to rest in peace.

Working their way through the crowd, Abby noticed how Jack kept her close, taking her hand in his. His warm, strong fingers wrapped around hers like a glove. Funny how natural it felt.

Abby shelved the ridiculous familiarity right alongside the pulsing lights and frigid breeze she had experienced earlier in her room. Forcing herself to focus on the here and now, she shaded her eyes and scanned the busy street. "Where's your car?"

"I thought it would slow me down, so I parked it and walked."

Abby moved to put the sun at her back. She looked up, wanting to see Jack's face, more exactly his expression, when he answered her next question. "You were in that much of a hurry to find me?"

"Damn right."

Satisfied, she gave an inch. "That's awfully nice of you."

"Nice, hell." Jack slipped on his sunglasses. "I was already late. I didn't dare give that Irish temper of yours time to build a bigger case against me."

"Irish? What makes you think I'm Irish?" Abby defied his slow head-to-toe appraisal.

Jack shrugged. "Must be the hair."

She self-consciously touched a long auburn lock. "A lot of people who aren't Irish have red hair."

Jack started to walk through the maze of people. "Name one," he challenged, working his way toward the sidewalk.

Falling easily into step, she shot back, "Howdy Doody."

Jack shook his head. "Doesn't count. He's made of wood."

As he maneuvered around two dangerously rambunctious preschoolers with noticeably melting, chocolate ice cream cones and a very pregnant mother, Abby smiled before deciding on her second choice. "Bozo the Clown."

Jack shook his head. "No way."

"Don't be so picky," she griped.

"Hey, his clown hair is literally attached to rubber scalp."

Laughing at the visual, she gave in. "Okay, then how about everybody's favorite redhead, Lucy?"

Before he could speak, she qualified, "You said name one. Technically, I named three. And there's not an Irishman among them."

Jack stopped and stepped closer. He took off his sunglasses, once again sliding one bow down the neck of his sweater. "Irish or not, your hair is beautiful." He wound a long curl around his finger as he spoke.

Something about the soft expression in Jack's eyes matched the gentleness of his touch. Abby suddenly felt delicate and cherished—two ungodly personal feelings, considering she'd known the man less than twenty-four hours.

"Where to now?" Abby asked, determined to get things back on track. One minute Jack was serious, and the next he was sexy. Not to mention this desire-thing that seemed to ebb and flow so easily between them. If nothing else, Abby knew she had to get a grip.

Jack checked his watch. "Unless you're hungry, we've got some time before lunch."

"Lunch? What happened to breakfast?" She poked him in the ribs with her elbow before she could catch herself.

He circled her. "I don't know, at first I thought it was the hair that made you sassy, but maybe it's heredity."

"You don't know a thing about my ancestry."

"Maybe not, but I know where heredity comes from." He gave her backside a quick look. "It's in the genes."

Abby groaned. "And this from a man with a law degree. That has to be illegal."

"Call a cop."

She shoved both hands in her pockets and increased the length of her strides. "You're criminal."

"You're gorgeous."

Abby couldn't even spell g-r-i-p right now, let alone get one. What she could do was file away his compliment and ask the one question that had been on her mind since yesterday. "I was just wondering. Have we met before?"

"No. Why do you ask?" As they walked, Jack eased Abby's hand out of her pocket.

"It's just—" she shrugged. "Honestly, I'm not sure." Strangely comforted by the gentle swing of their interlaced fingers, Abby couldn't help but notice the warm buzz she felt every time their skin touched. "Actually, I started to say that you look familiar, but it's not even that."

"What then?"

"I really don't know." Abby wished she had never brought up the subject. Right about now, she felt a little silly. Like earlier this morning in her room at the inn. Non-existent lights. Cold drafts from nowhere. Talk about stress induced anxiety.

"Well, do I remind you of someone you know?" he coaxed.

Matching his long strides, she looked up and studied his profile. Not remember a face like his? Fat chance. "Nope. I don't think so."

"How about someone you knew? Not recently, but in the past?"

"That's probably it." Apparently Jack wasn't going to give up and for some reason Abby needed a plausible link to explain their undeniable connection. Besides, his theory worked well enough for now. She had met countless customers and dealt with too many businessmen and sales reps over the last few years to count. Jack probably just reminded her of a prior acquaintance. That had to be it. So, why was she hearing the word *think* repeated over and over again in her head?

Like a one-two punch, a dog barked, and a cat hissed from nearby doorstep. Startled, Abby blurted, "Don't you feel it?"

"The familiarity?"

"Yes." The word escaped faster than a convicted felon—until a tourist let out a blood-curdling whistle that split the air between them like an ax. From behind a man raced past, coattails flapping, until he finally hailed a cab about two blocks further down the street.

Totally embarrassed, and at the same time relieved by the interruption, Abby immediately dropped talk of their kindred spirits like false charges. Whatever the two of them were feeling had to be hormones, plain and simple. There just wasn't any other explanation. She looked around. "Where are we headed now?"

"About what you said—"

Her head snapped up when he insisted on reopening the topic.

"I think some people just hit it off, that's all."

"Right," Abby agreed, a little too quickly. Her fingers slipped between his like the pieces of a puzzle.

"You never answered before. Are you hungry?"

She thought a moment. "I could eat."

Jack ushered her through the afternoon traffic to the colorful vendor across the street. He ordered without asking her, but Abby let it slide. Noting how the sky had clouded up, she pointed out an empty table beneath a huge multi-colored umbrella. Nestled between two gorgeous crimson maples, the view was perfect. She held up her sandwich. "You're lucky I like this."

He rested both elbows on the brightly striped, plastic tablecloth "I guess I never met anyone who didn't like a chili dog."

As the dark clouds grew darker, she sipped her drink, unwilling to say more about how familiar Jack seemed. "Ummm. This does taste like heaven. Do you know how long it's been since I had a black cow?"

"I didn't know anyone still called root beer floats that." He removed his straw and drank without it.

"See. That's how long it's been." Her laugh echoed the thunder that rumbled in the distance.

Jack polished off his first chili dog and without taking a breath reached for the second. "You know, I guess we never got around to it yesterday, but I don't even know what you do for a living."

Abby found it hard to believe, but thinking back she realized he was right. "Until a few weeks ago, I owned a shop called Aromatiques."

He blotted his mouth before asking, "Don't tell me you retired?"

"Not exactly. My building burned," she explained.

"I'm sorry." He grabbed her hand. "I hope no one was hurt."

"One employee." Abby inhaled deeply because that's the only way the words would come out. "Kat, my friend, died in the fire."

Jack placed his hand over hers. "Please accept my deepest sympathy, Abby."

"Thanks."

"I gather you two were close."

"We were friends." Abby struggled for control. "I always felt Kat was everything I wasn't. Resilient. Easy going. So much fun to be with…"

"She probably felt the same way about you."

"I hope so." With another big breath, she closed subject, because she had to—but she could never close the ache of her loss. That would be with her forever. "I lived above Aromatiques, so now I'm not only unemployed, but I'm homeless, too."

"That's terrible. What are your plans?"

Abby exhaled. "I haven't decided exactly what I want to do about either one. I hoped maybe some time away would help clear my head."

"Perspective is always good."

She reached for a napkin. "God, I hope so."

"So, Ms. Abby Corey is an entrepreneur."

"Well, I was. Technically, I guess I still am." She considered the concept, then added, "Mostly, I always wanted to be my own boss."

"What kind of shop did you have?"

She glanced around. "My place was similar to some of the boutiques here in Salem. I specialized in aromatherapy, candles, flowers, colognes, potpourri. You know, girly potions and lotions."

"Nothing for men?"

"In a manner of speaking we did sell something for that special man." She paused for effect…"We had some amazing sensual massage oils…" and saw his eyes narrow.

"I've been told they sell something like that around here."

She sipped her drink. "Just told about them, huh?"

Jack held up his right hand. "I plead the fifth."

"I'll bet you do," she agreed between bites. "They may have similar products here, but they're certainly not like mine."

"And what, may I ask, is so special about yours?"

"I make them myself." As Abby started to explain, a strong gust of wind fluttered their tablecloth, and she barely snagged her napkin before it blew away.

"Where did you learn something like that?" Jack wadded up all the paper wrappers and tossed them into the waste can next to their table. "Potions 101?"

"Nope. Just an old family tradition, I guess." As if from nowhere, dark clouds settled overhead. The wind kicked up and rustled through the maples, raining crimson leaves down around them. "The recipes I use have been passed down for generations."

"So, your mom made them, too?"

"I don't really know for sure."

"I see."

Certain the question was coming, Abby said nothing.

"Okay, I don't see."

And there it was. "I just hate discussing this aspect of my life, because it sounds like a soap opera."

Jack swiped his napkin across his mouth. "Hey, you don't have to explain anything to me."

"It's just that I was left in a basket on the doorstep of an orphanage." She held up one hand. "Swear to God that's the truth."

"Okay." He raked a hand through his hair. "Considering the bizarre circumstances surrounding the amulet inheritance, I guess I should ask who named you."

"A note with my name and birth date written on it was pinned to my blanket."

"And you were how old?"

"Two days."

"Then how did you find out about the recipes? You said they'd been handed down from your family."

"There was a book in the basket with me that was filled with recipes and what I've always called words of wisdom." She brushed a crumb from her lap. "Someone had written the word *Aromatiques* on the cover, but even then, the pages were fragile and had yellowed."

Jack thought a moment before asking, "Did the book burn in the fire that destroyed your place?"

"No, thank God." She tucked a windswept curl behind one ear. "Ironically enough I had it in my car that day."

"Lucky, huh?"

"You'd think, wouldn't you?" She saw the question in his eyes. The same one she had asked herself each and every day since. "Look, I have no idea what on earth possessed me to pick up the book that morning. I just don't know."

"If you had a reason, the trauma probably just blocked it."

"Maybe." That was as good as any explanation she'd come up with, and she had thought about it a lot.

He brushed an errant maple leaf from her shoulder and picked a smaller one from her hair. "So you really can't trace your heritage, can you?"

"Nope. I have no clue."

"Or, maybe you do. Considering your book of potions, maybe your ancestors were from Salem. Can't you imagine them bent over a big black cauldron, stirring up an old family recipe?"

"Caldron, huh?" Intrigued by his question, she thought a minute. "Did you know that in witchcraft, a caldron is an all-embracing symbol of Nature, the Great Mother?"

Jack shook his head and grinned. "I can honestly say I did not know that."

"As a vessel, it represents the feminine principle, and its three legs symbolize the triple moon goddess, Cerridwen." As certain of the specifics as she was uncertain where the information had come from, she continued, "The four elements of Life enter into it." Counting on her fingers, she listed, "Fire to boil, water to fill, green herbs to cook and fragrant steam that rises into the air."

Jack's eyes narrowed. "So, your ancestors *are* from around here."

"It's possible, I guess." Wouldn't it be something if her family originated from Salem? "At least would explain how and why I inherited the amulet."

"True. But as caldrons go," Jack pointed out, "you certainly seem to know your way around a seventeenth century stove."

"Not really." Abby shrugged, still surprised by what she'd told him. "I must have picked that up from some travel brochure or something."

"Probably just as well if your family wasn't from around here," he said. "Conjuring up exotic brews back then could have gotten them into a whole lot of trouble in Salem."

Dark eyes met green.

Thundered rolled in the distance.

And the rain began to pour.

Hand in hand, Jack and Abby raced down the street, rain soaking them to the skin.

"I know what we can do," he yelled.

"What?" Hardly able to hear above the thunderous downpour, she scrambled to keep up with his long, athletic strides.

"Ever have your fortune told?"

Abby's blood ran cold and not just from the storm. "No," she shouted back, every bit as much in response to his suggestion as it was an answer to his question.

"Great. That's what we'll do."

Thunder had clapped as he spoke. "What?" Abby asked, struggling to hang onto his water-slicked fingers.

"I said that's what we'll do."

Breathless at matching his sprint, she dodged umbrella-wielding tourists as he zigzagged down the crowded sidewalk. "You're kidding."

"I'm serious," he called over one shoulder.

Breathing heavily, Abby joined Jack as he turned a corner and ducked into the first available doorway. Her dark lashes blinked away unshed raindrops. Dripping, auburn hair deepened to match the cinnamon-colored sweater that had been plastered to her body.

The rain framed the two of them, splatting on the sidewalk at their feet. Its steady rhythm nudged her psyche, disturbing tucked away childhood memories. Not that Abby had forgotten. She'd never been that lucky.

Abby met his gaze and shook her head. "No fortune tellers."

"Why not?"

"Ever since I can remember, I've had these dreams," Abby confided.

"Well, that explains it."

She ignored his playful sarcasm and took a deep breath. "Most of the images I've seen have been very disturbing." Just like my nightmare last night, she added silently.

"That's not uncommon," he assured her. "Many people's dreams are vivid, even explicit."

She shook her head again. "When I have one of these, they're different. Nearly everyone I have that depicts some event that eventually comes to pass." She'd spent the better part of her life denying them, refusing them, chalking them up to coincidence brought about by an overactive imagination. Not telling anyone… until Jack. "So you can see why precognition, if that's actually what I experience, is not only unwanted but a little too close to having my fortune told."

"Are they bad things—the things you see in your dreams?"

"No." She offered a weak smile. "Not always."

"And you do realize these fortune tellers are not real, right?"

"Don't be ridiculous." Now she was feeling foolish. "Don't tell me. I can just hear my destiny now." Still holding Jack's hand, Abby turned it over and pretended to study what she saw there. In reality all she saw was one large, manly hand complete with long, strong fingers. The unexplainable familiarity made her heart smile; however, she continued the charade with a straight face.

Impressed by the strength she felt and the gentleness she sensed, Abby traced the lines then angled her glance as she slipped into a thick Gypsy accent. "I vill meet a tall dark stranger!"

"Well, that cuts it. If you don't know reading *my* palm won't tell your future, then you've got to go ahead with this. Besides, I already made an appointment with Sasha." Jack winked.

"You what?" Abby released his hand.

"Hey, I thought it would be fun. Besides, you don't really believe all that mumbo-jumbo, do you?"

"Let's just say, I believe in the theory of psychic phenomenon," she told him honestly. "I won't discount it, if that's what you're asking."

"It's pure hocus-pocus, nothing more," Jack swore.

Somewhere close by a car horn blasted and Abby jumped.

Jack grinned. "Hocus pocus got you a little spooked?"

She ignored her pounding heart. "Don't be ridiculous."

"Look, if you're really afraid, you don't have to do this."

Abby bristled at the implication. "Lead the way."

"Lucky you. We don't have far to walk." With a wide sweep of his arm, Jack gestured across the rain-puddled street. "Salem's premier fortune teller, Sasha, is set up right there in The Old Town Hall."

"Oh." She fought the urge to pull back. "Fine, let's go."

Chapter Thirteen

Abby found the building's dimly lit, cool interior only added to her uneasiness. Quick to blame the chill on her damp clothes, she gave herself a mental shake and turned her attention to Jack.

"This building was built in the early eighteen hundreds."

"The site of the Elias Hasket Derby mansion," Abby finished automatically.

"Right," Jack told her. "They did some renovation, and now the Salem Chamber of Commerce occupies part of the main floor."

"Makes sense," Abby admitted. "But what does that have to do with fortune telling?"

"During October this is where Salem conducts its famous Psychic Festival." His voice resonated in the historic silence. "You name it, they do it. I thought you'd get a kick out of it, so I called this morning and made sure Sasha would be here."

"Great," Abby muttered. She read the signs over the various doors: Fortune Telling, Palmistry, Astrology, I Ching, Tarot Cards, and Psychic Readings.

"Loosen up. It's just for fun." He poked her in the ribs. "All the tourists do it."

"Right." When her voice echoed, it dawned on Abby what was bugging her. They were the only people there. No picture-taking tourists, no shrieking children, nobody else. "If this is such a barrel of laughs, where is everybody?"

"Beats me." He leaned down and whispered, "It must be a trap."

"Very funny." She shoved him back. At that moment, the instant her hand pressed against his chest, something about Jack overwhelmingly reminded Abby of the tall, dark phantom from her dream. Not his face, because she hadn't seen the apparition's features. And not something bad. More Jack's presence than anything else.

Obviously, Hawthorne was human—a lawyer, in fact. Oxymoron or not, he was certainly no ghost. He was just a man... who happened to be a virtual stranger...dressed in black...the morning after her nightmare. She shivered.

"If you think fortune telling is such a crackerjack idea, have yours done, too," Abby challenged.

"I've already had mine done."

Hitching up her purse, Abby folded both arms across her chest. Finding no comfort in the still-soggy wool blend plastered to both arms, she eyed him. "Oh, all right."

After all, it couldn't it be any weirder than a three hundred-year-old inheritance bequeathed to a nonexistent woman living in a yet-to-be-built city? Could it?

• • •

Bridget handed the squat, old woman a crisp hundred-dollar bill. "That's for letting me know Mr. Hawthorne made an appointment. I just knew he'd show that bitch around."

Sasha tucked the Ben Franklin down the front of her shirt, between her hefty bosoms. "I did my part. Got anything for me?"

"As a matter of fact, I do. I have a recently widowed woman who would like to communicate with her dead husband, the poor dear."

"Has the poor dear got money?" Sasha mimicked.

Bridget's blood red lips curved. "Filthy rich."

The old woman's eyes widened. "When?"

Bridget thought a moment. "I'll send her by tomorrow night. Say eight o'clock?"

"Perfect." Sasha smiled. "The usual deal?"

"Sixty/forty split," Bridget told her. "And don't forget mine is the sixty."

The old woman cackled. "Works for me."

Extending one well-manicured nail, Bridget pointed to the restroom. "Now wait in there and stay out of sight until I come for you."

Taking Sasha's place, Bridget positioned herself behind the table and caressed the crystal ball as if it were the upturned face of a smiling child. Tenderly. Lovingly. Joyfully. She pulled the black candle and a match from the pocket of her long, flowing skirt. Striking a flame with the flick of her thumbnail, she lit the wick, whispering, "As this candle burns, so shall you, Abigail Corey, be cursed."

• • •

Abby assured herself that fortunetellers' visions were nothing more than money-driven hoaxes. Like magicians and illusionists, they were commercial con artists who had branched out from carnivals to those toll-free phone numbers on television. *For entertainment purposes only.* Wasn't that always the disclaimer at the bottom of the TV screen? So, why in the hell did the sound of the door opening make her heart clench?

After stepping into the dimly lit room, Abby took a seat in front of a striking woman with long, dark hair and pale, blue eyes. Dressed in black, except for a bright red bodice that matched her lips, and adorned with spangly gold jewelry, the seer's appearance was effective, to say the least. The silence, however, was eerie.

"My name is Sasha." Bridget spoke in a low, seductive voice as she walked around the chair and placed her palms on Abby's shoulders.

Abby stiffened at the strength of her touch.

"Please, relax."

Silently, she moved from behind Abby and sat down facing her. "Your aura is cool, a woman very smart in business." She paused before flashing a smile that made Abby feel as though they shared some intimate secret.

"There is another side to you. One you refuse to acknowledge. It is very strong, and very dangerous. You must fight it at all costs. You are of the Earth, the season. You do not belong here. Stay and you will destroy your past, your present, and your future. You will seal your destiny."

Placated by the generic hoodoo, Abby merely nodded.

"You had success, but it went up in flames," Bridget began.

Abby gasped.

Blue eyes locked with green.

"Like the full moon, life is a circle, so take great care," Bridget hissed.

When the expression on the seer's face dramatically changed, a tomb-like silence engulfed the room. "You have spent your life looking for something—yes? Someone?"

Abby shuddered, knowing she had spent her entire life yearning for something she'd never been able to define. Until now, she'd convinced herself the emptiness she felt was because she'd been orphaned. "No," she lied.

"Silence." Bridget's breath hitched. Her gaze widened. She leaned forward. "Believe me when I tell you someone has been waiting for you for a very, very long time. But beware. There will be grave danger if three paths cross."

Her lashes fluttered closed. "I need something—a piece of jewelry," she demanded.

"Alright." Abby started to slip off her onyx ring, when the amulet came to mind.

Without opening her eyes, Sasha ordered, "Give it to me."

Abby pulled the pine box from her purse and removed the lid. She noticed the red mark on the gypsy's upturned palm, much like a burn or brand of some kind before placing the amulet there.

When Sasha hissed and both eyes flew open, Abby's breath caught. Identical to her nightmare, she felt the sensation of being slammed back in time then immediately jerked forward into the present.

Sasha dropped the amber stone onto the table and fisted her hand.

"Dear God," Abby whispered.

When the black candle between them went out, Sasha's cold blue gaze turned to ice. The gypsy's voice whooshed from her lungs. "Beware."

Abby swore she saw a thin trail of smoke filter through the woman's clenched fingers. She blinked. The fumes had to have come from the extinguished candle, didn't they? Her mind screamed that this was not the first time she'd seen this. But that was ridiculous.

"I'm so sorry." Still concerned, Abby reached out. "Are you all right?"

Sasha snatched her hand away then pointed one blood red fingernail. "Never, ever wear that amulet, or you will die."

Chapter Fourteen

Abby seized the necklace, trying unsuccessfully to convince herself it did not feel hot to the touch. She'd simply been spooked by this overly theatrical performance. That was all. Barely convinced, she boxed the amulet and tossed it back into her purse, then stood. She heard her own breathless, "Thank you." Shaky legs nearly failed her as she made her way into the hall. It's only nonsense and gibberish, she repeated silently. Nothing more. The woman was just damned good, that's all.

When the door opened, Jack looked up. "Well?"

"Vague comments about success and family," she lied.

"See, that wasn't scary, now was it?"

"I never said I was frightened," she lied again. "I said I didn't believe."

Who was Abby kidding? The air around them seemed laden with foreboding. Danger? But what on Earth could be dangerous here? Duh. This was Salem, Massachusetts, a few days before Halloween. Some psycho passing herself off as a psychic had practically put a curse on her. Not to mention that ridiculous warning that she would die if she wore the amulet. What the hell was there to fear? Didn't matter. She wasn't sticking around to find out.

"Let's get out of here." Abby turned on her heels and headed for the door, and she did not wait for Jack to follow.

An invigorating walk to the car was exactly the diversion Abby needed to clear her head. As they made their way back, her long legs easily matched the rhythm of Jack's step. A scattering of rain-dampened leaves crushed beneath their feet, releasing the earthy smell of autumn.

The day had been surprisingly enjoyable, despite the downpour and the unnerving fortuneteller, and suddenly Abby dreaded for it to end. Amidst the surrounding beauty of the countryside, she needed time to put Sasha's strong reaction to the amulet and ridiculous warning, not to mention her own growing attraction to Jack Hawthorne, into perspective. As difficult as it was to believe, she was hard-pressed to say which bothered her more. But then her history of involvement with men named Jack or various forms of that name could probably defend her concern.

Jack pointed out a bright red cab. "Witch City Cab. Appropriate name, don't you think?"

Abby shrugged. "I think it's a clever advertising campaign, but it implies people still believe in witches."

"Many of the locals do." He checked the traffic and grabbed her hand, crossing the street before the light changed. "Haven't you seen the emblems and signs plastered all over town?"

She shivered. "That's what I mean." Fingers still linked through his, she hiked up her purse strap with her free hand. "The whole strategy is so obviously commercial."

"True." He sidestepped a big, blue mailbox where the postman was making the last pick up of the day. "But don't get the idea witches are a joke here."

"Well, maybe they shouldn't be," she insisted, not at all sure where she was going with her comment. "From what I understand, witchcraft is more a worship of nature than anything else. You know, the seasons, the circle of life, stuff like that." *Like the full moon, life is a circle.* The fact that her word choice mimicked Sasha's comment niggled at the fringes of Abby's mind.

"Oh, really." Jack gave her a sideways glance.

"Besides, you're just a little too well-versed on Salem," she insisted, needing but, for whatever reason, not wanting to forget the seer's words. "I still say you're probably a tour guide who poses as a lawyer on the side. You know, court for kicks."

"Like you, I'm just an avid history buff," he corrected. "In fact, you're looking at the newest board member of the Boston Historical Society."

"My mistake," Abby conceded, duly impressed. A gusty breeze ruffled the array of damp leaves covering the ground, and she brushed a wind-blown lock of hair from her cheek before looking up at Jack. Suddenly serious, she couldn't help asking, "How many witches would you say live in Salem now?"

"Rumor has it, several thousand."

"You're kidding."

"Nope. Even their police logo, The Witch City, pictures a hag on a broom."

Abby shuddered, trying to stifle the vivid images of her nightmare, as well as the pointed warnings of the fortuneteller. "I find that a little perverse."

Eager to change the subject, Abby glanced down the quaint street. There was something so welcoming and familiar about it. About the whole town, really. The streets in most cities could be interchangeable, but Salem didn't feel that way to her. She took a deep breath and really could imagine walking through this village over three hundred years ago on a day just like today with the intoxicating scent of autumn in the air.

"Earth to Abby." Jack snapped his fingers.

Shrugging off his smirk, she pointed to the nearby shops. "These boutiques look interesting. Want to—"

"Forget it. I don't shop."

"Well, I do." She headed straight for Wax 'N Wane. "Guess I'll just have to find another tour guide who does." Ignoring his low, contagious laugh, she walked through the front door without looking back.

Inexplicably drawn, she perused the rainbow of scented candles and oils. Without a thought about her aversion to fire in general and *the* fire in particular, she chose quickly. Working her way back to the front of the store, Abby had already carefully selected blue, gold, purple, yellow, and lavender votives.

"When's your birthday?" she asked, making her final choice—a pink one.

"June twenty-first."

Abby frowned at the pink candle in her hand and added it to the small wire basket hanging from the crook in her arm. She did not believe in coincidences. "Pink is for your zodiac sign of Cancer," Abby explained as she paid the clerk. "Your birthday falls on the summer equinox."

Jack opened the door for her. "And summer equinox is significant *because*?" he asked, drawing the word out.

She shrugged as they fell in step. "No reason, I guess. My birthday is September twenty-first, the day before the autumn equinox that's known as Mabon—the Harvest Festival."

As they worked their way through the throng of tourists, it was Jack's turn to shrug. "What the hell is a Candlemas?"

Abby blinked. "I'm not sure." The information came to mind slow and deliberate like long awaited, late-blooming flowers. She cleared her throat. "Wait a minute, it seems to me it's the four great feast-days of the Celtic year. I think there's one during each season."

Jack whistled. "Really?"

"Well, yeah. They were—" she took a breath "great Sabbats of the witches where they celebrated around a bonfire."

"Did your homework on Salem, huh?"

Abby offered a shaky smile. "Sure did," she lied, certain she hadn't, so she must have read about it. Just not recently. Of that she was also certain.

As they walked down the street Abby still couldn't shake the feeling of déjà vu. Something about the idea of Salem and bonfires and these houses seemed overwhelmingly familiar. Working their way toward the next intersection, she couldn't help but notice the residences off to the left. But one tall, cryptic house in particular stopped Abby in her tracks. Its peaks might have resembled steeples, but nothing else about the home felt church-like to her. Obviously several hundred years old, the charcoal color and thick iron fence added to its ominous presence.

Abby's sack from Wax 'N Wane rattled as a shiver yanked her to attention.

"Now there's a haunted house, if I ever saw one." Definitely not kidding, she continued, "You're the tour guide and I know this is Salem, but that place has to be inhabited by some infamous witch."

Jack coughed.

As Abby waited for an explanation, she unclasped her hand from his to instinctively touch the pine box in her purse.

"A woman by the name of Bridget Bishop lives there."

Abby's heart pounded.

"The house has been in her family for generations."

Abby's free hand slipped the lid off the pine box in her purse and located the amulet.

"As a matter of fact, Bridget is a friend of mine."

The stone heated in her grasp.

"So, in a word—no, it's not haunted."

When Abby's mind screamed, *that's what you think*, she filed it away with the fortuneteller's warning. *Believe me when I tell you someone has been waiting for you for a very, very long time. But beware. There will be grave danger if three paths cross.*

She jerked her gaze away from the house. "Which way?"

"I'm parked over there." He pointed to the silver B.M.W. convertible. As the light changed, they joined the rest of the tourists and crossed the water-puddled street. Jack held the door open and pointed toward the passenger seat.

"Next time. One rule," he told her. "No shopping. Now get in."

Abby slid onto the front seat. "Oh, you'll shop, Hawthorne."

She saw Jack laugh as he rounded the car. As he slipped behind the wheel, Abby laid her head back and stretched her legs the full length of the floorboard. In a day filled with unnerving familiarity, the engine hum released an unfamiliar feeling of contentment that could have lulled her to sleep had she not been so disturbingly aware of the man seated beside her.

She studied Jack's profile against the still blustery, late afternoon sky. Windblown hair, black as midnight, curled across his forehead. The impact of his disturbingly distinct features stirred something deep inside her. And the more time she spent with him, the more deeply she felt it. Despite her confusion, Abby gave in to the smile tugging at her lips.

Jack glanced her way. "What's so amusing?"

"Nothing." Abby focused her eyes straight ahead, but even the picturesque streets of Salem proved little distraction.

"If you say so."

Jack drove the last few blocks without saying another word, and as they pulled up in front of Hannah's Inn, Abby suddenly dreaded the long night ahead.

"Thanks for a wonderful day." Turning to face him, she deliberately reached over and laid her hand on his. The jolt was immediate, but she was careful to keep her palm in place. Studying his face, she was certain he felt the same sensation. "All kidding aside, you really are a terrific guide."

"My pleasure. How about dinner tomorrow night? I'll pick you up at seven-thirty."

Abby broke their unspoken connection. She grabbed her bag from Wax 'N Wane and slipped her purse over one shoulder before stepping out of the car. Facing Jack from the curb, she rubbed her tingling palm down one jean-clad thigh and saw the unmistakable recognition in his dark eyes.

Jack bussed down the passenger-side window.

"Sure, that'd be great." As Abby closed the door and watched him drive away, a little black kitten brushed against her leg and gave her a forlorn meow.

"Hey there, fella." She reached down and picked up the black ball of fluff. He was small enough to hold in one hand. Gently rubbing his head, Abby cooed, "You're just a baby. And so skinny. You must be starving." As she held him close and felt his little body purr softly against her neck, a verse popped into her head.

"Whenever the cat of the house is black, the lasses of lovers will have no lack," she recited quietly. "What in God's name?" Like too many other unexplainable insights today, Abby had no clue how she knew that phrase.

Overwhelmed by confusion and loneliness, she whispered, "Looks like it's just you and me tonight. So, here's the scoop. I'll get you something to eat, and you keep me company." She paused as if to listen. "You've got yourself a deal—" the named just popped into her head "—Shadow." Abby cautiously looked around the inn and shoved the furry creature in her shopping bag before slipping inside.

Chapter Fifteen

Salem, Massachusetts
1 October
Year of Our Lord, 1690

Darkness swirled around Abby much the way a cauldron's bubbling brew chases a wooden, shirring spoon. The gusty October breeze snatched at her bonnet and whipped the hem of her black cotton skirt. Her petticoats snapped around both ankles as she made her way down the narrow dirt path. Stumbling as she ran, Abby hurried home, glancing frantically behind her as though the devil himself was on her heels. Thunder rumbled in the distance, matching the pounding of her heart.

Relief, warm and welcome, washed over her as she finally spotted the small, log house. No candles in the window. No smoke curling from the chimney. No one there to greet her, but home nevertheless. Once inside, she fumbled with the door's heavy wooden beam, wrestling the rough-hewn barrier into place. Not at all eased by the makeshift lock, her breath still heaved as she lit a brass lantern and nervously peered out the window into the night.

Tall evergreens moaned and swayed, dancing helplessly to the rhythm of the eminent storm. Someone was out there, she had felt the eerie presence all the way home. Still could. As lightning split the sky in the distance, Abby saw the woman. Cape flying. Skirt flapping. Standing atop a hill at the edge of the clearing, her pale face shimmered in the wake of the electrifying bolt. Arms raised, her dark hair billowed around her head like an unholy halo.

Eyes riveted on the surreal figure, Abby's free hand instinctively sought the amulet that hung heavy around her neck. The smooth stone pulsed beneath her skin.

Thunder crashed, rattling the windows.

Lightning scorched the heavens.

Blinded by the glare, Abby blinked.

When she opened her eyes, the woman was gone.

Abby searched the blackness as the sky opened and rain unmercifully pelted the windowpanes. Heart pounding, she whimpered and backed away, planting her heels against the heavy wooden door. Like a bible to protect against evil, she clutched the necklace. Trembling fingers held fast the stone amidst the menacing gloom. One tiny beacon, shaking but steadfast in a terrifying sea of darkness.

• • •

For the second night in a row, Abby sat bolt upright in bed, an unspoken scream still lodged in her throat. Pulse pounding, desperate to get her bearings, her eyes darted wildly. No log cabin or driving storm. No spirits…past or present. No one outside her door.

As her breathing slowed, the serenity of Hannah's Inn bathed in the early morning light further calmed her. The exquisitely lush quilt. The enormous, down-filled pillows. The tiny kitten nestled beside her. Relieved, but not at ease, she laid back down, the amulet still unexplainably cocooned in her grip.

Shadow stretched himself awake and sidled over to Abby, looking her square in the eye. She scratched behind his ears and heard him purr.

"Breakfast, you say," she teased. "Why, yes, we have—" glancing at the tiny cans lining the dresser, she continued "— hearty chicken, tuna or salmon in rich gravy." When his tiny, rough tongue swiped her cheek, she nodded. "Salmon it is."

Abby scooped up Shadow and crossed the room. More than pleased by her makeshift litter/shoe box and gourmet cat food assortment, she opened the pop-top can and filled his bowl. A nearby shopkeeper had been more than helpful in supplying her new pal with all his personal kitty needs.

As the mantle clock struck seven-thirty, Abby nearly jumped out of her skin. Something about the chime struck an odd chord with her. Whether it was the plaintive sound or the essence of time itself, she realized there were twelve long hours to fill until she would see Jack again. What to do, she wondered, with half a day to kill?

The moment the question entered her mind, Abby felt ridiculous. After all, she was staying in one of the most historic, most sought after tourist sites in the country. This was autumn in New England, for God's sake, not monsoon season at Swamp Lake. Looking outside, the sun shined brightly and the cloudless sky was late-October blue. A beautiful fall morning surrounded the extraordinary countryside. With literally dozens of places to go and sights to see, why did she feel so uneasy?

• • •

Abby had returned from an afternoon of sightseeing, showered and dressed for dinner. Admiring the gorgeous amber stone, Abby was reminded that she had not only flown to Boston to pick up her inheritance, but she had come to contemplate her life. What it had been. What it is now. And what she wanted it to be. Having given it considerable thought, she decided to push aside her aversion to necklaces and wear the amulet. To hell with the stupid fortuneteller and her ridiculous warning.

Abby checked her watch again and noted she had well over a half-hour before Jack would arrive. Waiting patiently may not be her strong suit, but what she couldn't understand was why it felt like she'd been waiting for Jack Hawthorne for a very long time. That idea was not only impossible; it was downright crazy. Kind of like her inheritance. Regardless, unlike yesterday morning, she vowed to rein in her imagination and be calm. Besides, she wanted to make a quick trip to the drug store, and it was just around the corner. By the time she returned, it should be time to go.

• • •

In the lobby restroom, Bridget donned the maid's outfit then secured a short, gray wig as well as a pair of black horn-rimmed glasses. The bellhop she'd paid to let her know when Abby left the hotel had called right before he went off duty. He said Miss Corey had been dressed quite nicely when she left, and she looked like she would probably be out at least for dinner. Bridget may not be able to actually touch the amulet, but she had to retrieve it. She would try and use a pair of pliers to pick up the necklace, then slip it into the bucket that was underneath her maid's cart. Pleased at her plan, she used one long red fingernail to shove the fake front teeth into place, and the buck-toothed reflection that smiled back at her in the restroom mirror stood ready to secure her destiny.

• • •

As promised to Shadow, Abby returned within a few minutes. She had purchased the latest issue of "People Magazine," two packs of wintergreen mints, a Snickers candy bar and one adorable fake mouse cat toy. She smiled when Shadow snagged the toy and tossed it all over the room. When the doorknob rattled and a woman walked in, Abby's smile faded. Instead of Jack, she faced a tall, gray-haired maid.

"Can I help you?"

"Housekeeping," the woman said hoarsely as she backed toward the door.

"Must be another room, because I didn't call for anyone," Abby assured her.

"Sorry." The maid turned to leave.

"But, as long as you're here, could you do me a favor?" Abby approached her. "Could you fasten my necklace?" She dangled the amulet in front of the woman like a hypnotist suspends a pocket watch.

The maid jumped back so fast she nearly upended her cleaning supplies.

"No," the older woman croaked, holding up one hand in protest. "We're not allowed." She backed away, wagging one blood red fingernail at Abby. "Wrong room. Sorry."

Before Abby could say another word, the maid turned on her heels and hurried down the hallway with mops waving and buckets rattling as she pushed the overflowing, metal cart toward the elevator.

"Whatever," Abby muttered, confused that, once again, another perfect stranger reminded her of someone. A better question might be why so many people and places in this town struck her that way?

The old woman was a maid at the inn. Nothing more, nothing less. Abby had probably passed her in the hall. Or on the street. Or in a shop. And what difference did it make? She didn't know a soul in Salem besides Jack.

Closing her door, she gave the amulet's clasp one last try. It clicked shut without a problem just as someone knocked again. Abby grabbed her cape and hurried into the hallway as if the devil were on her heels. Instead, she found Jack. All six foot four of him. Black Armani suit. Crisp white shirt. And, for whatever inexplicable reason, *sooo* not a stranger.

Chapter Sixteen

In the restaurant parking lot, the cool night breeze whispered through the fallen leaves. As Abby stepped out of the car, her black cape fell open, and the pale moonlight shimmered the length of her chestnut-colored, beaded dress.

Once inside, she paused to stare at the unusual setting. "What on earth is this place; or, should I say what was it?"

"An old saw mill. After standing vacant for years, it was sold and converted into a restaurant by the new owners. The second floor is an inn."

She turned her attention to the huge, wooden paddlewheel in the corner of the lobby. A gentle trickle of water lazily turned the wheel, creating a tranquil, serene atmosphere. "It's lovely," she whispered, trying hard not to notice how the breeze had tousled his thick, dark hair.

"Not as lovely as you." He gestured around the room. "This is only scenery."

"You're too kind." *You're too kind?* Where the hell had that come from? Sounded like a line from a classic novel or a period movie. *Or what?* Her mind screamed the question. Why hadn't she just winked and said get outa town or something as simple as thanks?

Jack extended his arm. "Shall we?"

The restaurant's lights were dim. A blazing fire that roared in the stone fireplace on the far wall warmed the large dining room. Surrounded by the intimacy of the romantic New England Inn, Abby knew she dared not let down her guard, or Jack Hawthorne, like the phantom in her dream, would haunt her for eternity.

Jack ordered a Ben Nevis, neat, for himself and, again without asking, an Artesa Cabernet Sauvignon for her.

"Penny for your thoughts," he asked.

Abby leaned back. *Not even for your whole checkbook.* "I'm glad we came here," she hedged, her hand seeking the amulet.

"I thought you didn't wear necklaces."

"I don't." Abby touched it, enjoying the feel of it against her fingertips. She refused to believe the sensation had anything to do with the fortuneteller's warning not to wear it. "For some reason this piece just feels different."

"It does, doesn't it?"

"You know, throughout history amulets were thought to act as an occult shield to repel," she told him, realizing her explanation made the gypsy's warning not to wear the necklace all the more suspect.

"Like a talisman?"

"No, not really." Abby shook her head. "I know people think they're the same, but they're not."

"What's the difference?"

"A talisman is intended to attract some benefit to its possessor, not to protect." She heard herself differentiate between the two terms.

Jack leaned back. "Really?"

"Uh huh," she said, still holding the stone between her thumb and finger. "Amber—which is what this looks like to me—was called amuletum in ancient times, because it was believed to avert evil influence and infection. In fact, the word amulet is probably derived from the Latin amolior which means 'I repel,' or 'drive away'."

Abby's own words silenced her. She had no idea how she had come to know any of this. Just this side of being frightened, she decided being an avid reader had apparently paid off big time. After all, there wasn't any other explanation, was there?

Jack shrugged. "I take it you've done some research."

"Yeah," she lied, unable to explain what she'd told him.

"Sounds like you ought to be safe from the wicked folks of Salem," he teased.

"You'd think."

"What do you make of that mark in the middle?"

"I saw that." She nodded. "It's really interesting, isn't it?" Without waiting for his response, she squinted at the stone in the candlelight. "At first, I thought it was some kind of bubble, but I really think it's more tear-shaped than round, don't you?"

He leaned forward to take a closer look. "Yeah. Something may have been trapped in there, you know, like insects."

"Maybe." Green eyes met brown. "Jurassic Park wild, huh?" Abby released the stone and dropped the subject as well. She broke their gaze and looked around the large room. "This restaurant certainly is unique."

It wasn't until after the cocktail napkins and drinks had been placed on the table that Abby noticed the dance floor. Her heart nearly stopped. "Is that a set up for a band?"

"Yeah." Jack sampled his scotch. "Have you decided what else you would like to see while you're in Boston?"

"You're the guide. Just take me where the tourists go."

"Some sight seers have been known to check in and go upstairs."

There went her heart again. One slow motion somersault. Perfectly executed. For the first time in her life, she wanted to throw caution to the wind and live for the moment. The realization alone made her head spin. What she couldn't figure out was— why this man? Why was she so certain? Why were her feelings so strong?

Calling on every ounce of poise she could muster, Abby sipped her wine, then forced a coolness into her voice. "I'm sure the rooms are lovely, but I had something a little more *touristy* in mind."

"That should be an easy request to satisfy here in Salem." He sipped his drink. "In keeping with the seventeenth century theme, the community has restored everything to the period of time right around the witch trials."

Abby's fingers found her throat, and she absently fondled the amulet. "Then I'm surprised they have dancing here."

"Why?"

"Because dancing is an intricate part of witchcraft." When he just looked at her, she continued. "You know, the round dance. Like around a tree, a sacred stone or a bonfire. To raise power."

Still no response.

"Or, the witch's dance on riding-poles, leaping to make crops grow tall."

A blank look.

"Or the dance spiral where the witches dance into the center and out again to symbolize penetration into the mysteries of the Other World."

He shook his head.

"It was sometimes called the *Troy Town* after the old maze pattern, which was supposed to resemble the walls of Troy."

"Ya got me," he admitted.

Unable to stop, she heard herself continue. "Surely you've heard that witches traditionally dance back to back in a strange, but wonderfully diabolical kind of frolic."

"Never," he said. "So, what about you? What kind of strange, diabolical frolics do you like?"

Abby was speechless for way too many reasons to count at the moment, and Jack's expression was as dark as a cloudless sky at midnight and twice as mysterious. She didn't want to rattle off any more frighteningly unexplainable facts about witchcraft, let alone have him look at her that way again. Did she? Before she could answer her own question, or, for that matter, question her own answer, their waitress once more effectively interrupted them.

"Chateaubriand and two glasses of Gino's soft blush."

Again, he had ordered without asking, but ironically it would have been her choice.

Dinner conversation centered on a few more of the more normal get-to-know-you topics they hadn't taken the time to explore earlier. Reaching over to check his ring finger, Abby immediately pulled away from the warmth of his skin. Remembering yesterday and his side of the phone conversation with what sounded like a woman, Abby pointed out, "I should have asked before, but there's no Mrs. Hawthorne, is there?"

"No wife, no fiancée, not even a female pet." He tossed back the last of his Ben Nevis and set down the glass. "No strings."

Abby fought the persistent tug at the corners of her mouth. *Has fate really thrown us together?*

Now she fought the persistent tug at the corners of her mind. *Impossible. There's no such thing as destiny.*

Last, but oh-so-not least, she fought the persistent tug at the corners of her heart. *Unless kindred spirits really do exist.*

"How about you, *Miss* Corey?"

His obvious inflection didn't go unnoticed by Abby. "Did I say Miss?"

"No. I guess you didn't."

Abby smiled and shook her head. "I'm not married."

"I thought Maxine had mentioned that." Jack leaned back in his chair and traced the smooth skin on her ring finger.

Her hand tingled. "Ms. Spencer would have told you. She is one thorough woman."

"That she is."

Abby sensed Jack's move before he made it and began fiddling with her napkin to avoid it. Too close. Too personal. Too right? When the band began to play a soft, slow melody she added the beautiful surroundings to the soothing music and even without the handsome man seated across from her, they made a dangerous combination. Abby's intuition prickled and warned her the evening was about to take a definite turn. The most difficult part of it all was keeping in mind this handsome man was still a stranger even though he didn't feel like one.

"Dance?"

Dance with him? Was he kidding? Parts would touch. Like in her dream, the feeling of being backed in a corner washed over Abby. Silently she cursed the fact that every time he baited her she swallowed it hook, line, and sinker. With anyone else, tonight would have been nothing more than a harmless flirtation. But not with this man. Something about the look in Jack's eyes made her mouth dry and her palms damp. For an instant, she thought of her dream, the need to escape, and wondered if there was a back door to the restaurant.

"How about it?" He called her bluff. "Dance with me."

Abby slipped one foot out of her sleek brown pump and slid her toes along Jack's ankle and just a bit up his pant leg. She noticed his jaw clench and enjoyed a quick rush of power. "I'd love to."

"Let's have a drink first." He signaled the waitress, "Two Irish coffees."

Mission accomplished. Abby slipped her shoe back on and sat back in her chair as the waitress cleared their table. She wondered why it had been so long since she had relaxed like this? God, it felt good.

The next tune was lusty and slow. Jack stood and extended his hand. "Okay Lady, let's see your stuff."

Abby took a deep breath. Unwilling to back down, she winked. "I'll show you mine, if you'll show me yours."

"Deal."

Jack led her onto the dance floor. He had great rhythm and all the right parts fit. Being held by Jack felt like coming home. At this moment in time Abby didn't care how or why. She rested her head against his chest and eagerly inhaled the spicy scent...*that had always been him?* The texture of his jacket beneath her hand failed to conceal the strength of his muscled shoulder. Sensing his pulse pound, feeling the warmth of his touch, made everything she had tried to deny unbearably real. The music stopped and so did her heart.

Back at the table, Abby sipped the remainder of her coffee. "I haven't danced in so long I nearly forgot—"

"How nice it can be," Jack finished.

"Yes." She smiled. "Very nice."

"So, why haven't you?"

She frowned. "What?"

"You know, danced around a bonfire naked, chanting at the moon."

"How do you know I haven't?" Before he could answer, she corrected, "F.Y.I. that's skyclad, not naked."

"What is?"

"Spell casting in the nude." Abby had a quick flash—skyclad, casting a circle beneath the full moon—no doubt brought on by what he'd said.

"Now that's my kind of ritual. Seriously, you're such a natural. Why don't you dance more often?"

She thought a moment but couldn't come up with an answer. "I really don't know."

"Too busy?"

"Possibly," she considered, remembering how hard she'd worked to get her business up and running and knowing all of that was gone now. "Aromatiques demanded a lot of my time."

"Let me guess," he began, "you worked about ten hours a day, six days a week, right?"

"I did."

"And that worked for you?"

"Some days better than others," she admitted, surprised the words had come out so easily.

Jack shrugged. "I'm a confessed workaholic myself."

"Why?" she coaxed, watching the reflected firelight flicker in his penetrating eyes.

He shrugged. "I have a lot of work to do."

"And your social life?" she asked, for some reason not the least bit concerned about prying.

"Not much time for one," he confessed.

"Oh, I don't know." Thoughtful, she swirled her long-stemmed glass, then sipped the remainder of her wine. "You made plans yesterday."

"So I did." Jack leaned back in his chair. "That was just escorting an acquaintance."

"Escorting?" she echoed, "Kind of like this evening."

"No." He steepled his hands. "Nothing at all like tonight. Yesterday was just Bridget Bishop—"

Abby choked, quickly holding up a hand to show she was fine. "The woman who lives in that haunted house?" she asked, after catching her breath.

Jack nodded. "That's the one."

Torn, Abby couldn't decide if she was more shaken by the Bishop woman or the sudden, possessive rush she just felt toward Jack. Either way, something was way out of whack here. She needed time to think, and she needed it now.

"If you don't mind, I'm apparently still a little jet lagged."

"No problem." He paid the waiter and helped Abby with her cape. Then he took her hand and kissed it.

Exactly like the man in her dream.

She ignored the haunting similarity of his warm mouth against her skin.

"All set?" He gave her fingers a squeeze.

Abby nodded. She felt suddenly wary. As though she had been ready and waiting her entire life. For what, she wondered? For Jack? Impossible. Her free hand sought the warmth of the amulet as she followed him out into the cool, dark night.

The trip back to the Hannah's Inn was about as quiet as their ride to The Hideaway had been, but for an entirely different reason. Earlier, she had been uncharacteristically nervous. Now, she had become characteristically aware of Jack. More to the point—the way he made her feel. The uneasy comfort she experienced that niggled at her mind, raising more questions than she had answers for yet. Abby studied the set of Jack's jaw, his slightly narrowed eyes.

Thinking back, she had to admit the evening had been wonderful. Except for her unexplainable knowledge of witchcraft and her unreasonably strong response, again, to that Bishop woman. In fact, just the mention of her name made Abby's skin crawl. The magnitude of her reaction bewildered Abby.

He pulled up in front of the inn and cut the engine.

"I had a nice time, Jack." Brown eyes captured green.

"So did I."

Abby immediately recognized what was going to happen. Bound to happen. Had to happen. It was exactly what she'd been anticipating. *For so long?* Time stood still as Jack lowered his head. His eyes closed. Hers did not. For some reason, her need to see was too great. It felt like she had been waiting her whole life for this moment, and she had to make certain this was real. Not a dream.

Abby's heart fluttered expectantly against her ribs. As if she ended every evening like this, both arms circled Jack's neck in a familiar, easy way. She sighed, leaning into his broad, muscular chest. Lips touched. Barely. Like some warm, soft secret shared between lovers.

"Good night," Abby whispered, their lips little more than a breath apart. Whatever had just happened, she needed time to think about the kiss as well as her reaction to this Bishop woman. And she couldn't seem to do either right now. Not around Jack

She got out of the car before he had a chance to say one word. "Thanks for dinner."

"My pleasure." He buzzed her window down, reached across the seat and yanked her door shut. Still leaning, he looked up at her and smiled. "I'll be tied up first thing tomorrow—how about if I call you after lunch?"

"I had planned to rent a car in the morning and take a drive, so that works perfectly for me." She prayed her cape concealed her knocking knees. "Why don't you make it about two."

"Okay, but don't rent a car." He angled his head. "I'll drop off this one and leave the keys at the front desk."

"Oh, no. I couldn't—"

"I insist." He winked. "And don't rush back. If you're not there when I call, I'll just leave a message."

"Thanks. That would be great."

After he drove away, Abby's shaky legs gave way, and she collapsed onto a wooden bench in front of the inn. The sky was as black as indigo velvet and sprinkled with thousands of sparkling diamonds. A refreshing breeze sneaked beneath her cape, forcing her to pull it closer. Several couples passed hand-in-hand. Their muffled words and quiet laughter echoed in darkness. Abby had never felt quite so alone.

Chapter Seventeen

Salem, Massachusetts
15 October
Year of Our Lord, 1692

The night sky is dark, except for a brilliant, moon. A cool, fresh breeze billows through the carriage, caressing Abigail's skin, reminding her of the beautiful afternoon she spent with her beloved. They had met in the woods, surrounded by pine trees and the earthy fragrance of autumn.

Even now, thoughts of him warmed her cheeks. So tall. And handsome. So caring. She cradled the beautiful bouquet of burgundy mums in her arms like a babe.

Exhilaration coursed through her veins at the thought of becoming his wife. That's what today had been about, although she had not known. He had arranged a lovely picnic, supposedly for her birthday. Fresh flowers and red wine. Seated beneath the most beautiful crimson maple she had ever seen, he had sketched her picture, then promised to paint her portrait as a wedding present. Before she could catch her breath, he had called her "love" and eloquently proposed on bended knee. He confided already having asked her father for her hand and having been given his blessing.

Suddenly, the coach lurched, and the horses take off at break neck speed. Abigail cries out for help, and when no one answers, she struggles to her feet. Anchoring her bonnet, she shoves her head out the window. The driver is gone, and the bluffs are straight ahead.

•••

Unable to sleep, Abby awoke early, showered and dressed. She slid behind the wheel of Jack's silver BMW convertible and slammed the door. After having another dream last night, she was still trying to come to grips with the eerie sensation tweaking her consciousness. The very thought challenged her psyche, not to mention literally threatening her peace of mind.

Thinking through the details now that it was daylight, she understood the reference to burgundy mums. After all, they were her favorite flowers. As for the beautiful autumn setting—well, it was October in Salem. Can't get much better than that. And the handsome man? Well, there was a no-brainer.

"But the runaway coach," she muttered. "Now that's a real head-scratcher."

And, if having nightmares every night wasn't enough, there was this Hawthorne person. *The dashing man in her dream? Why not? Why the bloody hell not!* One minute he had her laughing; the next he made her pulse race. That said, neither of which were her major concern. What really bothered Abby was the unexplainable intensity of her feelings. So strong. So fast. *So right?* And so not like her. Trying to come to terms with such uncharacteristically strong emotions was the real crux of her problem.

Unlike yesterday morning, Abby tried to relax and simply focus on the scenery and the beautiful fall colors. The winding road cut through lovely neighborhoods that really got into the spirit when it came to decorating for autumn in general and Halloween in particular. On every street, there were pumpkin-lined porches. Doors dressed in crimson and orange wreaths. Yards costumed in bales of hay that hosted gourds, ghouls and ghosts in all shapes and sizes.

Unfortunately for Abby, all of the celebratory decorations Boston had to offer could not find a detour past the mental roadblock set up by her dreams. Scenes from the nightmare continued to flash through her mind. Relentless. Unsettling. Distracting.

It didn't take Abby long to realize that no matter how hard she tried, her heart just wasn't into sightseeing. Not today anyway. Or, maybe just not by herself. Or…well, she just didn't know. Something was out of kilter, but she couldn't put her finger on it. So rather than continue her drive, she decided to sort things out over a warm, cinnamon-spiced latte. She remembered seeing a quaint little café yesterday. If she could just find it again. Heading down a steep hill, she rounded a sharp curve a little too fast.

Abby eased her foot on the brake.

Nothing happened.

She tapped it again.

The car wasn't slowing down.

This time she stomped the pedal.

Again nothing. But it was picking up momentum—and fast.

Abby pumped the pedal.

Still nothing. But gaining speed.

This time as she slammed her foot down hard, the brake went straight to the floorboard without resistance.

Nothing!

"Oh, God!" she heard herself say.

The car was still accelerating. Abby's heart pounded against her ribs. Her breath came in short, hard gulps.

"Think, dammit!" she screamed.

Grabbing wildly for the emergency brake, her knuckles scraped relentlessly under the dash in a futile effort to stop. She fought to maintain control, swerving to avoid hitting an oncoming car. Somewhere nearby a horn blared and tires squalled.

Coming up fast on the rear end of a car, she jerked the wheel to pass but came face-to-face with a pickup truck. With nowhere to go she yanked the car back into her own lane and veered off to the right to keep from hitting the car in front of her.

A brick building loomed up before her eyes. She frantically laid on the horn, praying to God no one else would be hurt.

There was an explosive sound right before she heard a sickening thud. Then for a long moment everything was quiet. Why was her head pounding? Red-hot pain shot through her wrist. She struggled to get up, but the glass…there were jagged chards everywhere. There was something warm running down her arm. Blood! Lots of blood. What had happened? Had someone been hurt?

Faces loomed, seemingly from nowhere. Who were these people? Her eyes wouldn't focus. If only she could think, but her head felt like it was splitting. Voices. What were they saying? Why couldn't she make sense of this? Hands reached out. Panic set in.

"Don't touch me," Abby whimpered, fighting the sensation of overwhelming dizziness. Had her nightmare come true?

Like the cool October breeze innocently sweeping through the shattered windshield before moving on, she surrendered to the soothing, comforting darkness that beckoned.

• • •

Jack sat in his office, staring at his computer screen. He'd intended to take care of some work, but hadn't really accomplished much all morning. The shrill ringing of the phone sliced through his thoughts. "Hello."

He paused.

"Yes, this is Jack Hawthorne."

He listened.

"She what?" he shouted, impatient for information. His hands clenched into tight fists as he tried to comprehend the methodical voice from the emergency room.

"I'll be right there," he growled, cutting the caller off in mid-sentence.

He slammed down the phone and raced past Maxine without explanation, nearly tearing the door off its hinges. Barely behind the wheel, the Jeep's tires smoked as Jack screamed out of his parking space. The car lurched forward before he even yanked shut his gaping door. Jaw set. Eyes glued to the road. Accelerator to the floor. Jack rounded the first curve practically on two wheels. His thoughts ricocheted.

Darting in and out of lanes, horns blasted as Jack bullied his way through traffic. He recklessly took each corner at an increasing rate of speed, feeling the pull of the Jeep in direct proportion to the turn of the steering wheel. He jockeyed to maintain his position in the seat. Knowing he should slow down, but unable to push away his fears, Jack pressed his luck to the limit.

Abby had wrecked his BMW. Not just wrecked—totaled. Why the hell had he bought such a small car? No damn protection. His gut tied in a hard knot. He racked his brain to remember what the woman from the hospital had said. Abrasions? Head injuries? Dammit, he just wasn't sure.

The fortuneteller had predicted danger, and Jack had laughed off her warning. His mouth went dry. Why Abby had become so important to him, Jack didn't have a clue. Didn't need one. She was, and that's all that counted. From this moment on, he would make sure nothing bad happened to her. Absolutely nothing.

Chapter Eighteen

"I only gave you Mr. Hawthorne's name because I thought you might need some sort of, I don't know, credit reference or something. Not so you could call him." Abby gingerly touched both temples with the pads of her fingers and braced herself before continuing. "I'm perfectly capable of leaving on my own," she told the doctor, all the while trying to steady herself enough to sit up.

The tall, blond man waited patiently as she spoke. He laid a large hand on her shoulder and eased her back down on the examining table. "Are you finished?" he asked quietly.

Properly but nicely reprimanded, Abby nodded, then winced. Her head was pounding like a bass drum on Super Bowl Sunday.

"You sustained a scalp laceration that looked much worse than it was. That's where all the blood came from. You also have a bump on your head that would make Mother Goose proud, not to mention a badly sprained wrist. You're not going anywhere by yourself. Either Mr. Hawthorne keeps an eye on you, or I'm admitting you for observation," the doctor told her firmly.

"But, I—"

"No buts." He draped the stethoscope around the back of his neck allowing both ends to dangle on his chest. "When Mr. Hawthorne gets here, you're free to go," he insisted, brushing Abby's hair back off her forehead. "You're lucky these stitches are right at your hairline. They'll never show." He smiled warmly. "Relax. You're going to be just fine."

At that moment, Abby along with half the hospital staff and most of the first floor heard Jack's voice.

Storming through the doorway, he demanded, "What the hell happened?"

Jacket gaping, necktie over one shoulder, his presence filled the room. He wasn't the type to lose his cool, so the angry look on his face confused Abby.

"Oh, I'm feeling fine, thanks," she muttered. "If it's the car you're worried about, it looks worse than I do." Feeling tears well up, she turned her head and faced the wall.

"It's insured." Jack turned to the doctor. "How is she?"

Extending his hand, the doctor explained, "Still pretty shaken up. She's not quite herself. She's not to sleep soundly for the next several hours, so keep an eye on her."

"Okay, Doc."

"The nurse will bring in her prescription."

"Don't talk about me like I'm not in the room," Abby snapped, despite the fact it made her head throb.

The M.D. lowered his voice considerably, "She's still in shock, but she'll be fine. Just stay with her throughout the evening. Any changes and I want to know immediately."

"Thanks for calling me," Jack said, shaking the other man's hand.

The doctor inclined his head in Abby's direction. "Believe me, it wasn't easy."

As the door closed, Jack took a deep breath. He lowered his head to her ear, urging in a low, quiet voice, "Abby. Try not to sleep."

Her eyes fluttered open for a second, then slammed shut. "I'm not asleep," she whispered. Squinting, she tried to look up. Placing her free hand against his smooth, warm cheek, she responded to his tenderness. "My head hurts so badly, and that bright light makes it worse."

He flipped off the overhead fixture. "Better?" he asked quietly.

As her eyes adjusted to the dimly lit room, his concern moved her. Humorless, dark eyes dominated his features. Brows knitted together. The unusually hard line of his mouth. "Much better, thanks," she told him softly.

Aside from the pain, something deep inside violently tugged her heart. The fortuneteller had warned her not to wear the necklace. She'd said Abby did not belong here. Right now, looking at Jack, Abby could feel the corners of her mouth curve slightly at the thought. I must be delirious, she decided. That's what's causing these ridiculous thoughts. *Kind of like falling in love with your doctor.* Maybe illusions. Or delusions? Conclusions?

Jack's warm smile temporarily smoothed away the worry lines at the corners of his mouth, giving it that soft, kissable look. "You find something about this amusing?"

He laced his fingers through hers. "No."

Abby squeezed his hand.

The door swung open and a perky, dark-haired nurse bustled in, then stopped dead in her tracks. She reached for the light switch.

"Leave it off." Jack's curt words halted her hand in midair. "It hurts her eyes."

"Okay," she agreed, slipping momentarily back into the hallway before returning with a wheelchair. She carefully helped Abby off the examining table.

"Where's your coat?" she asked, easing Abby down.

Abby thought a moment. "I remember tossing it in the back seat of the car this morning. I guess it's still there." Jack immediately stripped off his jacket and wrapped it around her shoulders. It was still warm. She absorbed his body heat and caught the familiar, clean smell of his soap. "Thanks."

After a quick trip down the corridor and through the lobby the nurse handed Abby's prescription to Jack.

"I'll take it from here."

He had parked right by the door, so he helped Abby out of the wheelchair and into his Jeep.

"Take it easy," he crooned, slipping behind the wheel. "Everything's going to be fine." Buckling Abby's seat belt for her, he asked in a low soothing voice, "Trust me?"

She felt her bottom lip tremble at the simple question. "Yes." And she did.

Jack started the car. "Any dizziness?"

"No."

"Sick at your stomach?"

Abby relaxed a bit and managed a shaky grin. "Don't worry, Doc. Your seat covers are safe with me."

Returning her smile, he pulled out.

She settled back. Thank God the painkillers had finally kicked in. She was beginning to feel almost human again.

As they drove, brightly illuminated billboards promoting the annual Halloween Ball loomed up ominously at every turn. A brilliant harvest moon. Torch carrying pilgrims. Witches on brooms. Heart pounding, Abby closed her eyes. Why were these images every bit as familiar as they were disturbing? Typical Halloween dogma? Fragments of a similar gala? Incarnations flashed through her mind. *Her memory?* Ghoulish bits and pieces. Frightening glimpses. She tried to think—remember—but couldn't.

"Feeling any better?"

Abby started, her lashes flew open. "I'm okay," she lied. What else was there to say? *I'm just fine and dandy unless having flashbacks of witches and torches and angry mobs makes me crazy? Of course for some bizarre reason these actually feel like memories, not just Halloween hysteria. That's right, Jack, I'm apparently certifiable. The accident pushed me right over the edge and caused me to lose my ever-loving mind.*

"Are you sure?"

Abby laid her hand on his arm, more for her own reassurance than his. His well-muscled bicep felt warm and real beneath his crisp, white dress shirt. "Really, Jack, I'm fine."

Jack made one stop at the pharmacy before driving across town. Pulling in next to a beautifully built brick home, Jack parked the car and turned to face her.

"I may have been conked on the head, but this definitely isn't Hannah's Inn," Abby pointed out.

"The real question isn't what you see, but how many?"

Far from amused, she countered, "I see one lawyer who's definitely out of order—not to mention out of his mind. Now what's your point?"

"Is that any way to talk to your host?"

He jumped out of the Jeep before she could speak. Confused, she waited for him to open her door, then continued, "My what?"

"Host." He extended his hand to help her from the car. "You're staying here with me."

For support, Jack wrapped his arm around her waist and pulled her close. Resting her cheek against Jack's chest, Abby absorbed his warmth through the smooth material of his shirt. The regular beat of his heart echoed in her ear. All her life she had been waiting for someone. Holding her breath. Marking time. *Getting involved with the wrong Jacks?*

Jack stepped inside the house and flipped on the lights. "Are you all right?"

Abby nodded. She saw the deep concern reflected on his face. A fleeting glimpse of understanding that made her heart skip a beat. Did he sense her unexplainable fear? Had he experienced any of the same foreboding? Or was it just the accident?

"I can't stay here."

Jack checked his watch. "I wondered how long it would take."

She cocked her head slightly, then groaned at the consequences of her actions. "For what?"

"For you to start giving me a hard time."

She sighed. "It's not that I don't appreciate the offer, but—"

"But, what?"

"But, I don't need a baby-sitter. I can take care of myself. I'll be just fine at the inn." She clipped her words short to minimize the discomfort caused by speaking. *God, why can't that sadistic little bastard operating the jackhammer in my head take a break?*

"Maybe so. But, you're staying here."

She watched his playful look turn serious. He really meant to keep her here. Despite the underlying pain, she experienced a warm, pleasant sensation that made her feel safe and secure. "Just for tonight."

"We'll see." He crossed the length of the living room and turned on the soothing voice of Diana Krall. "Is that too loud?"

Already relaxing on the couch, the sultry jazz sounded heavenly. "Not at all."

Jack disappeared through a doorway and returned momentarily with a pillow and a blanket. He placed the pillow on the arm of the davenport and swiveled Abby's feet from the floor.

She watched in amazement as he deftly removed her shoes and covered her, carefully tucking the soft material around her legs. His large hands were gentle and giving and the smile she offered him in return was unconditional.

"Don't get too comfortable. You're not supposed to sleep just yet," Jack reminded in a low voice.

"I won't."

"Stay put. I'll be right back. Yell if you need me."

"I'm not going anywhere fast, believe me."

Abby leaned her head back on the soft pillow and listened to Diana's seductive rendition of "*Peel Me A Grape*."

Within minutes, Jack returned. He put his cup of coffee on the end table and handed Abby an earthenware mug of steaming soup. "Drink this."

Abby flinched inwardly at his order, but drank all the same. The creamy broth was delicious, and it warmed her spirit almost as much as Jack warmed her heart. *Must be the medication talking again.* She sipped some more then handed back the half-full mug.

"Finish it."

Abby didn't say a word.

"Please."

"Are you always so bossy?"

"Not always, no."

Abby tilted the mug and finished the soup. "Done."

Jack took her empty dish and handed her a glass of water and a small white pill. When she leaned forward to take her medication, he fluffed up her pillow.

"Rest, but don't sleep," he said quietly.

He smoothed an errant curl from her face before heading back to the kitchen. Calmed by his gentle touch, she willed herself to relax. She looked around the dimly lit room in an effort to take her mind off the accident, the pain and Jack. Not necessarily in that order. The entire ground floor of his home was one open space. Massive overstuffed furniture had been arranged around a rustic fireplace. Rough-hewn beams divided the cathedral ceiling, adding to the peacefulness and warmth Abby had sensed the minute she walked through the door.

Although it didn't help her headache, she strained her neck just enough to look over the back of the davenport. The fabulous upstairs loft was probably Jack's bedroom. For the first time since her arrival, Abby realized his stylish taste in homes had not surprised her in the least.

When Jack approached her makeshift bed, he was slipping into his jacket. "I'll be right back," he said quietly.

Abby struggled to sit up a little. "Where are you going?" Suddenly, the thought of being alone made her uncomfortable.

He held up a finger to silence her unspoken protest. "To pick up a few of your things." He dangled her room key in his opposite hand and smiled.

"I see you rifled through my purse." She arched one brow. "By all means, help yourself."

He smiled.

"So, you're telling me I don't have much choice—"

"No choice," he corrected.

"Fine. No choice," she conceded—well, not quite. With that in mind, she added, "As long as you're going, I do have one special request."

"Name it."

She conjured up her most earnest look. "If I'm going to stay here, I want Tom here, too." *After all Shadow was a tomcat.*

"And Tom would be?"

"Did I forget to mention he's staying with me?" Abby was barely able to keep a straight face as she watched him cram both fists into his pockets.

"You forgot?"

Convinced Jack deserved what she was dishing out, Abby ignored the twinge of guilt over the word game she was playing. "I just didn't want you to walk in and, you know, be surprised. That might be awkward."

Jack glanced over his shoulder, "Forget it. Looks like Tom will have the inn all to himself for a couple of days."

"I know he'll be there," she called to his back as he headed for the door. "Black hair, green eyes. You can't miss him. Please bring him back with you."

When the door slammed, she laid her head back down on the wonderfully soft pillow and laughed. The pain was worth it. Abby only wished she could be there when Jack met *Tom* for the first time.

Chapter Nineteen

Salem, Massachusetts
31 October
Year of Our Lord, 1692

"Protect my beloved 'til I return. Brand the hand of the one he spurned. Neither touch the stone nor cancel the spell, or the wicked one will burn in hell." Abigail's spell was quick. The merciless grip of the noose around her neck was not…

•••

There had never been an October wind frigid enough to cool off Jack right now. This was ridiculous. Abby had come to Boston alone. Hadn't she? So, who the hell was Tom? Not some guy she'd just met. Abby didn't strike him as the type. Maybe this guy had flown in to meet her? Then why hadn't she given the hospital his number? Itching to know, Jack headed straight for Hannah's Inn.

Jack couldn't find a place to park in front, so he drove around to the back. The parking lot was well lit, and he had just killed the engine when he saw Bridget and a burly, bald man exit the inn and get into her midnight black Porsche.

"I'll be damned." He leaned forward to be sure. "Gonna be in New York for a few days, huh? As they say—timing's a bitch."

Not at all surprised by how little he cared, Jack shook his head. Chalk up another one for Maxine, he decided. If the stock market was as easily predicted as the women he dated, Maxine could be his broker any day.

Filing away Bridget's lie, Jack hurried inside the bed and breakfast and unlocked room 204. The moment he flipped on the light, he stopped in his tracks. He didn't know much about Abby Corey, but he knew enough to realize she had not left her room like this.

Drawers half open with lingerie dangling over the sides.

Clothes on hangers tossed across the bed.

Suitcase linings slit.

He carefully backed out of the room into the hallway and shut the door. Pulling out his cell phone, Jack dialed the familiar number.

"Venucci."

"Lucky, it's Jack."

"Long time, no speak, Hawthorne. Sold any snake oil lately?"

"Besides your development, have you arrested anything else, Detective?" Same old Venucci who had kicked his ass in the eighth grade over Sandy…whatever the hell her last name had been. Regardless, Sandy had ended up liking some punk from St. Pat's and Lucky and Jack had remained friends ever since. "Kiss off, Venucci."

"Play nice, Jackie. You didn't call just to tick me off. What's up?"

Jack explained what he had found, assuring his difficult-to-convince friend—twice—that he knew a ransacked room when he saw one.

"I'm tied up on another case, but I'll send a squad to get the particulars. How's that?"

"No way, man. I'm telling you this room has been searched." Jack insisted. "Look, between her car wreck this afternoon and this mess, something stinks."

"She wrecked her car?"

"No. She wrecked my car. Said the brakes failed."

"And?"

"And I just had that car serviced last week. The brakes should have been fine."

"Gotcha. I'll be right there."

"Thanks."

Good to his word, Venucci arrived within minutes. His low whistle upon entering the room confirmed Jack's suspicions. "I'll say this joint was tossed." He walked to the dresser where lingerie dangled like Victoria Secret's Yuletide tinsel from five of the six half-opened drawers. Lucky extracted a black, lace teddy, then turned and grinned at Jack. "You said this Corey woman will be at your place, if I have any questions?"

"Get over yourself. She's a client from Illinois, and she doesn't know anyone else out here." The uncharacteristic silence caused Jack to pause. "Look, just call me the minute you hear anything."

"Will do." Venucci keyed his radio. "Central Ida Four."

"Ida Four, go ahead."

"Please dispatch the Crime Scene Tech to my location."

"Ten-four Ida One" the Telecommunicator responded adding, "Ida One requests a ten-twenty-five immediately at his ten-twenty."

"Advise Ida One I'm on my way."

"Ten-Four."

Venucci turned to the uniformed officer who had arrived on the scene. "Stay here until Jamison arrives." When the patrolman nodded, Lucky turned to Jack. "I've got another call, but the Crime Scene Tech is on his way. After he's done with the room you can take what you need."

Forty minutes later the technician had come and gone, and Jack began gathering the odds and ends Abby would need for the next few days. He couldn't help but notice how damn soft all of her *things* were. He shook his head and shoved some of her belongings into the slashed suitcase.

When a noise brought Jack up short, he stopped. Where the hell had that come from?

A small ball of fluff raced wildly across the floor and jumped on the bed, seemingly on tiptoe—tail erect—hissing like a cornered snake.

Jack's low laugh echoed through the otherwise empty room as he grabbed the cat and got a better look. Black hair? Green eyes? "I'll be damned."

Kitten in hand, he picked up the suitcase and headed home, muttering something about women in general, Abby in particular and the sweet revenge of paybacks.

Chapter Twenty

At the slam of the car door, Abby waited. She knew Hawthorne loved to dish it out, but couldn't help but wonder whether or not he could take it. The look on his face as he came through the door told her he could.

He stopped in front of Abby. "Tom, I presume?"

"Actually his name is Shadow, but he *is* a tomcat," she confessed. "No hard feelings?"

Jack set down her suitcase at the end of the Davenport and handed her the kitten. "Are you kidding?" He took off his jacket and tossed it over the back of the chair. "You owe me, Corey. You owe me big."

The twinkle Abby saw reflected in his dark eyes did more to ease the pain in her head than all the medication she'd taken. "You can't collect from someone in my condition, and you know it. Besides, what took you so long?"

"Look, there's something I have to tell you."

At the tone of his voice, she instinctively sat up a little straighter, pulling Shadow close. "What?"

"The reason it took me so long to get back was that your room had been ransacked."

"Ransacked?" she repeated, trying hard to wrap her mind around the concept. "Why on earth would anyone do that?"

"Good question."

"I have no idea." Abby thought a moment, then shook her head. Immediately regretting the gesture, she rubbed her throbbing temple. "First my home in Springfield and now my room here. What's going on, Jack?"

"When I saw what had happened, that's exactly what I thought. So, I called it in. Lucky Venucci is a friend of mine and he's a detective on the police force."

"He didn't want to talk to me?"

"In light of all you've been through today, I asked him to let you rest tonight, and he agreed." Jack shoved both hands in his pants pockets. "Unless you suspect someone in particular, he told me you could answer any questions tomorrow."

"Thank you." Abby swallowed hard. "I don't know anyone besides you in Boston, so what happened at the inn must have been a random act, don't you think?"

"I'm not sure," he said. "Can you think of any reason your belongings would have been tempting to the staff?"

"Not a thing." She thought, then shrugged, meeting his dark gaze. "I'm certainly not rich. What little cash I brought for my vacation, I carry in my purse. I have one Visa card and one Master card, both in my billfold. Other than that—well, you saw my stuff. Nothing worth stealing."

"Well, someone was definitely interested."

Abby frowned, but said nothing.

"Or, like you said, your room might have been selected by chance."

"Maybe." Remembering her unrequested visit from housekeeping the night before, Abby told him, "A maid did come to my room last night, right before you got there. But, I hadn't called housekeeping."

"What did she say?"

"Nothing much," Abby admitted, trying to remember. "Just 'wrong room,' I think."

"Your feeling?"

Abby considered the woman she'd seen. "Maybe a bit odd."

"How so?"

"I was having trouble fastening my necklace, and I asked her to help, but she refused. Said it was not allowed, but now that I think about it that doesn't sound right."

"But she saw your necklace."

"Yeah, but I certainly don't think she was interested in it." Abby sighed. "That was the weird part. You'd have thought I dangled a tarantula in front of her, not a pendant."

"Really?"

Abby nodded, immediately regretting the move. "She jumped back like I'd set her on fire and nearly overturned her cleaning cart hurrying back down the hall."

"That is strange. Be sure to tell the police when you talk to them, and they can at least check her out."

"I will." She offered a smile to counter the worried look in his eyes.

"Regardless, it's over and you're safe here."

Abby shivered without comment.

"Are you chilly?"

"A little."

"I know your shop burned, would a fire bother you?"

"I don't think so." Abby watched him cross the living room and kneel beside the huge stone hearth. She couldn't help but notice his broad shoulders and well-muscled back as he adjusted the logs.

Turning, he glanced her way. "If it does, tell me and I'll just kick up the thermostat instead."

"Thanks, I will." When he reached down and scratched behind Shadow's ears, she smiled.

Straightening, he asked, "How about some hot chocolate?"

She closed her eyes, contemplating the yumminess of his offer. "With marshmallows?"

"Is there any other kind?"

Jack's clattering in the kitchen gave her time to think. As comfortable as she felt in his house, Abby knew her stay in Salem would be over in a matter of days. Suddenly, the warm crackle of the fire chilled her to the bone. No Kat. No Aromatiques. No Home.

A bittersweet sensation of loneliness, the likes of which she had never felt before, swept through her. In her head, Abby knew, no matter how much she wanted to, she could not change what had happened. No amount of crying, praying or cursing could undo what had been done. Because she had tried them all. So at least for now, she forced herself to concentrate on the present.

As Jack reappeared, his tall, powerful form headed toward her, mugs in hand. Marshmallows bobbed in the steaming, rich brown drink as he eased his way back into the living room. She watched him with interest. Cocky attitude. Strong arms. Sexy mouth.

Accepting the cup, she was surprised when Jack sat beside her on the couch. "I feel awful about the car."

"Forget it."

When he pulled her feet into his lap and massaged them, ever…so…slowly, Abby's body hummed under his touch. "That's easy for you to say, you weren't driving."

"I can get another car, but you would've been a little tougher to replace—"

The phone rang.

"Rest," he said. "I'll take it in the other room."

When the ringing stopped, Abby couldn't help but overhear.

"I really didn't expect to hear from you tonight, Bridget."

Even the mention of that woman's name prickled the hair on the back of Abby's neck.

"So, tell me, how is New York?"

"That cold, huh?"

"No, I didn't get the message."

And Abby thought she couldn't feel worse. What was the old joke—did you get the name of that truck? Well, as far as she was concerned, that eighteen wheeler's name was Bridget Bishop. From Jack's side of the conversation, it sounded like her accident may have caused him to forget his date tonight. Even the thought made Abby shudder.

"—because I was with a client," he said. "How about you? What did you do this afternoon?"

What on earth had made Abby think Jack's generosity could or should be anything more than just that? He'd been taking care of an out-of-town client who'd had an accident. Doing his job. Nothing more. Nothing less.

"I don't know."

Jack slammed down the receiver.

The moment Jack walked back into the living room, Abby saw it. The laughter was gone from his eyes. Frustration or anger, she couldn't tell which, had taken its place. Stroking Shadow, she avoided his gaze.

"Why don't you just take me back to the inn? I'll be fine there."

"What?"

"I couldn't help but overhear. Apparently you had plans—"

"No. I didn't."

"Well, I want to go," Abby told him. "You've gone above and beyond your responsibility."

"Forget it. You're not going anywhere—especially there." He held up a hand. "You're staying here with me."

"Noble to the death," Abby muttered, suddenly too tired to argue. "Fine."

"What's wrong, Abby? Do you feel worse?"

"I'm tired," she sighed. "When can I go to sleep?"

Jack checked his watch. "Any time now."

Picking at the dried blood on her sweater sleeve, she asked, "Where can I wash up?"

"I'm sorry. I should have thought—"

"That wasn't your responsibility either." Jumping up a little too quickly, Abby faltered, and he scooped her up as if she were no bigger than Shadow. God, she was miserable. Aching bones. Pounding head. Throbbing wrist. Abby didn't want to wrap her arms around Jack's neck, but she did. She clung to him as he carried her up the spiral staircase and put her down on the bed.

"I'll be right back," he said.

Looking around, she noticed beautifully shuttered windows and a skylight directly overhead. Impressed by the bedroom, Abby wondered if that Bridget woman had decorated it. The pain in her head doubled.

"Here's your suitcase."

He looked like a fish out water. Poor thing acted like she was going to explode before his very eyes. "Thanks." Taking pity, she let him off the hook. "You go on. I'll be fine."

Jack pointed. "The bathroom is through there."

"Okay."

"The clean towels are in the linen closet." He gestured again.

She watched his hands slide into his pants' pockets. "Where are the dirty ones?" she asked, trying to keep a straight face.

"Huh?"

"It was a joke."

"Right," he conceded. "I'll be downstairs, if you need anything."

"I'm sure I won't." Abby watched him descend the staircase—finally. She grabbed her suitcase and that's when she noticed the slashed leather. Cringing, she found the bathroom, shut the door and waited until her heart stopped pounding. Someone had torn apart her room and sliced open her bag like a ripe watermelon. Looking for what? Unable to stand much longer, let alone think, she awkwardly stripped off her bloodstained sweater and jeans and opened the suitcase with her good hand.

"What in the world?" Abby muttered, digging to the bottom—her daintiest lingerie, skimpiest teddy and a sheer black nightgown. "I'll bet Hawthorne had a heyday picking out this stuff." He'd left her with some choice. It was either one of these or the street clothes he'd brought her.

After washing up, she slid into the nightgown and returned to find the room dark except for a tiffany lamp on a nearby pedestal table serving as a night-light. The bed had been neatly turned down, and Shadow already snoozed comfortably on one pillow. A wooden tray on the dresser held a pitcher of ice water, a glass, and one small, white pill. After taking the medication, she walked to the sleek wooden rail that surrounded the loft. The smooth rich wood felt solid beneath her hands.

The lights were out downstairs, and the dying firelight silhouetted Jack's broad-shouldered form stretched the length of the couch. Backing away quietly, she self-consciously slid beneath the soft, cool sheets, Jack's sheets, and snuggled under the covers. She gazed overhead at the skylight. The black velvet sky was sprinkled with a million stars. As her medication started to take effect, the shimmering night spiraled into images of Jack. Turning comfortably onto one side, she closed her eyes and smiled.

A little past twelve, Abby stirred only to find Jack standing motionless at the top of the stairs, checking on her. At two-thirty he stood beside the bed again. When she awoke briefly at five o'clock in the morning and found him sprawled in a chair next to the bed, she covered him with the plush, cotton throw that she hadn't needed.

Warm sunshine caressed Abby's face, slowly waking her. She opened her eyes and stretched, more than pleased to find the throbbing in her head had stopped. Shadow scampered across the bed, purring contentedly as he rubbed his furry face against her cheek.

"This is quite a bed, isn't it?" Turning her head to meet the sound of someone coming up the steps, Abby was quick to pull the covers under her chin.

"Morning," Jack said.

"Good morning." She watched him set down a tray on the dresser and approach the bed. He grabbed the other pillow and propped it in back of her head, enabling her to sit up. The aroma of bacon and coffee made her mouth water. "You shouldn't have," she lied, not surprised by the dark circles under Jack's eyes and the drawn lines around his mouth.

"I know, but I can't have you dying in my bed, now can I?" He looked up and smiled. "At least not from starvation."

"So this—" she gestured toward the breakfast "—more or less just protects your reputation?"

He balanced the tray on her lap. "Exactly."

Despite being a bit ragged around the edges, Abby thought he looked wonderful—charcoal sweater, sleeves pushed halfway to his elbows, stone washed black jeans. And he smelled as good as he looked.

"Far be it from me to tarnish your impeccable character." Adjusting her grip, a corner of the blanket slipped and exposed a portion of her nightgown.

"I think you already have."

"You mean this old thing?" She winked. "If you think this little number is something, you ought to see the rest. But then I guess you already did." She yanked the cover back up. "Like pilfering through ladies' lingerie, Hawthorne?"

"I usually prefer the woman to be in them at the time."

Abby ignored his comment and, instead, dug into the scrambled eggs, "Ummm. These are delicious. Thank the cook for me, will you?"

"Very funny."

"What?" she asked innocently. Taking a sip of coffee, she immediately peeled her lips from the cup. "Geez, Hawthorne, are you trying to scald me?"

"That's what you get for having such a smart mouth."

"Your concern is touching." Abby blew on the steaming liquid. Looking up, she found him staring. She enunciated as if explaining to a child, "This is what we do in Illinois when something is too hot."

"Someday, when you're feeling better, remind me to show you what we do in Massachusetts."

Abby watched Jack's lips curl into an insinuating grin before he turned and walked away. She muttered a string of oaths between bites as he descended the stairs. After finishing every bite, she struggled with her bandaged wrist to put the tray full of empty dishes on the floor. She swung her legs over the side of the bed, waited a moment to gain her equilibrium, then rested both feet on the soft, warm carpet. Standing tentatively, she balanced herself and checked for dizziness. Experiencing none, she headed for the bathroom.

Dressed in the jeans and sweatshirt he had packed, Abby applied a little makeup and brushed her hair before going downstairs. Much to Jack's disapproving glare, she'd managed quite well alone.

"What, no tray?"

"I think I'm doing rather well, thank you."

"So you are."

Uncomfortable with his sincerity, Abby turned her attention to Shadow who was wolfing down his breakfast in the far corner of the kitchen. "Awww. You bought him cat food."

Jack shrugged. "I fed you didn't I?"

"And a real litter box—"

"Which you can clean," he said matter-of-factly.

"Fair enough," she agreed. Stifling her pleasure, Abby reminded herself it was called keeping the client happy. She shifted her weight uneasily. "I'm ready whenever you are."

"Oh, really?"

Jack gave Abby a smile so suggestive that her knees turned to jelly.

"You know exactly what I mean."

Just the sight of him leaning against the cabinet, legs crossed at the ankles, arms folded across his chest caused her breath to quicken. His laugh was warm, catching. It erased the worry lines around his eyes and mouth, making him look years younger than he had earlier this morning. Just smiling at first, she couldn't help but join in. "Do you have to make something out of a simple request to go back to the inn?"

"Oh, *that's* what you were talking about."

"Yes." She rolled her eyes. "Besides, I have to talk to the police this morning."

He shook his head. "I already phoned Venucci and updated him. He knows where you are, if he needs anything."

"Thank you." Regardless of feeling a little steadier, Abby hadn't relished an interview—not that she knew anything. Because she didn't.

"You should stay here at least another day."

"Thanks, but no. You've already gone above and beyond."

"It wasn't a question." Jack shrugged. "You're staying."

"Says who?"

"The doctor. I promised him you'd stay forty-eight hours."

"You did not." Abby planted both hands on her hips, forgetting momentarily about her injured wrist. "Ouch!"

"See."

"Don't worry about me." She narrowed her gaze. "Tell me the truth. You didn't say that to the doctor, did you?"

"I meant to. Besides, I'm sure he'd insist." Holding up his palm to counter her protest, Jack continued, "I'll be at work all day. You'll have the entire house to yourself, and you'll be here in case Detective Venucci calls."

Well, she had to stay somewhere. And the police might need to talk to her. What could it hurt? "All right. Thank you."

Moving closer, Jack faced Abby. "Except for inheriting your necklace, you've had nothing but bad luck since you landed in Boston."

"That's an understatement." She watched his expression soften.

"Let me make it up to you."

The quiet emphasis of his words touched Abby. "How?"

"We'll call a truce. You rest and recuperate."

Hearing the challenge in his voice, she stepped back. "And?"

"And I'll take you to the Halloween Ball," he stated rather than asked. "It's the highlight of the season in Boston."

The sexy smile tugging at his lips may have been contagious, but in light of all that had happened to her in the past month, Abby wasn't really in a costume party kind of mood. "We'll see," was all she could promise.

• • •

"I'm going to the office now."

"Okay," Abby answered absently. She thought the view from the window was breathtaking…until she turned to face him. The man gave new meaning to the phrase tall, dark and impeccably dressed. "See you later."

"I'll be home about six."

"Don't go all domestic on me, Hawthorne. You sound like Ozzie Nelson." Truce or no truce, she couldn't help but remember Bridget Bishop's phone call last night. "I'm just a guest. Feel free to come and go as you please."

"On second thought, I may be late."

The front door slammed behind Jack loud enough for the neighbors to hear. It spooked Shadow so badly he hissed and raced upstairs, his hair standing out like a tiny black porcupine.

"Maybe he wanted to come home at six," she began, talking to herself. "Great. Now I can look forward to a long afternoon and a long evening." The cat peaked curiously around the corner to see if the coast was clear. "What am I saying, Shadow? We don't need Jack Hawthorne to occupy our time, do we?"

Chapter Twenty-One

Salem, Massachusetts
31 October
Year of Our Lord, 1692

Jackson could see Abigail's lips moving, surely saying what would be her last prayer. From where he stood, the torches blazed around her. Reflections of the flickering firelight cast a strange pulsing glow between her fingers.

Working quickly, a woman dressed in black except for a bright red bodice jerked Abigail by the arms and tied both wrists behind her back. The woman's strong, well-practiced fingers ripped the amulet from Abigail's grasp, then hissed as the smooth amber stone branded its shape in the palm of her hand. An oath escaped her scarlet lips as she threw the pendant hard and fast. Slipping the noose over Abigail's head, the woman moved closer.

"See you in hell," Bridget Bishop whispered as she yanked the cord tighter. "He's mine now."

"Never," Abigail swore as rough hands shoved her onto a frightened horse. "My spell will protect him from you until I return."

When ice blue eyes met green, thunder shook the earth and lightning slashed the heavens. The dark-haired beauty tossed her head back and laughed hysterically…

. . .

The house was dark when Abby woke up. Disoriented, the iridescent glow of the clock on the bedside table reflected seven-thirty. Flipping on a light, she made her way downstairs. Jack had cleaned the fireplace and set up new wood before he left, so all she had to do was strike one of the long matches and ignite the kindling.

Refreshed and hungry, she put together a ham and cheese sandwich and a glass of milk and ate her meal by the softly crackling fire. Looking around, Abby had to admit she was fascinated by Jack's home. Refined. Almost elegant. Yet comfortable. The man definitely had an eye for both shape and color. Paintings in muted earth tones hung haphazardly on opposite walls pulled the entire look together.

Suddenly aware of the silence, she flipped on the television. When was the last time she'd relaxed in front of the TV? Come to think of it, she didn't even know what programs were on anymore. And since when did silence bother her?

Irritated by her insistent soul-searching, she opted for a mindless hour soaking in a hot bath instead. No psychoanalysis. No self-criticism. No mind games. Indulgence, pure and simple, was what she wanted. Afterward, unwilling to parade around in her scant, black nightgown, she gave herself permission to search Jack's room for a robe. That seemed only fair since he was the one who brought her back as little as was humanly possible to wear.

She opened the closet door and found an array of neatly pressed suits, crisply laundered shirts and, voila, just as she'd suspected a wonderfully soft, kimono-style robe. Abby plunged her arms in and immediately recognized Jack's sent clinging to the plush, white terrycloth. She closed her eyes, inhaled, and hugged herself tightly. Forced to cuff the incredibly long sleeves several times, she crisscrossed the front before cinching the belt around her waist.

Curious, she continued to snoop around the huge walk-in. The man was disgustingly neat. His beautiful designer ties were precisely arranged on orderly rows of hooks. Abby was impressed by his taste, but more than that, she couldn't help but admire the fact that he didn't work at it. Whatever class this man had, he came by it naturally. And that's when she saw it...and smiled.

In the farthest corner of the closet she found a worn out, gray sweat suit, a pair of dirty Nikes and a badly scuffed basketball. So, Jack Hawthorne wasn't perfect after all. Thank God. Satisfied, she was able to shut the door and go downstairs with her piece of mind intact.

Abby stretched out the length of the sofa and allowed herself to be swept away by Clark Gable. Every woman, she decided, should see "It Happened One Night" at least once.

• • •

"You know, Max, I've never known you to become involved with any client." Without looking up from his computer screen, Jack continued typing as he spoke.

"Concerned. Not involved," she corrected. "After all, Ms. Corey was injured in a car accident."

Jack's fingers stopped mid-sentence, and he swiveled his chair to face her. He'd seen that look hundreds of times over the years, but today something else was there. Something he could sense but couldn't pinpoint. "Still, why so interested?"

"Your car was totaled."

Jack shrugged. "I'll buy another."

"Ms. Corey was driving."

"And we've come full circle." He crossed both arms over his chest. "Why so interested," he repeated.

"Pleasant woman." Maxine met his gaze. "Unpleasant circumstances."

"And?"

"And nothing." She stopped at the door and placed one hand on the knob but didn't open it.

"What is it, Max?" He used his understanding, soothing lawyer voice. The one that urged *trust me, and I can help you.* Difference was, this time he meant it as a friend, not a prosecutor.

She turned to face him. Paused as if to speak. Then shook her head. "Nothing."

"Okay." He shrugged. "But we've been together a long time, and you can talk to me about anything."

She pinned him with her gaze. "As can you."

He thought a moment but could find no concrete, logical place to begin. "I know," he said, wondering if that same feeling of uncertainty had anything thing to do with her decision not to speak.

Jack had learned a long time ago when Maxine was done discussing something, she switched gears without so much as a blink. And that was that. He might as well give up and go along with her. For the time being anyway.

Without a word, Maxine nodded, opened the door and left him feeling restless and frustrated. For a lawyer like Jack, unanswered questions gnawed a hole in his gut. What he had always trusted about himself, however, was his process. The way his brain worked. The way his mind sorted facts and connected the dots.

So, he made a conscious effort to spend the better part of his afternoon *not* thinking about Abby or Maxine or anything connected with either of them. Instead, he busied himself in the mundane, which unleashed his subconscious and allowed information to surface on its own.

During a trial, he would go for a long drive after work to clear his head. So, he decided today would be no different. Leaving the office, he settled behind the wheel of his Jeep. Content to head nowhere in particular, he laid the same mental groundwork that he would for any cross-examination.

Fact: Maxine does not pussyfoot.

Fact: Maxine deals solely in reality.

Fact: Maxine does not get involved in other people's business—except his.

As he wound his way down the scenic, tree-lined streets, Jack admitted just how much he trusted Maxine and her instincts. Engrossed in determining how this translated to Abby Corey, he didn't notice the rich autumn foliage illuminated by the setting October sun. Or the Halloween decorations. Or the jack-o-lantern studded porches. Instead, he concentrated on what he knew about Abby. The devastation she had experienced during the past month surfaced in his mind. The catastrophic fire. The death of her friend. The loss of her home as well as her business. And now all the misfortune that had happened to her since she arrived in Boston.

Jack would feel empathy for anyone under these circumstances. But his feelings went deeper than that. And what about Maxine? She was a rock. A no-nonsense woman who had never been at loss for words, much less an opinion, in her entire life. Yet neither he nor Maxine chose to verbalize why this virtual stranger had made such an impression on both of them.

Jack drove until his stomach insisted he stop to eat. He had never minded, and usually enjoyed, the solitude of a late night dinner. Until now. Tonight, visions of the red-haired beauty probably lying in his bed at this very moment teased and taunted him.

His smile faded when thoughts of Bridget intruded. He hadn't been at the office when she called the last time, but Maxine had taken a message. Max may have added her personal spin as to the amount of hostility evident in Bridget's tone, but he really didn't care. Again, he trusted Maxine's take on people.

Fact: Maxine does not like Bridget.

Fact: Maxine does not conceal the fact that she does not like Bridget.

Fact: Maxine's dislike for Bridget appears to be in direct proportion to her uncharacteristic fondness for Abby.

As far as Bridget was concerned, Jack sided with Maxine. It was over. Not that it had ever really begun. Seeing her with the guy at the inn had pissed him off, but only because he detested a liar. Not due to any feelings he had for Bridget. They just weren't there. Never had been. Maybe that was why her betrayal felt like more of a relief.

Pushing aside his barely eaten meal, Jack tossed down a twenty and left. Unfortunately, the drive home was every bit as frustrating as the trip there had been. Instead of finding definitive answers, he had succeeded in conjuring up more questions. Normally not a problem.

As a lawyer, there was nothing he liked more than the challenge of searching for the perfect angle or loophole. And he was damned good at both. However, that had not been his goal this evening. Tonight what Jack needed was rock-solid explanations. But as important as solutions were, and they seemed to be paramount, it was the sense of urgency brewing just below the surface that concerned him more. *The truth will set you free.*

Quietly entering the house, the sight of Abby sound asleep in the living room stopped him cold. The dying fire lent a soft glow to her face and heightened the purplish bruise on her cheek. His stomach tightened. The thunderous memory of her accident, not to mention her ransacked room, jabbed his conscience like a big thorny stick. He would check with Venucci first thing in the morning for an update on the investigation.

Mid-stride, Jack spotted his robe. He had to admit terry cloth had never looked that good before. Especially since it was tied loosely at Abby's waist where it parted, revealing what little there was of her black nightgown. Her hair hung enticingly over the edge of the sofa almost to the floor. Long, smooth legs stretched to their oh-so-impressive length.

Shedding his coat and suit jacket, Jack knelt down and gathered up Abby. As he started upstairs, her arms automatically curled around his neck. She felt small and fragile as she nuzzled her face against his shoulder. Her hair carried the fresh scent of his shampoo.

She only stirred for a moment as he carefully eased her onto the bed. "Jack?"

"Shhh," he spoke softly. "Go back to sleep." He saw her smile reflected in the moonlight that spilled across the pillow. One last look and he headed downstairs.

Abby Corey. Why did the sight of her just now make him want to put his fist through the wall? Where was his frustration coming from? How could his feelings be this intense?

I must be nuts. So she put on my robe. Big deal. Since when was that so damn special?

He paced. "Ever since she stepped off that plane…"

He yanked loose his tie and kicked off his shoes.

"…She's messed with my mind…"

He peeled off his shirt and ripped out his belt like a bullwhip.

"…She's disrupted my life…"

He dropped his pants, not to mention is guard.

"…She's…important to me."

But why? Jack swallowed hard. He crossed the room and poured a whiskey neat, a double. He downed it in one gulp and relished the path it burned down his throat as he swallowed. He poured another…

Maybe I can drown whatever's bugging me from the inside. Fat chance, pal. All you're gonna get is one helluva hangover.

… And another.

Feeling no pain, but far from anesthetized, Jack dragged out the bedding and made up the couch. Realizing part of what had him crazy, he pounded the suddenly uncomfortable pillow with his fist. He did not believe in coincidences—like one person experiencing an unexplainable car wreck and her hotel room being ransacked in the same day.

Was Abby in danger? If so, what kind and how much? How far was this person prepared go? Two incidents in less than twenty-four hours. That was way too far. As for the rest of what was making him nuts, his only clues had been bits and pieces. Scraps of some elusive feeling that tried his patience at every turn.

He angled for a more comfortable position. The bottom line—he would protect her whether she liked it or not. As for the rest, all the other explanations he needed, he decided time would tell.

Chapter Twenty-Two

A note scrawled in large masculine handwriting had been left on the kitchen table propped against a box of donuts. Jack had gone to work early and made several lurid suggestions about her feeling free to pillage his closet until he could stop by and pick up some more of her clothes.

Abby grinned; glad she and Hawthorne were back on speaking terms again. Suddenly famished, she ate a decadent donut filled with Bavarian cream, then another and felt more like her old self than she had since the accident. Enjoying a certain sense of freedom, Abby hit Jack's bedroom room like a Saturday morning garage sale. She grabbed a pair of black sweat shorts with a drawstring waist and a black and orange T-shirt with Salem's witch logo across the front.

"Can you believe it, Shadow?" she told the small furry cat who watched her every move with the utmost interest. "Even his grubby clothes match." The kitten fell headfirst into the dresser drawer she had opened. Hauling him out, she kissed his tiny head.

"Oh, no you don't. We're going exploring and see just how much we can find out about Jack Hawthorne. Come on. Wanna poke around a little?"

She began downstairs, assessing the kitchen as well stocked, but not fussy. Although a woman's touch wouldn't hurt, it was still very attractive. No plants. No cookbooks. No knickknacks. Plenty of beautiful granite counter space and every utensil in its place. The copper pots hanging over an island stove/sink combination were well used, not decorative. She marveled at the cleanliness and thanked God that Jack couldn't check any of those mystery containers in her refrigerator. Not that she even had a 'frig anymore.

Now more than ever, her life felt out of sync. And not just because of the loss of her friend and her shop. Those tragedies stained her past. Not to mention breaking her heart.

No, this felt different. More of a haunting sense of *something yet to come* that had actually followed her from Springfield. So, why had she experienced such an unexplainable familiarity in Salem? A sense of peace that resembled Shadow curling up in a warm spot of sunshine. After a silent vow to shelve her paranoia and take one day at a time, she decided today would be dedicated to exploring the world of Jack Hawthorne. Room by room.

Abby noted a stylish bar separated the dining area from the kitchen, complete with a wooden-shuttered pass through that could close off either room. Jack had left the morning newspaper and a half-cup of coffee behind. She admired the single pedestal design of his dining table, especially its massive ball claws. Like the rest of Jack's house his furniture was masculine, but beautiful.

As she wandered through the living room, the exquisite oil paintings caught her eye. Although each one was unique, the signature, if that was what you could call it, was the same. Every one of them had two solid black, inverted triangles side by side—points down and wide bases touching. Could that be an abstract W, she wondered? The seascapes were so alive you could almost smell the salt air and hear the unmistakable call of the gulls. The barns and landscapes were warm and earthy.

Behind the chair next to the television, she found something that revealed a side of Jack Hawthorne she would have never guessed in a million years. An Xbox. Her neighbor's son had beaten her into the ground playing Max Payne—at first. What the little darling didn't know was, after he had been sent to bed, Abby practiced that game until her thumbs were numb. Not that she was a sore loser or the least bit competitive.

Finding her way to the den, with Shadow in tow, the room smelled of leather, rustic wood paneling, and Jack. His desk was huge and damnably neat, and the extensive library awed her. Shelf after shelf of books lined the walls. Everything from *Wuthering Heights* to Stephen King and Lee Child. And, if his array of historical literature was any indication of his knowledge, it wasn't any wonder he'd been snatched up by Boston's historical society.

One entire corner of the room was an elaborate yet amazingly compact computer center. Just beyond the mini office complex, she found a niche that consisted of a telescope set up in front of a huge picture window and an easel situated off to one side. Careful not to disturb its alignment, Abby looked through the lens and found it focused on a lighthouse. The sketch on the canvas was an excellent likeness. So, that *W* had been Jack's signature on the paintings in the living room. Why W, she wondered? Regardless, Abby was genuinely impressed. Careful not to disturb his set up, she backed out of the small room and continued looking around.

Sidestepping the cat, who was grossly interested in playing with the fax machine's cord, Abby pushed aside a decorative louvered screen and burst into laughter.

"Looks like there's hope for Jack yet."

Neatly situated in the far corner of the room was a ginormous, glass and chrome jukebox complete with every rock n' roll hit imaginable. Unable to resist, she plugged it in. Iridescent neon lights blinked in progression, making Shadow head for cover under Jack's desk. Delighted, she punched a couple of buttons and smiled at the familiar voices of The Four Tops.

• • •

Nothing like an unmistakable Motown rhythm to rock Abby. Once she started to dance, Shadow raced out and jumped back and forth between her bare feet. She snapped the fingers on her good hand and in drunken Karaoke-style sang along, never missing a note. Whirling around, face flushed, arms spread wide and backfield definitely in motion, Abby froze, practically in midair, at the sight of Jack. She raced to unplug the jukebox.

"My God, don't you know how to knock?" she asked.

"That's funny, I thought I lived here." He dropped his briefcase and walked directly toward her.

Abby knew. His compelling look told her exactly what he wanted. What she had wanted since the day they met. The touch of his hands was unbearably tender as he gathered her into his arms. She could smell the cold October wind still clinging to him and realized how right this felt. Sighing, she dropped her chin to his chest.

His large hand took her face and tilted it upward. Standing on tiptoe, she was shocked at her eager response. He was surprisingly gentle. His mouth touched hers like a whisper, and she felt her body shudder at its sweetness.

His breath was hot against her cheek when he whispered, "I'll be home at six." His mouth brushed against her earlobe. "Make that five-thirty."

He was still way too close for her to think clearly. "I'll make dinner," she heard herself say.

Releasing Abby, he grabbed a file folder off his desk and snagged his briefcase. Before leaving, he gently lifted her hand to his lips.

She had never experienced such a sensation of relief as his mouth reassuringly touched her palm. His breath was warm, his lips soft and moist. She wanted to stay forever within this haven safety. Then he was gone. And just like in her dream, she was alone.

Blinking, she just stood there. "Shadow, did Hawthorne just rush in here, catch me making a total fool out of myself, then kiss me stupid and leave?"

The cat sat in the sun licking his paw and preening his face. He paused momentarily before continuing his ministrations.

"Did I just stand here and let him do that?" The sweet memory was enough of an answer for her. She plopped down cross-legged next to the kitten. "Did I actually say I'd cook dinner?" Shaking her head, she started to laugh. "Damn, Shadow, that man can kiss." *He always could?*

Finding enough ingredients to whip up spaghetti and a tossed salad, Abby headed upstairs and changed into a pair of khaki-colored slacks and an olive green sweater. Shadow followed close behind. Zigging and zagging, the kitten played with absolutely nothing or no one until he somersaulted to a sudden halt. He hissed at his reflection in the large cheval mirror in the corner.

"That's easy for you to say, but I've got a dinner to prepare." She scooped up Shadow and headed downstairs. "One kiss and I offered to cook for the man," she muttered. "Un-freaking-believable."

At five-thirty on the dot, Abby heard the front door open. She stirred the bubbling sauce that simmered on the stove. An unmistakable essence of herbs and spices mingled with the rich fragrance of scented candles.

"Judging from the delicious aroma, it's probably a good thing I picked up a little something for the cook." Standing in the doorway, he offered Abby a huge spray of burgundy mums and baby's breath.

Turning to face Jack, Abby realized tall, dark and handsome might have been a cliché, but in his case it was such an understatement. That prickly sensation nipped at her toes again when she saw the luscious bouquet of her favorites. "They're beautiful, but maybe you should wait until you taste this before you pass out too many compliments."

He inhaled deeply. "I don't think so."

She gestured around the kitchen. "Got something to put these in?"

Jack loosened his tie and gave his collar a yank before handing her a tall, cut glass vase from the cabinet over the sink. He lowered his face to her ear and inhaled deeply. "Anything that smells this good has to taste even better."

Abby didn't want to admit just how good Jack's warm breath felt on her neck, so she sidestepped him and filled the cut-glass container with water. "You've got a few minutes before dinner."

Jack peeled off his jacket and tossed it over a barstool before unbuttoning his cuffs and rolling up both sleeves.

"Want some coffee?" she asked, pointing to the freshly brewed pot.

He washed his hands before grabbing two mugs and filling them. "Black, right?"

"Right." She eased the flowers down into the water and found herself smiling at his easy charm. "These will look great in the dining room."

After placing the bouquet in the middle of the candle lit table, Abby returned to the kitchen. There Jack stood, slicing the French bread. His tall form was bent painstakingly over a granite cutting board as he slathered each piece with butter and garlic powder. She watched him carefully re-form the loaf and wrap it in aluminum foil before popping it into the oven.

"My God, he cooks."

He met her gaze. "I thought you figured that out this afternoon."

"You're not referring to that little," she shrugged her shoulders, "peck on the mouth you gave me on your way out, are you?" she asked without as much as a glance in his direction.

"You're absolutely right. That's all it was."

Looking up, his dark eyes searched too deeply. Said too much. Weighing the possibility of Jack's statement, she swallowed hard and maneuvered around him to remove the salad from the refrigerator. "Ready for dinner?"

He brushed a stray lock of hair off her cheek. "I'm starving."

When Abby slipped past him, his low whistle followed her out of the kitchen. As they ate, Abby wondered why looking at Jack through the warm glow of candlelight during dinner didn't seem the least bit awkward or strange? After all, she didn't even know him—not really. It made no sense that she felt so at home with him or in his house.

Jack pushed his empty plate aside. "I definitely owe you more flowers."

"No, you don't. It was my pleasure." And that was the truth. "After all, you remembered burgundy mums are my favorite."

"You really shouldn't have gone out for the candles though," he pointed out. "You're probably still a little shaky."

"I didn't." Was he kidding? After that so-called little peck on the mouth, she couldn't have even dialed 911.

"Oh, that's right. You bought some in Salem."

"I did, but not these. They were in my suitcase."

"You carry candles with you?"

"I—"

"No. Don't tell me. I don't want to know."

"You brought it up."

"Got any stakes of holly, silver bullets—"

"If you'll knock off the sarcasm, it's really quite simple." But it wasn't, not really. In fact it still confused her a little, too. "I love candles," she lied, knowing she'd always had an aversion to fire.

"And after your shop burned, they don't bother you?"

"Not these," she told him, certain that was the truth but not certain why. "The gold ones symbolize protection."

"From what?"

Abby hiked both shoulders. "Evil, I guess," she told him, bracing for the smirk that never came. Instead, she watched him grab the bottle of wine and both of their glasses from the table.

"They're nice. Let's drink this in the living room," he suggested.

"Okay. I'll just clean up first."

"Leave it."

Jack moved Abby's candles to the coffee table. "Mind if I make myself comfortable?"

"Su casa is, after all, su casa," Abby reminded him.

"Right."

When he eased off his shoes and stretched out both legs, Shadow jumped from beneath the sofa and attacked his feet. Scooping up the little furball, he stroked the kitten. Purring, the small creature ritualistically turned around three times before settling down on his lap and dozing comfortably.

"Speaking of your house," she began, "I really do like it, but I'm kind of surprised that you bought a home."

"Why?"

Abby swirled the wine in the delicately stemmed glass as she spoke. "It just seems like most men prefer to rent an apartment."

He shrugged. "I wanted my own place. Something to focus on besides work."

She sipped her drink and watched him absently pet Shadow. "Work and home sound pretty good to me right now."

"I'm sure they do," he said. "Have you decided what you're going to do?"

"Not yet." She sighed. "It's still so hard to believe. Kat. My apartment. My shop."

"I can't imagine—"

"Hey, enough about me," she insisted, cutting him off. She refused to let a pity party ruin such a nice evening. "Did you paint these?" she asked with a wide sweeping gesture toward the pictures on the walls.

"Guilty as charged."

"Why the *W* signature?" Before he could answer, she realized, "It's the *W* you added to the Hathorne name, isn't it?"

"Well, not me personally, but yes."

"They're wonderful. You have a great eye. Well, actually two," she observed, without cracking a smile.

"Thanks. On both counts."

"No portraits?" she asked, remembering the man in her dream who promised her portrait as a wedding present.

"Never found a face interesting enough to paint—until now."

She willed away the dream—her beloved's promise of a portrait for a wedding present. Just as quickly, she ignored Jack's compliment as well as the slow somersault her heart did. "Were you always interested in art?"

"Yes," he said. "Tell me. What do you lose yourself in? Something that puts you in the zone."

She took a frank, admiring look at Jack. Feather-like laugh lines crinkled around his eyes, softening his sometimes disturbingly intense appearance. "I walk."

"Your dog?"

"I don't have a dog."

"Cat?"

She shook her head.

"No pets?"

"Nope."

"Let me get this straight," he began. "You don't have a pet back in Springfield, but you adopt one while you're on vacation?"

Abby's eyes widened as she pointed to Shadow. "You mean him? Oh, I'm not taking him home with me."

"Then why am I feeding him?"

She scooted closer and whispered into his ear, "Because you're such a nice guy?"

He turned his head quickly to prevent her from moving out of reach. His lips brushed hers as he murmured, "Damn right I am."

Abby enjoyed the feel of his strong arms. Her body told her so. Timidly, she splayed her fingers across his broad back, savoring its warmth. The only aspect of Jack more powerful than the strength simmering just below the surface was the tenderness he tried so hard to hide.

Abby could feel Shadow at her back, slapping at her hair. Reaching around, she tried to shoo him away with one hand. The more she waved her fingers, the more he wanted to play.

Raising his head a whisper, Jack asked, "Are you always this flighty when you're being kissed?"

Unable to suppress the laughter, Abby pulled Shadow from behind her. "Blame your cat." She eased herself back against the davenport, just out of Jack's reach and watched him refill their glasses before saying, "I can't stay here indefinitely, you know." She'd always prided herself on her strength, but living under the same roof with Jack was becoming too much of a challenge, even for her. The physical attraction between them was undeniable, and it was growing. Abby decided it best to leave while she still had the inclination.

"Sounds like you've already decided."

Abby nodded, accepting the wine Jack offered. She focused on Shadow and ran a teasing finger along the couch to encourage his playfulness. Without looking up, she answered, "Yeah, I think it's for the best."

"Not Hannah's Inn though."

Even though Abby thought Jack would agree with her decision to go, she wasn't prepared for the hurt that followed his easy acceptance. Abby uncurled her feet, planting them squarely on the floor. She set the wine aside. "No, I'll find another bed and breakfast or a nice hotel." Standing, she started toward the kitchen. "I'll get us some coffee."

"Whoa." Jack caught her about halfway. "You sit. I'll pour."

"I'm not an invalid," she insisted. "After all, I made it."

"Exactly," Jack grinned. "So, don't overdo." He gently shoved her in the direction of the couch. "Go."

"To hell," Abby muttered as she headed back into the living room.

In less than five minutes, Jack handed Abby a cup of coffee. "You realize that what happened today wasn't some prank. Someone is after something, and whoever this is, they think one of us has it."

"Maybe," she agreed half-heartedly.

When the phone rang, Jack turned his back to Abby as he spoke. "What have you got?"

"What's the bottom line?"

"Thanks. Keep me posted."

He hung up the receiver and faced Abby.

"What?" she asked, bracing herself for the inevitable.

"Just let me handle this, will you?"

She bristled, then spoke with quiet firmness, "First of all, this is not some legal case. *This* is my life—and yours. Secondly, you are not my employer; therefore you cannot dismiss me like some kind of servant. In fact, now that I think about it, technically I'm your employer. You're my lawyer."

"Your room at Hannah's Inn being ransacked may have been the result of a nosy maid who was baited by a beautiful necklace," he began. "My car, on the other hand, may have been deliberately tampered with which makes this *my* problem and my decision."

Abby struggled to maintain an even, conciliatory tone. "Not when it comes to me," she insisted, observing his dark eyes flash a gentle but firm warning.

"Damn it, Abby, can't you get it through your head whoever is behind this is playing for keeps." He shoved his hands deep into the pockets of his pants.

"Then we'll just have to check into it."

"What do you mean *we?*"

"What do you mean, what do I mean? You know very well what I mean. Someone has targeted one of us. My room. Your car. So like it or not, we're in this together."

Jack shook his head. "Not anymore."

Determined to beat him at his own game, Abby lifted her chin, meeting his icy gaze straight on. "You're right."

"Forget it. You're not playing Nancy Drew…I'm what?"

"I said you are right." Abby enunciated as though she were speaking to a small child. She slipped past him muttering hostile, unintelligible expletives and nearly ripped the pages out of the phone book, searching for the number of a cab. "You believe you're the target," she hissed at Jack, pounding the touch-tone at the expense of her still sensitive wrist. "So, I'm sure you'll want me as far away from you as possible." She switched hands. "For my safety, of course."

"You're not going back to Hannah's Inn," Jack stated.

"I'll go where I please," Abby insisted, not that she would return there, it was just the principle.

"Not there you won't. I checked you out."

"You what?" She slammed her free hand on her hip, wincing at the pain in her wrist. "And just when were you planning to tell me?"

"When I didn't take you back," he said matter-of-factly.

"Of all the impertinent, presumptuous, egotistical—no, no not you," she apologized into the receiver and glared at Jack. "I'm sorry. I'd like a cab."

She shot him a look that would have dropped a bull elephant at a thousand yards. After the quick phone call, she tore the address of a motel from the phone book and spent the next few minutes stuffing her suitcase.

Jack never made a move to stop Abby. Instead, he stood motionless in his very empty, very quiet house as the cab's fiery taillights disappeared into the darkness. She was gone and he was alone.

Chapter Twenty-Three

Lashed to a nearby tree, Jackson watched in amazement as a woman deftly intercepted Bridget's throw and snagged Abigail's amulet from midair. Careful to stay behind the crowd, the tall, thin woman wove her way through the shadows and dropped the amulet in the dry grass at his feet.

"Maxine?—"

"Hush," the woman ordered as she slipped behind the tree and shoved a folded sheet of paper into his hand.

"What's this?" Sweat stung his eyes as he ground both arms against the tree's rough bark to give Maxine as much slack as possible.

"Abigail had another dream last night. About a witch hunt. Fearing it would come to pass, she wrote out instructions for me to give you, so listen carefully. First, I've dropped her necklace at your feet. You must take it with you. Second, you must read what she's written and do exactly as she asks."

"Why?" Jackson felt her bony fingers nimbly working at the knot that bound his wrist.

"There's no time to explain," her thin lips warned. "Just do as I say…"

●●●

Before daylight, Jack stood impatiently in the hallway outside the entrance to his office. Head pounding and sleep deprived, he had tossed and turned all night, tormented by the haunting Bill Withers' song that had relentlessly played in his head. He shoved his key into the lock and, once inside, he slammed the door shut behind him. The deafening quiet screamed at him like a jealous lover and somehow managed to further tick him off, if that were even possible. Whatever the hell was going on, one of them was in danger. Him? Or her? That was the real question. The jump ball as it were.

The past few days had been a nightmare, and his gut reaction to each incident had erupted like a bleeding ulcer. Jack was used to taking control, being in charge. For him, the law had always been black and white, and that was the concept he liked most about it. Inside the courtroom he was damned good at calling the shots, but this was different. Suddenly, he was up to his eyeballs in gray areas. Jack hated gray areas.

He flipped on the lights, wishing his thoughts were as easy to illuminate. As he crossed the beautifully polished floor, his shoes echoed in the otherwise silent building. Wasn't this the same maddening quiet that had driven him from his tomb-like house at the crack of dawn?

"Dammit." Jack slammed his fist into the wall. How in the hell could he protect Abby…*this time?* Those two words didn't even make sense to him. Jack's heart beat hard against his ribs, like a mother shaking a child from a fitful dream. Only for Jack the implication merely teased at the edges of his mind like an unspoken threat. His consciousness refused the warning, but something deep inside sensed some kind of an awakening.

"Bring it on," he whispered to no one.

• • •

"Hurry, Midnight, he's right behind us." Abigail held on for dear life and begged her horse to gallop faster. Whispering in his ear, cooing and pleading, she ducked the tree branches and woody vines that canopied the well-worn, dirt path. Abby dug her heels into his flanks and prayed her beloved animal could hold his pace. As she hunched over the pommel, his thick, dark mane whipped against her cheeks the same way her petticoats and her long, black skirt's hem slapped his heaving sides.

Careful to keep her head down Abby stole a glance over one shoulder. The man in the red cape was gaining on them. His horse's hooves pounded the barren trail, gouging chunks of earth and spitting them in his wake. Whip in hand, the rider lashed out, pushing the animal harder. As the stranger's fearsome silhouette thundered through the sun-dappled forest's path, light and shadow alternately flashed across his features, scrambling his identity in what could otherwise be considered broad daylight. The black, pilgrim-style hat he wore stayed put, unlike the scarlet material that billowed behind him like great devil's wings…

• • •

Splashing water in her face, Abby regarded her reflection in the tiny hotel mirror. "Not too bad for only a couple of hours sleep and a nightmare that would have made Rosemary put her baby up for adoption."

Dabbing extra concealer under both eyes and gingerly tapping some on her bruised cheek, she put the finishing touches to her makeup and decided it was good enough.

Despite another bad dream, a ransacked room, and checking into what might as well have been the Bates Motel, Abby had made it through the night on her own. However shaky, she had stood her ground and still had no intention of letting anyone dictate what she could or could not do.

As she stepped into the hotel parking lot, the brilliant October sun felt warm on her back but only for an instant. A black cloud appeared from nowhere, blocking out the daylight, shadowing her every move. And with it came a chilling breeze that swirled around her ankles, shackling them with chains of dried leaves. Her blood ran cold. She shook each foot as if to break some invisible restraint.

Fighting the uneasy sensation of being watched, Abby walked back to where she'd parked the black Ford Taurus she had rented on her way to the hotel last night. As she pulled away from the curb, that uneasy feeling she couldn't shake shrouded her consciousness like a pall. Not just the creeps. This was different. Intense. Over and over, she sensed some kind of warning. But what?

Several blocks later, Abby checked the rear view mirror and her breath caught in her throat. Was that the same red car that had just been parked across the street from the hotel?

Talk about paranoid. Be realistic. How many red cars, she glanced again, are there in a city the size of Boston? Only one? Don't be ridiculous.

Abby decided to double back to the hotel just to satisfy the knot in the pit of her stomach and to see if he was really following her. Several turns later, the red car was still a good block behind her. But he was there. She accelerated and veered into the hotel parking lot. Rushing inside and down the hall, she slammed the door behind her. It took two tries before her shaky fingers finally secured the chain lock. Aggravated at having knees that felt like Jell-O and hands that still trembled, she sat down at the small desk next to the bed to catch her breath. Unable to remain seated, she stood and began pacing.

This was not only absurd, but returning to the hotel hadn't proven a thing. Ever since that stupid nightmare, these eerie feelings had plagued her. Irritatingly persistent and scary as hell. Red cape. Red car. Red flag? If that weren't bad enough, the deadly silence of this damnable room was driving her over the edge, but—oh, that's right—because of her hissy fit last night, she had no other place to go…

She glanced toward the window.

...*Except back out there.* She shivered. "No way," she whispered.

That increasingly familiar niggling in the pit of her stomach started again. She took a deep breath and tried to will it away. As she sorted through the facts, she had to admit whatever was going on here didn't look good. The wreck was bad enough. She had been driving, but it was Jack's car. Someone pilfering her room at Hannah's Inn pointed directly at her. And now the red car—*her* again. For the first time in her life, Abby was truly frightened.

• • •

Zeke pulled into the hotel lot and parked. He drummed his fingers on the steering wheel. What to do? Following the Corey woman had definitely spooked her. Hell, she couldn't get back to the hotel fast enough. Panic. He liked that in a woman. He would definitely use that against her. He grinned. Maybe, if she left in enough of a hurry, she would leave the necklace behind. His grin widened. He got out of the car, careful to stay close to the building, and picked a spot behind some thick evergreens where he could remain hidden and still see her when she left. And she would leave; he would see to that. Pulling out his cell phone, he dialed the hotel and asked for room 114.

She answered. He could hear the dread in her voice. He said nothing. Rewarded by another tremulous *hello*, he waited a beat then breathed into the receiver. Why that freaked out chicks he didn't know. What he did know...it worked every time.

• • •

As tired as Abby was, she knew sleep was out of the question. Instead, she just lay down on the bed. Maybe she could rest and think. Possibly contemplate going home. Back to Springfield. Not that there was any home to go home to. The shrill ring of the phone nearly sent Abby into orbit. She fumbled for the receiver.

"Hello."

Silence.

She waited a beat. "Hello."

Nothing.

But someone was there. Abby heard breathing. She held her breath to make sure what she heard wasn't coming from her. It was not. Her mind searched for logic. Jack was the only person she knew in Boston. She had ripped the page from his phone book, so he may have figured out where she was staying. But he didn't play games. So, if it wasn't Jack, who the hell was it? The desk clerk probably rang the wrong extension, that's all. She exhaled.

Or, maybe it was the driver of the red car?

The hair prickled at the base of her neck. Abby eased the receiver back in its cradle and raced to the window. Was that the same red car on the far side of the parking lot? Thank God her car was right by the exit. She ran across the room as fast as her trembling legs would carry her. Fumbling, she finally tore free the locks and slammed the door behind her.

• • •

Unlike Hannah's Inn, this time Zeke had been instructed not to toss the joint. Bridget had ranted and raved because he trashed the last hotel room. So, instead of ripping the place apart, which he had always loved doing, this time he would be careful. Not that he liked it, because he didn't. Zeke took great pleasure in doing things his way. Always had. But, as Bridget had so often reminded him—the bitch was the boss. So, he would play along for now.

First, the closet. He searched each pocket thoroughly. Nothing. The dresser drawers. He painstakingly sifted through every one careful to replace each piece of neatly folded clothing. No necklace.

And finally, her suitcase. The one he had nearly shredded the other night. He wondered what there was about gutting something—anything—with a knife that turned him on? Controlling the urge to tear out the zipper, sweat beaded on his forehead. Instead, he followed his instructions and unzipped the side pocket.

"Bingo." He pulled out the wooden box and smirked. "Pay dirt." He started to shove the case into his jacket pocket then hesitated. Instead, he opened it and removed the necklace. Slipping the amulet into his pocket, he shut the lid and replaced the wooden box exactly where he had found it. Walking to the door, he turned. Everything looked exactly as it had when he came in. Successful but sure as hell not satisfying to him. Not in the least. What to do? What to do? He thought a moment.

Question. Should he shut and lock the door behind him, like Bridget had insisted. Or, should he ignore Her Highness and do at least one thing as he damn well pleased? Why the hell not? After all, that Bishop chick was a psycho if he had ever met one. And he had met some real freaks in his time. Some of them good psychos, like Layla. Real good. His mouth watered at the thought. But some were bad. Really bad. Scary bad. Like Shanti. Now that was one twisted sister.

He was sick to death of Bridget's bossy mouth and her flunky jobs. Once this was done and he was paid, he was through with her. But not with the redhead. Oh, no. He liked her looks way too much, and she was already set up for it. He had heard it in her voice. She was scared shitless. Just the way he liked his women.

Decision made. He could leave the door ajar to give the chick's paranoia another nasty little poke. Besides, he loved the upper hand way too much not to. If he couldn't trash the place to show her who was boss, why not at least leave a calling card to let her know he had been there before he paid her another visit. What the hell. On his way out, Zeke eased the door closed—almost.

Chapter Twenty-Four

Salem, Massachusetts
31 October
Year of our Lord, 1692

"Hawthorne," a burly man heading Jackson's way yelled.

"Luke?" Jackson felt Maxine's frantic effort stop. Knowing she had slipped away, but failed to free him, Jackson raised his tear-stained face. "For God's sake, Luke, untie me," he pleaded.

"Watch," Luke ordered, desperate to save his longtime friend. "Watch her hang, and it will break the witch's spell."

"I am not bewitched." Jackson swore. As he writhed furiously to free himself, his captors' ropes sawed through the tattered waistcoat and the torn sleeves of his loose, white shirt, biting into the exposed flesh of both arms. "I love her," he bellowed.

Compelled to meet Abigail's gaze, his head snapped up, and dark eyes met green for the last time. So powerful was her stare that he dared not breathe. Time stood still…

...

"Let me get this straight." Jack tossed his pen aside and folded both arms over his black and gray herringbone jacket. "After storming out last night, you came here to offer your services?"

"Why not?" Abby skirted the obvious load of crap she was dishing out. "When I was here the other day, Maxine told me about your plan to redecorate."

Jack's eyes narrowed. "She did, did she?"

"Uh huh." Abby nodded. "I thought you might need some help putting things back together."

"I believe you made it crystal clear last night that I work for you. Not the other way around."

Abby couldn't argue that point, so she didn't even try. "Just call this a little thank you for your generosity. After all, you did go above and beyond after my accident," she insisted.

"And what about your adamant rejection of *said hospitality* last night?"

"My reaction had nothing to do with 'said hospitality,' and everything to do with personal boundaries. You know, the ones you completely disregarded."

"Believe it or not, even I can understand gratitude."

At the arch of Jack's eyebrow, she amended, "Look, I don't have any plans this afternoon—that's all—and regardless of what you think, this car wreck ordeal may still be tied to me. I guess I just feel responsible for dragging you into it." She met his blatant stare and saw the hint of a smile tip the corners of his mouth.

"You just don't give up, do you?"

"I assume that's a rhetorical question." Sensing the change in Jack, Abby took the seat opposite his desk.

"I guess it was," he admitted. "And you're just here to help straighten up my office out of undying gratitude?"

"That's right," she lied. For whatever reason, Abby knew she needed to be close to Jack. "So, where do we go from here?"

"I, for one, have work to do," he told her.

"Just tell me where to start."

He leaned back and stared. "Like a Kelly girl?"

She sidestepped his question as well as the mess that covered the floor. "Looks like the painters had a fit in here."

Jack eyed the index cards scattered on the floor beside his desk. "Derailed my Rolodex."

"I can't believe you still use one of those," Abby muttered as she leaned down and scooped up the errant cards.

"Just a backup."

She straightened the mishmash in her hand, then shot back, "I assume these were in some sort of order."

"Not really." He shrugged, handing her the small metal wastebasket at the side of his desk. "Normally, I just keep those in here."

She ignored his sarcasm as well as the trashcan. "Alphabetical?"

"No, numerical." He set the can back in its place without cracking a smile. "Of course alphabetical. Or, was that your version of a rhetorical question?"

For meanness, she shuffled the array of cards then offered, without as much as a blink, "Maybe you'd like a shot at these yourself."

"Not me." He stopped at the doorway and turned to face her. "I don't suppose you make coffee, too?"

She placed the empty Rolodex in the middle of Jack's desk and simply looked at him.

He shook his head. "Black, right?"

She nodded. "Coffee would be nice, thanks."

After Abby made short work of the cleanup, she joined Jack and Maxine at her desk in the outer office.

"Can I get you anything else?" He reached for Maxine's phone. "Chinese Food? Pizza?"

"Cut the bull, Hawthorne. Don't you have something else constructive I can do?"

"Let's see." He refilled his mug. "Maxine has a '68 Mustang out back that can use an oil change."

"Cool car." Abby didn't even blink. "I'll check it out before I leave." She ignored the priceless look on his face and winked at Maxine.

"He knows good and well I change my own oil," she told Abby. "Always have."

"Me, too," Abby lied then winked. "I have to say that you did a super job on the redecoration, Ms. Spencer. The place looks great."

"Maxine," the older woman corrected. "And thank you."

"Maxine," Abby repeated with a nod. "And you're welcome."

Jack glanced from one smiling female to the other, but decided he did not have time to psychoanalyze their strange but obvious bond right now. "They'll be back this evening to paint the filing cabinets and by tomorrow it should be business as usual." He double-checked with Maxine. "That meeting still on with O'Malley tonight?"

"He just called. Seems he had to take a later flight, so he should arrive about eight o'clock tonight. I rescheduled him for nine o'clock, allowing eleven minutes for flight fluctuation, twenty-one minutes for luggage retrieval and a twenty-eight minute cab ride."

Maxine looked from Jack to Abby and back again.

When neither spoke, she added, "I have an errand to run, but I'll be back." Without waiting for a response, she turned and walked away.

"Amazing," Jack muttered, turning his attention to Abby. "Care to squeeze in dinner about seven?" he offered. "It's the least I can do to repay you."

Abby checked her watch—almost four—and forced the panic from her voice. "Did you say seven?" she asked.

"Yeah."

Dread coiled in the pit of her stomach. Just the thought of that hotel room and the wrong number, or whatever it had been, made her skin crawl and the pulse pound in her ears. The last thing she wanted was to sit alone in that hotel room and watch the clock—not to mention the phone—or, the window.

"What am I supposed to do for three hours?" she blurted.

Jack searched her face, then offered, "I won't be home, so if you're looking for a way to kill time, you could stop by my place and feed *your* cat."

At the mention of Shadow, Abby's heartbeat steadied a bit. At least he would be company, albeit feline companionship, and that was a helluva lot better than being alone.

"Okay." She felt better already. "But your favors are really piling up."

"And I'll bet you're keeping score." Digging into his pocket, Jack pulled out his keys and handed her the one to his front door.

Abby stared at the key. Just a chunk of metal. Nothing more. Right? Wrong. Dead wrong. It was a whole lot more than just a hunk of metal to her. When she walked through Jack's front door, the furniture and pictures would be familiar. The house would remind her of coffee brewing and Jack's after-shave. She knew what drawer his underwear was in. She knew exactly which cabinet held the chocolate fudge cookies. She knew the feeling, the smells, the sounds of home.

"Thanks." She offered a shaky smile.

"Are you okay?"

"Sure," she lied. "I'll meet you back here."

"No need. I'll pick you up."

"Thanks, Jack." She gave him a long, hard look and stood very still.

Jack laced his hand through her thick hair. He cupped her chin and lowered his head. He kissed her sweetly.

Abby saw it coming. He was going to do it again and she was going to let him. His touch was almost unbearable in its tenderness. She parted her lips ever so slightly and raised herself just enough to meet him. His mouth touched hers like a whisper. The hint of some trusted secret. She sighed.

Deep inside a haunting restlessness stirred. Not passion. Not desire. More like a fierce protectiveness she couldn't explain. *Or could she?* The all-too-vivid mental image of Gallows Hill clouded her thoughts. Like distant thunder rattling the windows of her mind, it warned that a storm was brewing. Shaken, she pulled away. Something was gathering force. And fast. She could feel it.

Chapter Twenty-Five

Abby spotted Maxine in the lobby, waiting by the door. Pristine navy blue suit. Her thin lips pursed. And something important on her mind.

"Thought I'd wait and walk out with you," Maxine told her.

As little as she really knew about the older woman, Abby understood this was not social. And that fact did not offend her in any way. On the contrary, one detail she had picked up on about Maxine Spencer—when this woman talked, Jack listened. And that spoke volumes to Abby.

"Sure. I'd like that." Abby followed her through the huge revolving door and out into the afternoon sunlight. She inhaled the sweet scent of autumn in the still-warm breeze and smiled. "Fresh air feels great."

Maxine nodded.

"I've got a feeling there's something you'd like to talk about," Abby told her.

Maxine pulled herself up a little taller. "I'm a very private woman, Ms. Corey—"

"Abby," she said quietly.

Maxine nodded. "I have no family and no close friends. She cleared her throat unapologetically. "No one with whom to confide."

"I see." Abby could tell the woman would not be placated, so she simply waited for her to continue.

"If you have the time," Maxine began, pointing to the Star Bucks across the street, "I would like to speak to you."

...

Shortly before seven, Jack and Abby arrived at The Grotto, a quaint little neighborhood restaurant nestled between a bakery and a candy store, both of which smelled like heaven on earth. Hurrying inside, she shivered and pulled her coat tighter against the cold night air, or whatever had suddenly chilled her to the bone. Jack? Her conversation with Maxine? The almost full moon? Abby just wasn't sure.

Seated in a booth, they were situated just far enough from the kitchen to avoid the ever-swinging door yet close enough to appreciate the mouth-watering aromas of sizzling steaks and simmering sauces. Candlelight flickered across the well-worn wooden tabletop as busy waiters and waitresses hurried past, taking and filling orders.

"Feeling better tonight?" Jack asked as he considered the menu.

Abby looked up in time to catch Jack watching her. Unceremoniously breaking the mood, her stomach growled, so she straightened her sweater, hoping he couldn't see her unsteady hand in the candlelight. "I feel fine," she lied.

He met the uncertainty in her gaze. "I meant better than this afternoon?"

"I felt fine then, too," she lied again, certain he must have picked up on her…hysteria, or whatever the hell had come over her earlier in the day.

Interrupted by the waitress, Jack waited until they had ordered to continue. "Want to talk about it?"

"Look, I said I feel—"

"Fine," he interrupted. "Yeah, I got that. But I'm a lawyer, Abby, and I do have a certain ability to read people. What I saw this afternoon, was not a woman who felt fine."

Something about his even gaze and steady tone relaxed Abby. "I don't really know," she began honestly.

"Well then, are you ready to tell me why you really came to my office this afternoon?"

Abby should have known better. After all, Hawthorne was a lawyer. He lived for details, facts and questions. But most of all for answers. Too bad she didn't have any. So, as the food arrived, she decided to stick with her story. "Like I said, I really was grateful for all you've—"

Before she could continue, Jack's cell phone rang, nearly stopping her heart.

Jack ended his conversation quickly. "O'Malley's flight was cancelled, so there's no rush," he told her. "Sorry, you were saying?"

Between bites and after careful consideration, Abby decided not to tell Jack about her conversation with Maxine, nor would she try and explain the man who may or may not have been following her. Much less the creepy phone call or the red car in the hotel parking lot. After all, she couldn't be sure it was the same car, and wrong numbers happen all the time.

"Actually," she qualified, "I was just repeating what I told you earlier. I just stopped by to say thanks." She folded both arms across her chest, careful to protect her injured wrist and end the cross-examination.

Thirty minutes later, still unable to get the truth out of Abby, Jack shoved his empty plate aside and laid down a fifty before shrugging into his jacket. "Ready?"

Outside, they hurried back through the blustery shadows to the car. The moment Abby realized Jack's next stop would be her hotel, she froze.

"What?" Jack asked.

She just stood there, a gust of wind whirling dry leaves around her feet. Like they had before. When had she become such a coward? This whole cloak-and-dagger routine was ridiculous, and she wasn't about to let some bizarre, over-blown, non-incident spook her any longer.

But what about the red car that followed you?

Must have been my imagination.

You saw it.

Boston is full of them.

And the mysterious phone call. What about that?

A wrong number.

Someone was there.

A childish prank.

If you say so.

Abby willed her practical side to shut up and go away as she faced Jack. "What do you mean—what?"

"You stopped right in the middle of the parking lot."

Abby just looked at him.

He held up both hands. "Forget it." He headed for the car and opened the passenger's door. "Get in."

She slid onto the seat. "Only because you asked so nicely."

Once inside, Jack fired up the ignition then faced Abby. "Look, I don't know what the deal was this afternoon, and apparently you're not going to tell me. But just for the record, I don't think you should go back to that hotel."

Relief battled pride. "If you won't take me, I'll just phone for a cab." So how in the hell had stupidity won out over both of them?

Jack didn't say a word.

"Your call." She reached for the door handle.

"Sit still." He accelerated just to make sure. "You're not taking a damned taxi."

"Adam's Inn. It's on—"

"I know where it is," Jack snapped.

When they pulled into the hotel parking lot, Abby swallowed hard. They had passed several billboards along the way advertising the Halloween Ball. Something about the vivid images tweaked her consciousness. It seemed to whisper, *tag you're it!* Like coming to Boston, this elusive challenge simply refused to be ignored. For whatever reason, she felt an overwhelming, unexplainable need to attend the gala event.

Content, for now, to know at least that much, she took Jack's hand and entered the hotel. As they walked down the dimly lit hallway, doubt smirked at her through long, sharp teeth from every dark corner. Why on earth had she ever insisted on coming back to this place?

That's when she noticed it.

She grabbed Jack's arm to stop him and whispered, "My door's not shut."

Jack pushed her behind him and slowly eased the door open. Little...by...little. Pitch dark.

He loosened the death grip she had on his bicep and mouthed, "Stay here."

"No way," she muttered, following right behind him.

Jack flipped on the nearest light and crept silently through the bedroom and bath. Satisfied no one was in her room, he turned on Abby. "Don't you ever do what you're told?"

"Not really." She pretended not to understand his thunderous look.

He raked frustrated fingers through his hair. "Any idea who was in here?"

Abby's chest constricted as she felt the demons of the afternoon rear their ugly heads. She forced herself to ignore them and, instead, to look around paying strict attention to detail.

Personal items—untouched.

Suitcase—zipped tight.

The amulet's box—right where she left it.

Everything else seemed fine. Nothing out of place. Neat and clean. Convinced all was well, her fear dissipated. "It doesn't look like anything's missing, and I did leave in a hurry." Boy, was that an understatement. She had raced out of there on a dead run. "Maybe I just didn't pull the door shut."

Jack eyed Abby. "Maybe's not good enough. Either you closed it, or you didn't," he said. "And, don't give me that look."

"What look?"

"You know," he said. "That don't-you-dare-tell-me-what-to-do look."

Abby turned toward the dresser and proceeded to re-straighten her already meticulously lined up cosmetics. "I don't know what you're talking about."

Jack rubbed the back of his neck. "Look, Abby, this isn't a game. Don't make it one."

Abby hadn't realized how serious Jack was until she faced him. His dark eyes mirrored every bit of the concern she had heard in his voice. "I'm not taking this lightly," she insisted, desperate to ignore the sinking feeling in the pit of her stomach.

"Good," he said. "Then you're coming home with me."

Abby shook her head. "I said I wasn't playing a game, and I'm not, but, I am staying here."

"Suit yourself." Jack stalked past her. Turning the knob slowly and deliberately, he added through clenched teeth, "Don't forget to lock the door behind me. Wouldn't want your room to be open all day and all night, too. Would you?"

Abby secured the lock behind him and leaned heavily against the door. She knew, without a doubt, her arrogance and foolishness had just crossed the boundary of common sense. Restless, she roamed the perimeter of the room. The more she thought about it, the more convinced she became that she had pulled the door closed on her way out. *I did shut that door this afternoon.* Hell, thinking back, she even remembered hearing it slam.

But, nothing in the room had been disturbed. If they weren't looking for some*thing,* what were they looking for? Some*one?* Her? She spent the remainder of the night fully dressed and sitting in the chair. Eyes glued to the doorknob, she cursed Jack Hawthorne for all he was worth, but not half as much as she cursed herself.

Chapter Twenty-Six

In the hallway outside Abby's room, Jack fumed. Not only was she keeping something from him, but she was too damned stubborn to admit or give into the fact that she may very well be in danger. He looked around the semi-darkness. Damned, skanky hotel. He should have just thrown Abby over his shoulder and taken her back to his house. Now there was a thought. His mouth curved in a grin.

One thing was certain. He sure as hell wouldn't leave her here. Since she refused to come with him, he would just stay. He plopped down in front of her door and wadded up his jacket, tucking it behind his head.

An hour later, Jack stretched his cramped legs and cursed his numb butt. The floor was hard. The door was hard. And all the physical evidence pointed to the fact that his head must have gone soft. He punched up his jacket and gritted his teeth certain this was going to be one damn long night.

Suddenly, he heard the side door to the hotel slam shut. Its metal frame echoed in the confines of the entryway. In the dim light, he saw a man round the corner then stop short and stagger slightly, heading toward him. Jack pretended to sleep.

"Hey, boy," the man drawled as he nudged Jack's shoe with his foot. "You okay?"

Jack opened his eyes. A dusty pair of snakeskin boots stared back at him—extremely large boots. Standing over him, with a twelve-pack of long necks under one arm and a chip cocked forty-ways-for-Sunday on his broad shoulder, there stood one big, drunk biker.

"Yeah, I'm fine. Just ticked off." Jack jabbed his thumb toward Abby's door. "My old lady threw me out, can you beat that?"

"Women." The man shook his bald head and hefted the Coors. "Wanna beer?"

"No, thanks," Jack said. "I can barely handle this one when I'm sober!"

"I hear ya," the man slurred sympathetically. "But you ain't plannin' on sittin' here all night, are ya?"

Jack's internal radar went off like a lie detector. "She'll cool off later."

"Maybe." The biker grinned and gave one side of his mustache a thoughtful twirl. "Then again, if she was to come out and find you gone, that'd really teach her a lesson."

Jack's eyes narrowed. "Think I'll just hang around—"

"Hawthorne, is that you?" someone called from halfway down the hall.

As the man approached, Jack recognized the familiar face. "What the hell are you doing here, Venucci?"

Lucky openly eyed the biker. "I was on my way home and got a silent alarm call from here, but it turned out to be false. I was just coming in to get a cup of coffee."

Without getting up, Jack shook the large hand the man extended.

"Enough about me." Lucky poked his finger in Jack's direction. "There must be quite a story behind this."

"You could say that." Jack shifted his weight, reluctant to continue in front of the stranger.

Lucky inclined his head, "A friend of yours?"

"I just met Mr.....?" Jack waited.

"Smith," the biker offered.

"Mr. Smith stopped to see if I was dead or alive."

"Is that so?" Lucky turned to the big man, but neither one extended his hand. "Funny, at the first sign of trouble, most folks would've run the other way."

"Oh, hell, no." The biker shrugged. "Trouble's my middle name."

"I'll bet," Lucky said, a trace of an edge to his voice. Staring down the other man, he didn't turn away to ask, "Mind if I join you, Hawthorne?" Without waiting for a reply, he slid his massive form down the wall. He elbowed Jack in the ribs. "How about it? Want a cup of coffee?"

Jack licked his dry lips. "Sounds great."

"No problem." Lucky flipped out his cell phone. "What do you think room service—or in your case hall service—is for?"

"How about you, Smith?" Jack leveled a steady gaze. "Coffee?"

"Too tame for me, Pal." The biker shifted his twelve-pack. "Well, since you two are fixin' to guard that door all night, I'll just be on my way." Halfway down the hall, Jack heard him cut loose a slightly off-key version of a classic country western song. "Somewhere on earth Garth Brooks has to be howling at the moon." Lucky's eyes narrowed. "Wonder what room that guy's in?"

Jack shrugged. "Just check the register under Smith."

"Yeah, right, like I've never heard that one before." Lucky shook his head.

"You don't believe that any more than I do."

"I sure as hell don't." Lucky shook his head again. "Must be the country way of saying none of your damned business." He settled against the wall. "So, what gives with your little camp out?"

Jack laid his arm on the other man's bulky shoulder. "It's a long story."

Lucky checked his watch. "What the hell. I've got all night."

Shortly before dawn, Lucky headed back to the office. Within minutes, Jack dozed off, then jolted awake, disoriented and feeling downright nasty. It took a moment before he remembered why he was sitting in the hotel's hallway, and he realized the night had passed without incident. He sat up and stretched then walked out a few of the kinks. Every bone in his body ached as he limped into his car.

Halfway home, he rubbed his stiff neck and swore that anyone who was stupid enough to want Abby Corey was welcome to her. Unfortunately, the shrill ring of his cell phone drowned out the only pleasant thought he'd had for the past three hours.

"Hawthorne."

"Are you still at the hotel?" Lucky asked.

"Nope. I'm on my way home," Jack told him. "Why?"

"When I came in this morning, I talked to the patrolman working your accident—"

"And?"

"And the mechanic that checked out the car noticed the brake lines had been cut."

"Sonofa—"

"Somebody tampered with the brakes, so whoever was driving that car was one screwed pooch."

"Abby." Jack wheeled into a U-turn."

"I need to talk to her."

"I'm on my way back. I'll let her know."

"I want to talk to you, too. How about ten o'clock?"

"We'll be there."

•••

A thunderous, nonstop pounding on her door shattered the otherwise quiet crack of dawn, not to mention Abby's brittle nerves. For one timeless moment, she just sat there. This was the bitter end. Thoughts of her damnable dream or vision or whatever the hell she'd experienced last night hadn't given her a minute's rest. Abby couldn't shake the image of seeing herself so clearly…it seemed like a memory.

The year had been 1692. She had been enjoying herself at Salem's Harvest Festival. A full moon had hung in the dark autumn sky like a huge paper lantern. One minute she had been dancing and laughing with a man—the same handsome man who had proposed in her other dream.

The next instant their rollicking good time had turned into terror. The once friendly faces of the town's people had become distorted, angry. Separated from her fiancé and frightened, she had fled. This time, when the evil man in the red cape had followed her, Abigail instinctively knew she must run for her life. The brute had easily overtaken her, but seemingly from nowhere her fiancé had reappeared. The two men had struggled violently—and then she had awakened or snapped out of it…or whatever.

"Abby, open up." Jack shouted, stilling banging hard with one fist.

Checking the peephole, she opened the door. "Good morning to you, too."

"I didn't come here to exchange pleasantries." He shoved his way into the room.

"Obviously."

"I have something to tell you."

Abby stared at his unshaven face, his crumpled clothes. The same clothes he'd had on yesterday? Where had *he* spent the night? She gave him a second look. Rumpled, dark hair. Five o'clock shadow turned to stubble. Red, irritated eyes. Not to mention his lousy disposition. "The only thing I want from you—"

"You're coming with me." He stopped directly in front of her.

Abby hesitated, but like last night, she pushed her better judgment aside. "I'm not going anywhere—"

"Just once, will you shut up and listen," he shot back, barely able to resist the itch to clamp a hand over her mouth—hard.

She pursed her lips and swallowed the brash comment that teetered dangerously on the tip of her tongue. His eyes flashed an unmistakable warning that told her it was the smart thing to do. He really didn't look like a man to be reckoned with.

Nevertheless, she struggled to temper her anger and settled, instead, for a hostile glare. The scary thing was, in her head, Abby knew Jack wasn't the type to get this irate over nothing. So, what could possibly have him so agitated? God, she was tired, maybe she didn't even want to know. Not true. Abby believed in facing everything head on, so she took a deep breath and braced herself. "I'm listening."

Jack looked her square in the eye. "You're going home with me." He pointed toward the suitcase in the corner. "Now pack."

Chapter Twenty-Seven

Salem Massachusetts
31 October
Year of Our Lord, 1692

The instant she looked away, the wind moaned and the frightened horse pranced. Amidst the brewing storm, Jackson hung his head. Unable to free himself, tears from his dark lashes splashed onto the amber stone at his feet. He watched in disbelief as the amulet hissed like a red-hot branding iron immersed into a trough of ice water.

Abigail's screams ripped through his heart, each one draining more of his life's blood than the last. As the remainder of the mob caught up, the crowd circled her like starving vultures. In the light from their torches, he saw their hideous, hate-filled faces as the rope was tossed over the dead oak's barren branch.

"Bridget! Stop them!" When the raven-haired beauty only smiled, Jackson raised his dark head to the sky, howling his beloved's name like a wounded animal. "Abigail…"

...

Abby's mouth fell open. Had Jack just ordered her to pack? She planted both hands on her hips. "Excuse me?"

"Get out of my way."

Today, her eyes burned from a self-induced insomnia and her back ached from sitting ramrod straight in the plain, wooden desk chair all night. She was definitely not in the mood for this. And as if that wasn't enough, she glared at Jack, it looked like the better part of her punishment, all six foot four of it, wasn't over yet.

Jack pushed past her, grabbed her suitcase and tossed it wide open onto the bed. He yanked the drawers out of the dresser and dumped them into the gaping luggage.

"Stop that!" She snagged a lacy teddy in midair and stepped between Jack and the dresser.

"Well, I told *you* to do it."

"Exactly." She watched his eyes narrow.

Jack stood very still. "Look, Abby, I'm through arguing with you."

She snatched up her leather bag from the corner and began packing her cosmetics. "I'd like to keep my breakables in one piece," she arched one brow, "that is, if you don't mind."

Jack shrugged. "Be my guest. But get the lead out."

"Just back off," she warned over one shoulder, "I said I'm going with you. Don't push it."

He jammed both fists into his pants pockets. How on earth could getting one woman out of a hotel room be so difficult? He should have gone with his gut instinct and just yelled fire. A twisted smile quirked his lips.

As Jack stepped back and watched Abby gather the last of her belongings, he couldn't help but notice how pale her cheeks had become. Unshed tears had welled up in her eyes. Her hands were shaking so badly she fumbled as she jammed the bag full of bottles and containers. His grin faded.

That was his undoing. He could handle her strength. He could go head-to-head with her stubbornness. But, what in God's name was he supposed to do when she looked so defenseless?

Dammit, he had always tried to protect her, keep her safe. Always?

Where the hell had that come from? His vision? Or mind flash? Or whatever the hell you called it? The hanging at Gallows Hill flashed through his mind and just as quickly he pushed aside the disturbing scene. He hadn't known this woman more than a couple of days, so she couldn't possibly have anything to do with that. Regardless, from the look on her face, whatever protection he had offered hadn't been enough.

Then or now.

When, his mind ranted? When exactly was *then*? Never, he insisted. They were strangers—period. Regardless, she was in over her head, and he had to help her get to the bottom of whatever was going on. Had he tried, even once, to understand how scared she must be? Hell, no. He'd just bullied his way into her room and ordered her to pack.

"Abby, we need to talk," he began, then stopped. There she stood, wide-eyed and innocent, expecting him to say something, anything…except that someone had tried to kill her. He cleared his throat and looked away. "I'll be damned if I'm going to discuss this here." He grabbed her hand. "Let's go home."

Abby took one deep breath and gave Jack's hand a squeeze. "Let's go."

Jack didn't say a word, and the quiet ride gave Abby a chance to think. What concerned her now was the reason for his visible edginess. Hard lines creased his forehead. The tenseness in his jaw betrayed deep frustration. Determination cast a harsh shadow across his features. Was it possible his expression mirrored the same turmoil that churned inside her? *Not much consolation there.*

As they pulled into the driveway, Jack parked and took her bags to the loft. He heard the soft music Abby had turned on before he saw her curled up in his favorite chair, eyes closed and feet propped up on the coffee table. He scraped a hand over his day-old beard and cleared his throat. "I'm going to jump in the shower, then we'll talk."

Abby looked up and offered a shaky grin. "Okay, want me to make some coffee?"

Jack returned her smile. Just having her here made him feel so much better. And from the look on her face, he wasn't the only one who felt that way. "Sounds good."

The early morning sun stenciled a warm pattern across the dining room table. Abby leaned back, drawing comfort from a strange sense of familiarity. Without a second thought, she'd gone straight to the coffee canister, knew right where the sugar was kept, and filled Shadow's dish with dry cat food. He purred his utmost appreciation before cuddling up under the table next to her feet.

When Jack walked into the room, she merely stared. The shower had washed away his tension. The grim lines around his mouth had vanished and the creases across his forehead were gone. He eased into the chair beside her, smelling of spicy after-shave and shampoo.

"Feel better?" she asked, fascinated by the way his damp hair curled on the neck of his sweater.

"Much."

"Me next," she said, heading for the bathroom.

He drank the coffee and tried to organize his thoughts while she was in the shower. Unfortunately, a weird sense of urgency nagged at his consciousness, picked at his psyche and undercut his concentration.

Jack's logical, legal mind wanted to dissect the irrational decision he had made on the way home. He had offered to take Abby to the Halloween Ball, but it made no sense. One of them was definitely in danger, so the last thing they needed to do was show up at such a high profile event. The thought was ludicrous, and the timing was ridiculous.

Besides that, Jack didn't even like Halloween. In fact, he'd always had an intense, albeit unexplained, dislike for the legendary holiday. So why had an overwhelming need to accompany Abby to the ball hit him like a sucker punch? Never one to run from a fight, Jack decided round two would definitely be his.

Abby reappeared a few minutes later, refreshed and relaxed by the comforting warmth of the shower. She took the seat opposite his. "Now, what did you want to talk about?"

"It's about your car wreck," he began.

"Okay." She sat up a little straighter. "What about it?"

"It was no accident." He paused and let the meaning of his words soak in. "My friend, Detective Venucci, called first thing this morning and confirmed it."

"So…" Abby thought a moment. "That's why there weren't any brakes."

"Exactly."

"That's why I hit the phone booth," she said, reliving the blind terror.

Jack nodded.

"I thought it was just an accident," she whispered. "But it wasn't." Unable to stay seated, she stood.

Jack's gut tightened. Why would anybody do that to her? The hint of a bruise still remained on her cheek. He remembered bringing her home from the hospital that night. Even the thought of such a deliberate act could outrage him all over again, so he worked to keep his emotions in check. Anger would only slow him down. He knew that. With his control hanging by a thread, he had to dig deep to find enough discipline to ensure his advantage. He wanted a full head of steam, but he had to keep a lid on his temper to deal with this situation. And he would deal with it. "I don't suppose you'd consider going back to Springfield and leaving this to me?"

She steadied herself before stepping out of his reach. "I can't."

"That's what I was afraid of," he admitted, impressed by the proud, albeit forced, tilt of her chin. He moved to her side and warmed her icy-cold hands between his. "Okay, then. Here's the deal. You stay with me for the remainder of your vacation, and we'll try to get to the bottom of this."

Considering the source, Abby knew she was being offered one hell of a compromise. She paused. There was something in Jack's expression—a soft, understanding look in his eyes—that rushed in and filled the emptiness that had threatened to devour her. "I can live with that," she answered quietly.

He pulled her into his arms. His lips brushed against hers as he spoke. "Can you really?"

Abby stared wordlessly at him. Filled with fear and doubt and need, her heart pounded. "Yes."

Jack rested his forehead against hers and groaned. Abby wasn't a woman who offered anything casually. And, she was giving him her trust. Jaw clenched, he closed his eyes and swallowed hard. As he rubbed his cheek against hers, he felt her body mold to his, yielding and pliant. He laced his fingers through her hair and tilted her head back.

Jack's steady gaze bore into Abby with silent expectation. His invitation was a passionate challenge, impossible to resist. She could feel his uneven breathing, the beat of his heart. Her body felt heavy and warm against him. His lips met hers and melted her weary resolve. Time ceased to exist.

He pressed his mouth to hers again, this time teasing and enticing, coaxing her emotions to the surface, leaving her no choice. His teeth nipped and tormented. His tongue probed and plundered. Her unsteady hands found their way beneath his sweater to the warm skin of his well-muscled back. His body shuddered in response, filling her with exhilaration.

Abby's delicate fingers against his bare flesh were Jack's undoing. He swept her into his arms and his long strides consumed the distance between the dining room and the stairway.

Stunned by the magnitude of her own desire, Abby realized how desperately she needed more from Jack. She buried her face in his neck and breathed a kiss there. The sensation of his pulse beating hard and fast beneath her lips empowered her.

Jack took the steps two at a time.

The bed was warm and inviting. Sunshine streamed through the skylight. No darkness. No shadows. No secrets. But, just for a moment, he couldn't help but wonder if she would have preferred moonbeams.

Jack lowered Abby onto the bed and felt her tremble beneath his touch as he traced her delicate features with his fingertips. He buried his face in her hair and inhaled the intoxicating scent of her. She sighed. He took her face in his hand and parted her lips... ever...so...slowly...with his tongue.

His mouth did not become softer with each kiss, but more demanding. He tempted and taunted until a need, so strong, so violent, ignited like a flame in her belly.

Jack pulled Abby to her knees in the middle of the bed. His erratic heartbeat matched her passion-darkened eyes. He eased her out of her clothing, leaving her fiery auburn mane to tumble around her bare shoulders and tease across each breast. Bathed in sunlight, her creamy skin took on a magnificent golden glow.

Abby ran her palm down his chest and, with shaky fingers, unsnapped his jeans.

Swearing an oath, he grabbed her wrists. His voice was hoarse. "Careful, love, or this will be over before it begins." He peeled off his jeans and tossed them aside.

Abby felt Jack's urgent fingers dig into her arms as he laid her down. She met his blazing stare, the cords in his neck standing taut against his skin. Perspiration beaded his forehead. *So, this is the dark side of love—where the animal lives. Crouched and hungry, waiting for me. And I for him.* She raised her arms, offering, inviting.

Raw, primitive desire thundered through Jack's body like a stampede. He laced his fingers through hers and pressed them over her head, her arms beneath his, sinking into the lush covers. Lowering his lips to hers, his tongue plundered the soft fullness of her mouth. God, she was sweet. Teasing, but not satisfying, his teeth scraped a path down her neck. He nipped at the tender skin on her shoulder, leading her, showing her. She wrapped her arms around his neck and pulled him closer. How could he possibly know every sensitive spot on her body? But he did. With each sigh that trembled past her lips, she craved more. His hands roamed freely, seeking, finding. She gasped for air, writhing beneath his touch. When the first shudder hit, she reached out, desperate to hold onto something. Her hands slipped off his sweat-slicked shoulders to grab wildly at the bed covers.

Jack moaned through gritted teeth. This is what he had wanted, what he had dreamed about, what he had waited for. The passionate, demanding side of Abby that could—that would— let go. His control exploded. In a tangle of arms and legs, they frantically rolled across the bed. Jack steadied himself over Abby and her shaky smile was all he needed. Heart to heart, they left the rest of the world behind. For now, everything else could wait.

Exhausted and clinging to one another, Jack shifted his weight. He lay down beside Abby and pulled her close. Her head rested on his shoulder, and she draped one arm across his chest.

Abby snuggled closer, trying hard not to think about the overwhelming familiarity of making love with Jack. "I suppose you're pretty pleased with yourself?"

Fighting the gut feeling that he and Abby had danced this dance before, Jack's grin widened. Hair tousled, he propped himself up on one elbow and faced her. "Only if you are." He pressed a kiss to her hand.

Abby traced the hollow of his cheek with her fingertips. As chiseled and striking...*as ever?* She shoved the unsettling thought aside and stroked his jaw line. His skin was warm—but then, so was hers. Since the fortuneteller had been right about her wild, sensuous side, had she been right about belonging here, too? She looked at Jack, sunlight glinting off his damp body, and wondered.

Her soul-searching ended the moment she looked around and realized they were at the foot of the bed. She couldn't help but laugh. "How'd we get down here?"

Eyes bright, face flushed, lips pouty, she ignited the fire in him that still smoldered just below the surface. "Give me a couple of minutes and I'll show you," he promised.

Abby leaned up and lazily kissed Jack. "I have to warn you," she began, nibbling his lower lip, "sometimes," she tickled his earlobe with the tip of her tongue, "I can be a…very…very. . . slow…learner."

Jack struggled to listen to every delicious syllable, each wistful sigh.

Put your pants on so you can think straight, pal. Either you can play 'circus act' again from one end of this bed to the other, or you can keep your appointment at the police station. What's it gonna be?

Jack sat up and checked his watch. "Damn." At her confused expression, he continued. "I nearly forgot. We have to meet with Venucci."

Abby's heart sank. "About the accident?"

Jack nodded.

As casually as she could manage, Abby asked, "When?"

He sat on the edge of the bed and watched her expression crumble. Once again, tense lines creased her forehead and bracketed her mouth. God, he'd wanted to spare her all this. "About an hour and a half."

She gathered her scattered clothing like a tiny bundle of courage and shot him one brave smile before disappearing into the bathroom.

"I'll be ready in fifteen minutes," she shouted through the closed door.

• • •

Waiting for Jack and the Corey woman to arrive, Lucky tapped his pencil. He had shut his office door to drown out the incessant squad room noise. Ringing phones. Clicking computer keyboards.

Occasional outbursts. Sometimes good. Sometimes not good at all.

Following up on the break in at Hannah's Inn, Lucky had put the word out on the street. He had a couple of reliable snitches that he could count on for leads. If there was any information to be had. And he still wasn't convinced of that. After all, Jack had just met this woman. How could he be so sure she wasn't playing him? The fact was—Jack couldn't.

Regardless of how sure Jack was, Lucky was not. He respected Jack enough to take his opinion into account, but he would maintain his objectivity. Had to in order to get to the bottom of it. For Jack. He owed the guy. Big time. And he would damned well make sure this Corey woman wasn't dragging Jack into some pile of shit. That sure as hell wasn't going to happen on his watch.

Chapter Twenty-Eight

Jack waited for her by the front door, but the look on his face did not reflect the passion they had just shared. His dark, somber expression spoke volumes, and none of it was good.

"What?" Adjusting the collar of her jacket, she took the envelope he handed her.

"Someone slipped this through the mail slot."

Abby didn't recognize the ornate handwriting, but her name had been scrawled across the front. She looked from the writing to Jack and saw every one of her concerns mirrored in his eyes. Someone not only knew she was staying here, but they were bold enough to come to the house in broad daylight to deliver a message.

With shaky fingers she pulled out the single sheet that had been tucked inside and read the message. "If you want your amulet, meet me at the Halloween Ball. Eight o'clock sharp. I'll be the clown."

Without a word, Abby raced upstairs and yanked open what remained of her shredded suitcase. Digging through her clothes, she grabbed the pine box and fumbled it open.

Hurrying back downstairs, she confirmed, "The amulet's not there."

"Sonofabitch." Jack scrubbed his face with one hand.

"It must have been stolen from my room at Adam's Inn. The box was right where I left it, so I just figured the necklace was inside. But I never looked."

"Let's go. At least the timing's right. We can show this to Lucky."

As they drove, Jack tried his best to relax Abby with easy conversation. And, despite her cool, calm demeanor he noticed how tightly her hands were clasped in her lap. Dammit, he didn't want her to think about thievery or deceit much less murder. There would be time enough for all that. But right now, after making love with her, he wanted to take all of her burdens away. Not that he could, but he could try.

When the car veered into an unfamiliar parking lot, Abby asked, "Why are we stopping here?"

Jack pulled the key from the ignition and pointed toward a slatted wooden sign: Ye Ole Costume Shoppe.

"I know, because of that note, we have to go to the ball, but we can't do this now. We'll be late."

"Relax." He came around to the passenger's side and took her by the hand. "We've got plenty of time."

Abby hesitated. "So you do think we should go to the ball."

"What?" He looked around innocently. "Oh, you mean because we're here?"

She said nothing.

"No way." He winked, trying his best to make her smile. At least for a little while. "This is for later."

"I don't play dress-up, Hawthorne."

"I don't remember asking, love." He reached across and opened her door. "Now let's go."

Love? Jack had used the same endearment the man in her dream had spoken. Abby shook her head. Such a common term simply meant coincidence, didn't it?

When she didn't budge, he added, "Look, we're going to show the note to Lucky and fill him in on what little we know. We'll see what he says." He took her hand and helped her out of the Jeep. "I trust him."

The shop's plank floor shined like rich, umber satin and smelled of lemon-scented wax. Potpourri, soft and spicy, mingled with the cool afternoon breeze. An endless display of brightly colored costumes filled the store. Sequins and pearls. Feathers and beads.

Tatting and lace. Some were exquisitely elegant, others tastefully authentic.

And the minute Jack walked through the door he knew he'd made a mistake. In the midst of all the charm and enchantment, he watched Abby's smile fade the moment she saw the display suspended from the ceiling; the one that had been saved for the macabre.

Painted masks stared. False faces watched. Severed heads gaped. Grotesque facades with one sole purpose. They had been designed to horrify. Each one fascinatingly different. Every one mindlessly the same.

As quaint as the shop appeared at first glance, it gave Abby the creeps. Even the friendly white-haired owners reminded her of the vivid nightmare she'd had. Unlike the dream she'd had at Adam's Inn, the striking array of costumes were nothing more than illusions. One may have been of the mind, but the other was definitely of the body. The fear coiling deep inside was of the real world, and no sleight of hand or vanishing act could make it disappear. For whatever reason, Abby's dream been a warning. The autumn festival had to represent the Halloween Ball.

Despite that, something deep inside insisted she and Jack had to go to the ball, because she had to get the amulet back. She just didn't know why it was so damned important. At least not yet. What she did know was that staying away was not an option. Of that she was certain. For now the explanation eluded her, but she knew in time all the pieces of the puzzle would fall into place. They had to. Until then, she had to pay special attention to her instincts, and right now they were centered on Jack.

Jack slipped up behind Abby and wrapped his arms around her waist. "Hey, pretty lady," he whispered.

"Yes," Abby sighed, relaxing against him and placing her hands over his. She rested her head against his chest, grateful for his strength. When she felt his warmth seep through her clothes, she smiled.

Everything between them had changed so quickly she hadn't had time to sort through any of it. And she still didn't. As much as she would like answers, right now, something told her personal relationships of any kind would have to wait. The sense of urgency hovering over her heart like a thundercloud insisted the storm would break and soon. What that would mean to her and Jack, she wasn't sure.

Jack pulled her closer.

"Do you think Detective Venucci will agree that we should go to the ball?"

He gave her hand a quick squeeze. "Like I said before, I trust Lucky. Trust me, he won't pull any punches."

Abby tilted her head back and looked up at Jack. Had he been the nameless, faceless man in her dreams? Her lover? Her protector? Something deep inside her soul whispered, *Yes*.

"And I trust you." Her smile matched his.

"You should."

Abby held on just a little tighter.

"Don't get me wrong. This situation is serious, and I would never play it down by taking you to the ball unless Lucky okays it," he assured her.

"I know you wouldn't put my life in danger," Abby told him quietly. And she did. For now, that fact, in itself, was enough for her. "Looks like we'd better find costumes, just in case." Unable to shake off a nagging sense of foreboding, Abby decided to do what she could to lighten the mood. She tugged him close enough to whisper in his ear. "Guess what, Hawthorne? You're shopping." His hearty laugh took the edge off her nerves. At least for the time being.

"Renting is not the same as buying," he insisted as she dragged him arm-in-arm down the first aisle.

"Is, too."

Jack refused to be baited. Instead, he pilfered carefully through the outfits. He slipped one off the rack and held it under Abby's chin—by way of both breasts.

"Bo Peep?" she gasped. His choice in costumes hadn't surprised her nearly as much as his intimate touch, however well-disguised it had been. She was lost in the sensation until the door to the shop banged shut. Untangling her arm from the curved wooden staff, she immediately batted away the layers of organdy ruffles, along with his hands. Finding her voice, she whispered, "You mean to tell me that after this morning…you see me as a little girl?"

"Only you, Corey." Jack shook his head. "Only you."

Abby heard him mumbling something about simply thinking she would look good in pink. Perusing the rack, she hauled out an Indian garb and inhaled the sweet smell of the leather. Her lips curved in response. "Now *this* is you."

"A warrior, huh?" He smiled.

"Savage," she clarified in a sultry voice.

"Yeah." He leaned down and whispered. "I can do uncivilized." His cheek rubbed hers as he spoke.

"Then you'll take it?" She swallowed hard, wondering exactly what kind of bargain she'd just made.

"Can't." Jack shook his head.

"Why not?"

"I don't do makeup."

"War paint." She tried to ignore the tip of his tongue teasing her earlobe.

"Close enough."

"Actually, I was referring more to this." Abby dangled a tiny loincloth from her finger. Her cheeks warmed at the thought of just how delicious he'd look with or without it.

"I'll wear that if you'll wear this." He held up a mermaid costume.

Abby's eyes widened. "That's nothing but a fish tail!"

"I know." He didn't blink.

Abby recognized the passion in Jack's eyes. Memories of lying naked in his bed. The warm tangle of arms and legs. Skin on skin. "You know, the faster we find our costumes, the faster we get our interviews over with and—"

"The faster we get back home," he finished.

She flashed him a provocative smile. "Exactly."

"Five minutes," he warned. "That's all you've got."

Abby grinned. "Let's not show each other our costumes. We'll either wear them to the ball if that's what the detective suggests, or—"

"Deal."

"You don't even know what I was going to say."

"Or we'll wear them at home," he finished.

She turned to walk away, then paused and lowered her voice. "Make it three minutes."

Chapter Twenty-Nine

Stale cigarette smoke followed Jack and Abby down the dingy corridor of the Twelfth Precinct like a specter. The sound of ringing phones seemed to come from every direction. Bits and pieces of a heated discussion escaped as a nearby door momentarily chinked open, then closed.

They stepped into the squad room just in time to witness two policemen drag out a burly biker in handcuffs. Amid the tap of computer keys and milling officers, a lonely-looking woman sat, cradling a Styrofoam cup of coffee between work-worn hands and weeping softly.

Abby's nerves relaxed a fraction when a tall, striking man smiled and gestured to them from a nearby office doorway.

"Detective Venucci." He shook the hand Abby offered. "Just call me Lucky."

"Abby Corey."

The police officer nodded. "Hey, Jack. Come in and sit down."

Abby took the seat next to Jack and waited while Detective Venucci shut the door and sat down behind his desk. His office was modest. To his right, there was one metal, three-drawer filing cabinet. A gunmetal gray cabinet with two doors that opened from its center occupied the opposite wall. One window behind him provided the only natural light in the room, and the Venetian blinds covering it had been closed. Accordion folders were stacked haphazardly on the floor around his chair, and papers, faxes and files covered every inch of his desktop.

"Looks like I'm the new kid on the block," he began, "so you're going to have to fill me in. I don't know anything about you, your background or your business, but what I do know is that there has been an attempt on someone's life." He paused and grabbed one of the legal pads and a pen before continuing. "It's my job to determine if you're the target, Ms. Corey, or if you were just in the wrong place at the wrong time, and it's Jack they're after."

Jack reached out and gave Abby's hand a squeeze.

"I'm sure you're a very busy man, Detective," Abby pointed out. "Thank you for taking the time to see us on such short notice."

"No problem. And call me Lucky."

Abby nodded.

"I'm going to ask you a lot of questions and some of them may seem a bit personal," Venucci continued. "I want you to know up front this is strictly standard procedure."

"I understand." Abby tried to clear her mind and focus on the individual circumstances that had brought them here today.

"Okay then. Let's start at the beginning."

Abby took a deep breath. "I received a call from Mr. Hawthorne's office informing me of an inheritance. I'm here in Boston to pick it up."

"How much and from whom?"

Abby turned toward Jack. "No money. Just a necklace and the benefactor is unknown."

"This necklace has been passed down from law firm to law firm since the late 1600's," Jack added.

Lucky leaned back in his chair. "You're kidding?"

"Nope. The note requested the pendant be given to Abigail Corey by October 31, of this year."

Lucky frowned. "Come on, Jack. How's that possible?"

"Beats the hell out of me," Jack told him honestly. "All I know is that I have the directive. It's documented and authentic."

"Right." Lucky waited a beat. "Well then, how valuable is this necklace?"

"I don't know. I haven't had it appraised," Abby pointed out. "I'd say the stone is amber, but there's a flaw or what looks like a teardrop-shaped mark in the middle, so whatever it is, it's certainly not perfect."

"Not valuable enough to kill for?" Venucci continued, taking notes as he spoke.

"I can't say for sure," Abby admitted. "But it doesn't appear to be."

"Okay. Then let's take the necklace out of the equation." He swiveled his chair slightly to face Abby. "If this was an attempt on your life, Ms. Corey, can you think of anyone who might want you dead?"

"No." Abby answered without hesitation.

"So, exactly who knows you're here?"

"No one, I guess." Abby thought a moment. She had mentioned to Jacques and J.T. she'd be going out east, but she had never been specific. "I can't think of a soul who knew I was coming to Boston."

"No one? Not family or friends?" he probed.

Saddened by the realization, she merely shook her head.

"Have you made any enemies through your business? Maybe disgruntled employees?"

"No." Abby began, picking absently at the gauze wrap on her injured wrist.

"Any problems with debt? Unpaid suppliers? Anything like that?"

"Not at all. My accounts are paid in full and always have been." Meeting his gaze, she added, "I've actually thought about this a lot the past couple of days, and I really can't remember having problems with anyone."

"What about a boyfriend?"

"No."

The detective scribbled as she continued. "Have you broken off any relationships recently?" the detective asked.

"No."

"Do you know anyone here in Boston besides Mr. Hawthorne?"

Abby shook her head. "The only people I've even come into contact with are the employees at Hannah's Inn and the hotel I stayed at last night." She turned to Jack. "What's the name of that place?"

"Adam's Inn.

"Oh, yeah." Venucci nodded then repeated with a smirk, "Adam's Sin."

Abby cringed. Remembering her hasty departure from Jack's house, she clarified, "It was the first one listed in the phone book."

"Okay." The detective paused momentarily. "Who knew you would be driving Jack's car?"

"No one." Abby looked at Jack.

Venucci momentarily shifted his gaze. "Anyone?"

"I didn't tell anyone." Jack thought a moment. "Well, someone did stop by trying to catch me before I went to the office, so I bummed a ride to work."

"Name?"

"Bridget Bishop. But she doesn't even know Abby." Jack ignored the instant knot in his gut.

Abby felt the cold rush of dread at the mention of the woman's name and turned to Jack. "You mean the woman from the haunted house?" She remembered the creepy, unearthly home she had seen the day they spent in Salem. The same house that literally vibrated with palpable malevolence. Emanated with enough evil to stop her dead in her tracks. Bridget Bishop…Maxine's conversation flashed through Abby's mind.

"Yeah." Jack would have laughed at Abby's description if not for the sincere look in her eyes.

"Oh." Abby heard the hollow ring to her response but could not conceal it. Her physical reaction insisted this woman was connected somehow.

Lucky redirected his attention to Abby. "Have you noticed anything suspicious that we haven't discussed? Anything at all, no matter how insignificant it seemed at the time."

Abby sighed. "That's the really weird part," she began, shifting uneasily in her chair. "There have been…I don't know…little things. Just stuff that I can't quite put my finger on."

"Such as," the detective coaxed.

Abby felt uncomfortable and shrugged. "It's more of a feeling. I don't know. Maybe like someone's watching me."

"Have you seen anyone strange hanging around?"

"Well," Abby hesitated. "I could have sworn this car was following me yesterday, but I talked myself out of it."

"Where did this occur?"

Jack butted in. "Why didn't you tell me?"

Abby ignored him and sat up a little straighter, directing her answer to Venucci. "When I left the hotel—Adam's Inn," she clarified. "Yesterday morning."

"Why didn't you tell me?" Jack repeated.

This time it was Lucky's turn to ignore Jack. "Approximately what time?"

"Early." She thought a moment. "About eight-thirty."

"How long did the car follow you?" Venucci asked, jotting down details without looking up.

Abby didn't hesitate. "It stayed with me long enough for me to notice. Quite a while. So, I doubled back. As I turned into the hotel parking lot, it was still with me but kept on going. I'd say a good fifteen minutes."

"Could you I.D. the make and model?"

"I'm sorry." Abby sighed, fully aware that Jack was glaring holes in her but refusing to face him. "I don't know much about cars, and I wasn't close enough to read the plates. The only thing I remember is that it was red."

"That's a good start. The fact that you were aware of the car in the first place probably means you saw more than you realize." Lucky held Abby's gaze. "Can you tell me anything at all about the driver?"

"Well, it's hard to say." Abby tried desperately to remember. "He stayed far enough behind to keep me from getting a really good look."

"He?" Detective Venucci repeated. "So, the driver was a man."

"Some man was following you, and you just didn't bother to tell me," Jack said, flailing both hands in the air in disbelief.

Neither Lucky nor Abby looked at him.

Despite the interruption, Abby had gotten the gist of Venucci's questioning. "Definitely a man." She paused to conjure up a clearer image in her mind's eye. "In fact he was a bald man," she stated deliberately. "He had a—"

"—bushy, dark mustache?" Jack's blood ran cold.

Dumbfounded, Abby merely nodded.

Jack jumped up. "That son-of-a—"

"You know him?" she asked.

"Dammit, Abby, did you really think that I would leave you at that hotel alone after coming back and finding your door open?"

"What?" Flashes of sitting miserably in a chair until dawn, ramrod stiff, staring at the doorknob—scared to stay, but too scared to leave—leapt through Abby's mind, immediately switching her confusion to anger. "Well, if you were there, where the hell were you?"

"Sitting on the floor outside your door."

"What?" she repeated.

"Her door had been open?" Detective Venucci interrupted, this time looking directly at Jack. "You didn't tell me that."

"We went in and looked around, but she said nothing had been taken and insisted on staying." Jack shrugged. "I figured the latch just didn't catch when she left."

"Where had you two been prior to this?" Lucky asked.

"We ate dinner at The Grotto," Jack told him.

Abby added the scant details of the unsettling phone call she had received after being followed by the red car, if, in fact, she had really been tailed.

Jack jumped to his feet. "Why in the hell didn't you tell me any of that?"

Unintimidated, Abby looked up and shook her head. "I figured it was a wrong number, and for crying out loud, Jack, how many red cars are there in Boston?" Without waiting for his answer, she added, "Besides, I felt embarrassed enough without pointing my finger at thin air."

Jack paced then faced her. "I do not believe in coincidences. Someone has been close. Way too close. He not only phoned your hotel room to scare you off, but he stole your amulet."

"So, he already had the amulet when he came back, and we saw him in the hall," Lucky pointed out.

"That doesn't make sense," Abby countered. "If he already had the necklace, why—"

"Why?" Jack's voice bounced off the walls. "Don't you get it Abby? He came back for you!"

Abby swallowed hard, but the words couldn't pass the lump in her throat.

"That's right," Jack told her. "And it's a damned good thing Lucky and I spent the night outside your door."

"Thank you." Her voice was small. Clearing her throat, she glanced at Lucky. "Thank you both."

Lucky nodded. Jack did not.

Jack tore the envelope from his jacket pocket and handed it to Lucky. "This was slipped through the mail slot in my door. I found it right before we left the house to come here."

As Lucky read the note, Jack asked, "How the hell has someone managed to stay one step ahead of us at every turn?"

Venucci leaned back in his chair. "That's a damn good question." The detective threw down his pen and flexed his fingers. "Looks like you two should have spoken up sooner. From the sound of things, I'd say you've been very fortunate."

"Maybe so," Jack said, placing his hands on Abby's shoulders. "But luck has a way of running out, doesn't it?"

"Unfortunately, Jack, it does just that."

"Hell, it's a wonder Abby hasn't gotten herself killed, several times over, no thanks to me." Jack stood behind her and gently massaged the tense muscles in her shoulders. "That's exactly why I'd like some police protection for her."

Tapping the notes he'd taken with the tip of his pen, Venucci shook his head. "Convincing or not, we don't have that kind of manpower available."

"Dammit," Jack began but stopped himself. "I don't agree, Venucci, but I understand." Jack pulled Abby to her feet.

"Go home and let me think this over," Venucci told them. "I want to check things out, put out some feelers, and I'll get back to you."

Jack shook his hand. "You've got my number."

Lucky winked at Abby. "Hell, I've had Jackie's number since junior high." He rounded his desk. "If you think of anything else, Ms. Corey, call me."

Leaving the police station, Abby had never felt such an overwhelming sense of urgency. Her mind raced a mile a minute. Who had stopped just short of murder? And why? To scare her off? Her brain short-circuited, and it felt like her heart was going to have to handle the overload.

She searched Jack's face and examined the steadiness of his gaze, the determined set of his jaw as he drove. His white-knuckled grip on the steering wheel was the single clue that he had only harnessed his emotions.

Abby was still shaky from the statements she and Jack had given Detective Venucci. So much of what they'd experienced individually had seemed harmless until they had compared notes. Once the sequence of events had started falling into place, their stories had fit together, like a hand in a glove.

Curious as well as desperate for ordinary conversation, Abby asked, "Why is it that you trust Detective Venucci so much?"

"We go back a long way." Eyes straight ahead he continued, "A few years ago Lucky was really jammed up on the job. Evidence had been planted, and he was framed. I represented him at trial, and we won."

Sensing there was more, she asked, "And?"

"And I not only saved his reputation, but I saved his job." Lucky glanced sideways at her, then back at the road. "Lucky's connections in the case gave me one of the biggest mob busts in years. Let's just say that big break didn't hurt my career either."

Abby shivered. "Sounds dangerous."

"I knew he was innocent." Lucky shrugged. "That was the hard part."

"The hard part?" she repeated. "Wouldn't that make it easier?"

"Hell, no. When it's someone you know, a friend, there's a whole different kind of pressure. Then add to that the fact that you know he's innocent. It's like that scene in The Godfather when you only see Michael Corleone's feet, and they're trudging along."

"I remember that."

"Well, that's the way I felt. Like I had the weight of the world on my shoulders."

"But you won."

"Yes, we did."

That was exactly the kind of story Abby wanted to hear right now. Knowing good could win over evil, she needed to replace her fears with faith in the system and force her thoughts elsewhere. This time when Abby glanced at Jack, all she saw was the magnificent man who had swept her off her feet. Had that only been hours ago?

She could almost feel the warmth and comfort of the pliable bed beneath her back as he had lain her down. Dark, penetrating eyes. His masterful hands had teased and tormented away all her inhibitions. Achingly tender kisses. Powerful legs and arms wrapped around her—controlling and demanding. For that moment in time she had belonged to him. Only him. And so it would be. Satisfied, she leaned her head back, closed her eyes, and sighed, content for the moment to enjoy and maybe for the first time not to question the haunting, uncanny feeling of familiarity.

When Jack and Abby returned to his house, they went their separate ways. Abby headed for the living room and sank decadently into the *overstuffed* sofa. God, she was so weary. The moment she surrendered to the lengthening afternoon shadows, the tension of the day began to melt away.

• • •

The sun has just set, and twilight is settling over the woods like a misty, silver blanket. Walking down the familiar path, Abigail realizes a man is following her. He stays just far enough behind that she can't get a good look, but she can see he wears a red cape. She doesn't fear for her life, because she knows he can overtake her, but for some reason, he chooses not to. Frightened, she wonders what he wants. To scare her? To watch her? To follow her? When her fear turns to panic, she lifts her long, dark skirt and runs. She doesn't stop until she sees familiar windows filled with the soft light of candles. Once inside, she bolts the door and leans against it, breathing hard, wondering if she has been foolish coming home. After all, the man is still out there somewhere…waiting. And now he knows exactly where to find her.

Chapter Thirty

Jack found Abby dozing. Careful not to disturb her, he struck a match to the kindling and sat down on the floor in front of the fireplace. Content to lean against a chair and watch her sleep, he realized there was no point denying what an important part of his life she'd become. It didn't matter that it had happened fast, like being struck by lightning, he was glad she had come along. He needed her every bit as much as he wanted her and judging from the way he felt now, that was one helluva lot.

* * *

Abby awoke with a start, momentarily disoriented by the darkness. When she recognized Jack's silhouette in front of the blazing fire, she willed away the unsettling dream and offered a shaky smile.

"Are you awake?" she whispered.

"Yeah." His tone was quiet and his mood, he realized, was peaceful. It had been a long time since he'd enjoyed such a feeling.

"I can't believe I fell asleep," she yawned, praying the man in her dream had been just that, a subconscious fear, nothing more.

"You needed it." He watched as she sat up and swung her long legs onto the floor. "Hungry?"

"Uh huh," she nodded.

"What sounds good?"

Abby thought a moment. "How about pizza?"

"My kind of woman." Jack grinned. "No muss. No fuss. No dishes."

She flipped on the light, slid down the front of the davenport and landed derriere first on the floor right in front of him. "Just order."

Dialing the number he had taped above the phone, Jack asked, "Preference?"

Abby shrugged. "I have never met a pizza I didn't like."

"*The Works* it is."

Less than an hour later, they sat cross-legged before the fire, the flat, cardboard box between them with a silver ice bucket and long-stemmed glasses set off to one side. Jack smiled as he wrestled the cork free.

Champagne bubbled dangerously close to the lip of the glass as Abby accepted the frothy flute. "Trying to ply me with liquor?"

He sipped slowly and considered her question. "That depends."

"On what?" she challenged with an uninhibited drink and a provocative smile.

"On whether or not alcohol would work."

She raised an eyebrow.

He grinned.

The fire's glow defined the angular planes and distinct lines of Jack's handsome face. Abby wondered how many sides there were to this man? At the police station, she'd heard the fierce protectiveness in his voice when he'd blurted out that he'd spent the night in the hallway outside her hotel room door. She'd seen concern blacken his expression at the hospital after her accident. Through it all, he had undoubtedly saved her life by taking her in when her nightmare had somehow crossed over into reality. Right now, Jack Hawthorne was the one person in the world she could trust. Maybe the only one. "Your pizza's getting cold."

Abby watched Jack toss the half-eaten piece in the box and shove it clear across the floor. The look of surprise that flashed across his face when he saw her reach for the lamp had definitely been worth the price of a ticket.

This time when Abby went to him, she was as much the seducer as the seduced. When she touched his face, her cool hands against his warm skin, she watched his eyes close. As she planted kisses along his well-defined jaw, the tiny lines creasing his forehead and punctuating the corners of his mouth relaxed. He pulled her to her feet and wrapped his strong arms around her, and they stood together in front of the fireplace, casting a single shadow on the wall behind them. Abby reached out. She slid his sweater over his head and ran her curious palms along the solid planes of his chest.

Jack groaned.

His muscles twitched beneath her touch, but it was the passion darkening his expression that urged her on. She unzipped his jeans and slid them over his hips…and waited.

"Do you know what you do to me?" he whispered through clenched teeth. Without waiting for an answer, he slid the slender ebony straps from her shoulder. The silky material trembled past her breasts and puddled at her feet.

She offered him a wicked smile as she slipped her panties down around both ankles, and kicked both undergarments aside. He fisted his hand in her hair and pulled her head back. His mouth moved freely over her lips and down her neck. His hands kneaded and soothed until every muscle in her body relaxed. Abby's knees began to buckle and she instinctively wrapped both arms around his neck. "I want you, Jack."

He lowered her to the floor. His lips tasted of cold champagne. The incredible fire in his eyes defied the heat of his passion. She cried out each time he discovered some treasured, secret place. Demanding, she rolled over him to seek and taste and explore until she thought her lungs would burst and his body would fly into a million pieces. In one deliberate movement, Jack eased Abby onto her back.

Passion and madness had ignited between them this morning, but this was different. Lust had deepened to desire. Demands had shifted from physical to emotional. Yearning had replaced want. His needs were hers. Her desires were his. For this moment in time, they would be one.

So, was Jack Hawthorne the man Abby had been waiting for all her life? Was he the reason why her relationships had failed? Why she never *really* let herself become involved with a man? Jack, with his arrogant charm and brooding good looks, his laughing eyes and tender touch. With the scrape of his teeth. His teasing lips. The flick of his tongue. She reveled in a whirlwind of newfound emotions. He may have led her to freedom, but she would be bound to him forever.

Abby snuggled closer, her head resting against his shoulder, her hand splayed across his heart. A log hissed as it shifted in the fireplace, shooting sparks up the chimney and sending shadows dancing around the room. The turbulent October wind gusted and moaned and slapped a solitary branch against the window, a sound that might have ordinarily spooked her. But not tonight. She'd never felt as safe and secure as she did at this very moment.

Jack pressed one hand over Abby's and brushed a stray tendril from her flushed cheek. He smiled. "And I thought being with you couldn't get any better." He trailed a lazy path down her arm with his fingertips. "Boy was I wrong."

She pushed herself up on one elbow and brushed a hand through his hair. For once, she refused to weigh her words. This time, she had to say exactly what was in her heart. "Can I tell you how happy it makes me to agree with you?"

Jack smiled. "Does it?"

Abby pressed a kiss to his neck. "Yes." One minute she was sharing pillow talk with Jack, then next an instant, overwhelming sensation rocked her so hard, she had to reach out and steady herself. Panic gripped her by the throat, cutting off her air as surely as a…hangman's noose? Barely able to breathe, she fought the sickening flood of emotion, determined not to drown in her own fears. "Jack?" she finally managed.

"What the hell was that?" Jack had already sat up. His eyes darted around the room.

"You felt it, too?"

"Damn straight."

"Maybe it was some kind of earthquake or tremor." Abby scooted closer.

Jack slipped one arm around her. "Whatever it was, it's over now."

Abby looked up at him. "I thought for a minute it was inside my head. It felt like I was falling off the face of the earth."

"So did I." He pulled her closer and whispered, "Stay with me, Abby."

She took a shaky breath. "You're serious, aren't you?"

"Yes, I am." He caught her chin and steadied it in his hand. "Stay here in Boston."

Before Abby could open her mouth to speak, the buzz of the doorbell broke the tenuous silence.

"Who the hell—" Jack swore, yanking on his jeans.

Abby jumped up and made a mad scramble, as much to gather her composure as her clothes.

Jack blocked her path. "Relax." he assured her. "No one's getting in here tonight." He framed her face with unsteady hands. "Grab my robe and get back down here. We're far from finished."

Abby bit her lip, knowing this discussion had been inevitable since the day they met. Jack's solemn expression told her he knew that, too. She nodded before hurrying past him.

The cold October wind that blew in when he opened the door couldn't have chilled him any quicker than the sight of Bridget sashaying into his living room. With her flawless, mask-like skin, sleek designer clothes, frosty smile.

"Whoa!" He hooked his arm through hers and spun her around.

Tipping his chin with one blood-red fingernail, she flashed him a cover-girl smile and eased out of his grip. "You haven't returned my calls since I got back from New York." She slipped out of her cape and tossed it to him. "Shame on you."

Teeth clenched, he instinctively snagged her wrap. "Look—"

"Believe me, I am. But darling, you'll catch your death running around half-naked this time of year." She paused long enough to survey his muscular torso and smile approvingly. "Not that I mind, of course."

"What are you doing here, Bridget?"

She dismissed him with the wave of one perfectly manicured hand. "Really," she tapped the pizza box with the toe of her Manolo Blahnik, "you'd be better off eating out, don't you think?"

Jack increased his stranglehold on her cape. "Dammit, Bridget—"

"I was kidding, silly," she interrupted.

"I'm not."

"Oh, I know," Bridget sighed, raking her nails down his chest.

• • •

Abby took the steps to the loft two at a time. Once she had slipped into Jack's robe, she turned back toward the stairs, but her feet seemed rooted to the spot. Suddenly and without reason, she felt overwhelmingly compelled to light one of the candles she had purchased at the Wax N Wane.

She heard the doorbell ring again.

Unable to shake the fierce sense of need that bordered on panic, Abby remembered that historically the gold candles were used for protection. Unexplainably drawn, she pulled one golden candle from the shopping bag. Shaking, she steadied her hand and lit the complimentary matches the sales clerk had included.

When she heard the front door open, Abby said quickly and quietly, "As this candle melts today, make this stranger go away, protect the man, the house and me, this is my will, so mote it be."

She stood there a moment—speechless. What had she just done? And why? Better yet, why didn't the ritual seem the least bit strange? Unable to answer any of these questions, Abby realized she really didn't care why she had done it. She might not understand her actions, but she felt certain what she had done had been right. Content, she descended the stairs and walked back into the living room. The sound of the other woman's voice struck such an unrelenting chord; it took Abby's breath away.

The moment green eyes met blue, she was overwhelmed with emotion. Red hot and intense. A gruesome combination of dread, sorrow and hate. Without being told, Abby knew the woman facing Jack was Bridget Bishop. Her very presence rocked Abby so hard she had to lay one hand on the back of the chair to steady herself.

"Excuse me, Jack," Abby finally managed. "I didn't know you had company."

Jack's head snapped around.

There stood Abby. The sleeves of his robe had been cuffed-up to accommodate her size. Belted at the waist, one leg showed provocatively through the front split. Cheeks flushed. Eyes bright. Shiny, auburn hair falling past her shoulders. She was magnificent.

He winked at Abby. "Bridget was just leaving."

The distance between Abby and Bridget crackled with intensity.

"And believe me when I tell you, darling, so is she," Bridget warned.

Maxine's words echoed through Abby's mind as she saw Bridget glance at the loft where she had lit the candle then narrow her striking blue eyes. In an instant, the air turned so thick you could slice it with an athame. She snatched up her cape, drilled Abby with another scathing glare, and raised one, disapproving eyebrow in Jack's direction.

"Have fun with the help, Darling." Switching her gaze to Abby, she added, "Enjoy him while you can."

The door had barely slammed behind her when Abby found her sea legs. "So, that's Bridget Bishop. The woman one who knew I'd be driving your car."

Jack rubbed his jaw. "I see where you're going with this, but she doesn't even know you."

"Of course not." The question remained—why did Abby feel she knew Bridget, at least on some level, all too well.

Jack rested his forearms on Abby's shoulders. "Forget it. She's gone now."

Surprisingly, Abby felt that, too. When Bridget left, the overwhelming feeling of dread simply vanished. Abby sighed against him. "I know."

"Remember when you told me about your dreams," he began, "and that some of them came true?"

"Uh huh."

"Do you ever get flashes like that during the day?"

Abby thought of the oppressing sensation she'd experienced in Bridget's presence. "Sometimes."

"Do they mean anything?"

She angled her head to get a better look at his face. Serious. He was dead serious. "They're usually significant, if that's what you're asking. Why? Do you get flashes, too?"

He broke their connection long enough to pace. "Just lately."

"What kind of images?"

Jack cleared his throat then turned to face her. "I see a woman being hung on Gallows' Hill."

Abby's knees buckled, but she locked them. Her hand instinctively went to her throat. "Who is she?"

"I can't see her face, but it's not like some reoccurring dream. The scene keeps progressing. Every time it returns there's more to it." He shrugged. "This last time there was a dark-haired woman waiting and watching. I still couldn't see the face of the woman being hung, but there was such a sense of urgency. More powerful than anything I've ever experienced. Crazy, huh?"

"No, I don't think it is." Abby's throat burned. "Anything else?"

"Well, there was one other thing. But it wasn't a flash or anything like that."

"What was it?"

"This sounds so ridiculous." He paused a moment, and when she didn't placate him, he continued, "I had a sense of writing."

"A book?"

Jack shook his head and thought a moment. "More like a journal."

"And?" She could tell there was more. Knew there was more.

"Through the Boston Historical Society I heard about a recent acquisition of some seventeenth century documents," he explained. "They're on temporary display at an antique book store owned by one of the society's members. I think the shop is called *Pages From The Past*."

"You think the journal you *sensed*, if there is such a journal, is there?"

Jack considered her question. "Don't ask me why, but I feel sure of it."

Without hesitation, she grabbed his hand. "Then let's go."

Chapter Thirty-One

Twenty minutes later, they parked on the quaint, tree-lined street and got out in front of the shop.

"Dammit." Jack pointed to the *Open by Appointment Only* sign in the window.

"Now what?" Abby asked.

Jack pulled out his cell and punched in the phone number listed on the sign. He listened, then flipped shut his phone.

"What?" Abby asked.

"He's out of town today. He'll be back tomorrow."

"Tomorrow?" she repeated. "We can't wait until—"

"I know."

Jack scanned the neighborhood. Late afternoon shadows shaded the leaf-dappled brick sidewalk. A dog barked in the distance. There was no one out and about. He went to the door and found the top half was a glass panel. The bottom was solid oak. He took off his jacket and wrapped one arm, and in one swift motion he broke the window with his elbow. Knocking away the jagged shards, he slipped his hand inside and unlocked the door.

"Jesus! What do you think you're doing?" Abby asked, glancing up and down the street to make sure no one was around.

Without a word, he opened the door and motioned for her to follow.

Abby hurried across the glass-splintered threshold and, for what it was worth shut the door behind her.

The shop was much larger inside than it appeared from the street. A familiar old-book smell permeated the air, mingling with the scent of aged leather and furniture polish. Dust-free shelves lined the walls from floor to ceiling and were flanked by tall, rolling ladders for easy access. In the fading daylight, faux candle night-lights enhanced the rustic look of the rough-hewn floor and paneled walls, creating a relaxing twilight atmosphere.

Abby caught up with Jack halfway through the shop. "What are we looking for?"

"I'm guessing a display case." As they walked, Jack slipped on his jacket and continued to explain, "From what I understand, this guy wanted to premier the documents in his shop then donate them to the Historical Society next month."

"Jack, look." Abby pointed straight ahead.

At the back of the store, there was a huge display case filled with books, documents, papers, and journals. Even from this distance you could see everyone was yellowed with age. Fragile. Antique.

Abby's breath quickened and her palms grew damp. Whatever Jack was looking for, it was in there. She could feel it.

Scanning the length of the case, Jack pointed to a leather-bound journal in the middle of the second shelf. Stepping behind the counter, he slid the glass sideways and reached in.

Abby held her breath as Jack eased the journal from the case. Opening the book, his fingers were cautious, turning the first few pages with care. He stepped to her side, so they could read together:

October 31, 1692

I must guard Abigail's amulet with my life. I must ensure its safe delivery into the future for it is the tether to her soul. When the time comes, we will need this necklace. On that fateful date we must have the amulet to succeed or, God help us all, we will unleash an evil, the likes of which the humanity has never seen.

"Oh, Jack," Abby whispered.

He met her gaze. "Oh, shit."

Turning the page, they continued:

November 15, 1692
It has been 15 days since the death…no, the murder of my beloved. I rage. I cry. I curse. And still I find no relief. I went to her grave again today and sat on the stone bench by the big tree. If it were not for the promise of our next meeting, I would surely die.

Abby squeezed Jack's arm as he flipped the next page…

December 1, 1692
I have discovered something very important, indeed. Maxine came today to make sure I still had the amulet, and that I fully understand its importance. She is not an easy woman to convince, but I assured her that I did. What she told me next is every bit as important as the amulet itself. By the time Abigail and I experience our "coming together," Bridget's powers will be waning. This, coupled with the amulet, may give us a fighting chance. And fight we shall.

Jack turned to Abby. "Maxine?"

"Bridget," she hissed.

The steady ticking of the old school clock on the wall behind the counter punctuated the silence.

Jack Hawthorne—speechless. That not only was a first, but it said so much more than words could ever say.

"Maxine and Bridget?" Abby finally repeated.

He shook his head. "No way in hell."

"But—"

"But nothing. That has to be a—"

"Coincidence?" she finished. "I thought you didn't believe in coincidences."

"I don't." He maintained eye contact.

"Well," Abby began, dragging the word out on purpose. "We're here in the present, aren't we?"

Jack raked his fingers through his hair. "So, what you're saying is that there might be more of…*us*."

"I don't know." Abby shivered. "What do you think?"

Jack took a moment to consider the thought. Meeting her gaze, he answered, "I honestly don't know."

She sighed. "This journal, if it was your journal, mentions women named Maxine and Bridget. Don't you find that highly suspect?"

"I do," he agreed without hesitation. "Logically, if we're here, it would seem possible there could be others."

"Others?" Her voice was little more than a whisper. "What are we doing? Playing out some modern-day, X-Files scenario from 1692?"

"Prior to today, I'd have said absolutely not." He shook his head. "Right now, it beats the hell out of me."

Abby pointed to the yellowed pages. "Maybe you should read on."

December 15, 1692

I have spoken again with Maxine, and I now understand the possibility of Abigail and my "coming together" will not be in this lifetime. So, this day I will ensure the amulet's passage through time by making Maxine its keeper, and I will write instructions for its safekeeping. As much as it saddens me, I will gladly wait as long as it takes for the heavens to align and give us the chance to make it so.

Having read the journal thoroughly three times and carefully replacing it, Jack left several hundred dollars in the display case. From a nearby payphone he anonymously called 911 and reported the shop had been vandalized. Breaking the law had gone against his grain, but in this case his hands had been tied. Hell, the situation itself had demanded immediate action. A question of life or death had given Jack no choice.

On the drive back to Jack's house, talking was not an option, and the unnerving quiet that ensued was deafening. Silence screamed in Abby's ears all the way home. As they walked through the front door, the shrill ring of the phone nearly sent Abby through the ceiling.

"Son-of-a—" He stalked toward the telephone, snagged the receiver and barked, "Hello."

When Jack's voice abruptly changed from homicidal to serious, Abby held her breath until he hung up. "What is it?"

Jack rolled his shoulders restlessly as he crossed the floor to stand beside Abby.

Her stomach tightened. "Well?" His expression didn't give her a clue, so she waited for him to answer.

"Nothing to worry about." He enfolded her in his arms. "The police have just rounded up some men, and they want you and I to have a look at them."

Abby tensed. "A line-up?" The knot in her stomach hitched.

Jack's silence answered her.

She instinctively moved closer to him. "When do they want us?"

"Now."

Abby stood beside him in the dying firelight. Again the two cast one single shadow. Something once-in-this-lifetime had happened between them tonight, and she refused to let anything take that away from her. "Let's get this over with," she whispered.

"Yeah." He pulled her closer. "Then, we need to talk."

• • •

"That Corey bitch and Jack better play house while they can," Bridget spat. "As if I care. I've had over three hundred years to get over Jackson Hathorne. The fool, however, is necessary for my plan." She paced the confines of her parlor, her scarlet robe flowing about her feet.

"Let me see," she mocked, her low, menacing laugh resembled a growl. "In order to banish the lovely Abigail Corey back in time and inherit her powers, I need three things." She ticked each item off with her blood-red fingernails.

"A loyal man who is pure of heart—check."

"That miserable amulet—check."

"And Abigail Corey on All Hallows Eve, present day—check."

She parted the curtain and smiled at the almost full moon. "This time tomorrow, Abigail Corey will be no more. I will have her man—*if* I want him. But most important, I will have all her power. Her pale blue eyes narrowed in anticipation. "Then nothing can stop me."

Chapter Thirty-Two

Salem Massachusetts
31 October
Year of Our Lord, 1692

The slap on the horse's rump echoed through the suddenly quiet night. As Abigail's lifeless body dangled from the tree, a cheer rose from the mob. Jackson closed his eyes. Sealed his heart. Released his soul.

"I will find you, Abigail. I swear. I will search eternity until I do!"

• • •

Neither Abby nor Jack had been able to identify the biker from the line-up at the police station, and he watched her edgy frustration settle into silence once again on the ride home. Jack respected her need for space and didn't push, but didn't like what he saw when the click of the deadbolt behind them didn't ease her concern. Seeing the undisguised fear still present in her eyes, Jack would be damned if he slept on the couch tonight. He took her hand in his, and, side-by-side, they walked to the loft.

Within minutes, Jack was settled beneath the soft, feather comforter with Abby nestled in the crook of his arm. He lifted her delicate fingers and kissed their tips before releasing her hand to rest comfortably on his chest. Unlike the law, he couldn't offer her justice tonight. He couldn't cite concrete facts as to what was going on. He couldn't even assure her the bald man would be arrested and everything would be all right. But he could hold her. Protect her. Defend her with his life.

Jack's heart thudded beneath the palm of Abby's hand. Lulled by its slow, steady rhythm, he sensed her relax. His blood began to pulse in sync with hers. Two hearts beat as one. She snuggled closer to him, and he felt her surrender to sleep.

"Per chance to dream," a voice whispered crisply and clearly, waking Abby with a start.

She raised herself on one elbow and checked Jack's face in the moonlight. Not that she believed for a moment he had spoken, because she didn't. It simply hadn't sounded like Jack. Making sure he was all right, she also realized he apparently hadn't heard it either, because he was still sleeping soundly. When Abby replayed it in her mind, she realized it hadn't been the words that had scared her as much as the voice. The voice had been edged with enough hatred to turn Shakespeare's promise into a deadly threat. Abby knew sleep would not come easy tonight just as surely as she knew the telltale nightmare was on its way…

Jack tossed and turned as the reoccurring dream reared its ugly head, scratching and clawing at his subconscious like a starving animal waiting to be fed…

Despite being fast asleep, Jack and Abby's hands reached out. Their fingers entwined. Their past unfolded…

•••

Jackson Hathorne raced through the darkness like a thief in the night, dragging Abigail Corey behind him like a rag doll…the hounds of hell hot on their heels…frantic barking…tracking beasts…horses' thundering hooves. coming closer.

Abigail's lungs burned…she struggled to keep up…she scrambled on shaky legs…she held fast to the amulet. "I'll…die…if…if we don't stop."

"You'll die if we do." Jackson fought his way through the overgrown path. The mob is catching up…so close…pouncing like lions, the frenzied riders ripped Abigail from Jackson's arms.

"Satan's whore," one man shouted.

Closing her eyes, she murmured frantically, as there was not much time.

Bridget tied Abigail's wrists behind her back…ripped the amulet from her neck…hissed as the stone branded her palm… she threw the pendant hard and fast…slipped the noose over Abigail's head. "He's mine now."

"My spell will protect him 'til I return…Jackson, wait for me—"

"I'll find you, Abigail. I will search eternity until I do. I swear."

•••

Jack bolted upright in bed. Abby sat straight up beside him.

"Abigail?" he asked, desperate to clear his head.

Abby could hardly breathe. "Jackson?" she whispered.

Unbelieving, Jack turned to face her. Bathed in moonlight Abby sat wide-eyed and pale beside him. "I had this dream."

"Me, too." Her hands were trembling. "You were in it." She thought a moment. "At least he looked like you would have in the seventeenth century."

"The hanging dream on Gallows Hill—"

"It was me, wasn't it?" she asked.

"Or a likeness of you back in the *burning times*." Jack tried to whitewash his use of the phrase, and when he couldn't, he turned on the bedside lamp. "The woman's name was Abigail Corey."

"And his was Jackson Hathorne—without the W." Grateful for the light, Abby still shivered. "Bridget Bishop was there, Jack, in my dream. And the amulet. And even Maxine."

Now it was his turn to say, "In mine, too."

They compared identical details, then sat in silence for a long time.

"Weird, huh?" Abby asked lamely, simply not knowing what else to say.

"Having the same dream?" Jack pointed out. "Yeah, I'd say that's pretty damn weird. I can see how all this could fit into one of our dreams."

"But not both," she finished. "Unless…"

"What?" Jack demanded.

"Unless…" Abby hesitated, knowing how crazy what she was about to say would sound.

"Go on."

Regardless of the absurdity, she just looked him in the eye and said it. "Unless they truly are memories and not dreams."

"Like the journal," he agreed.

"Yes, exactly like that. Only not in writing."

He said nothing.

"Look," she began, running a frustrated hand through her hair, "all my life I have felt like there was a piece of the puzzle missing. For whatever reason, coming to Salem for the amulet fit. You fit. Hell, Maxine even fits."

"And Bridget?"

The air between them took on a frosty haze. "After tonight, I think she fits most of all." Once the words were spoken, the pall dissipated into thin air.

Jack pulled Abby close. "You realize that we have to go to that Halloween Ball and get the amulet." He leaned back and looked into her eyes. "We don't have a choice."

"Yes, I know." And somehow she did. Wrapping her arms around his waist, she said as much to herself as to Jack, "God help us."

Chapter Thirty-Three

Abby had agreed with Jack's decision that they must attend the Halloween Ball…this morning…in the sunlight.

But, tonight? Hours after sunset on All Hallows Eve? Dreams or no dreams, she wanted desperately to skip the ball and hole up in Jack's house. Unfortunately she knew they had no choice in the matter. Both she and Jack were remembering, for lack of a better word, bit and pieces of a grotesque puzzle. Tonight was the one and only window of opportunity they would have to stop Bridget. And not just for their sake. For the sake of all who would ever know her wrath.

They must retrieve the amulet. That much they knew. She prayed to God whatever else they needed to defeat her would be revealed.

When the antique clock on Jack's dresser chimed seven-thirty, Abby's jumped. Her nerves stretched even thinner, if that were possible. So much had happened in such a short time. The parts she seemed to understand made no sense, and the pieces she couldn't figure out defied logic.

Reality insisted the bald man was still out there. Somewhere. Waiting? Watching? Biding his time? And tonight she and Jack were deliberately planning to leave the house and meet the person who stole her amulet. She glanced anxiously toward the bedroom window. Something powerful and commanding told her to cast a circle. She did so, lighting two gold candles. One for her and one for Jack.

"Protect us tonight at the Halloween Ball. Free us from danger and lift the pall. Neither Bridget Bishop nor the bald man let in. Ostracize them and their ways of sin. This is my will, so mote it be."

Satisfied, she buried her fears and started for the living room When she reached the rail at the top of the stairs, Abby froze.

As if sensing her presence, Jack looked up.

He took her breath away. His tall muscular body was clothed all in black. Leather boots encased his legs up to his knees. His face was hidden by a phantom's mask, and his aura was as dark as the cape hanging wildly about his broad shoulders. Jack Hawthorne was the man from her nightmare.

He watched Abby slowly descend the staircase. His gaze wandered from the tip of her pointed hat to the fascinating green eyes that sparkled behind her sultry satin mask. The neckline of her sleek, raven-colored dress was cut to the waist and barely laced up the front. But it was the delicate silver, satin ribbons that crisscrossed the creamy vee of skin exposed from the middle of her breasts to her belt that seduced a devilish smile from his lips. Her tattered hem dipped gracefully with each step and waves of auburn hair swayed halfway down her back as she approached him.

In an attempt to postpone the inevitable task at hand, Jack tried to lighten the mood for Abby. With one elaborate gesture, he bowed ceremoniously. "Madame, you are truly bewitching."

"Thank you," Abby said quietly, still in awe. "And you, Sir, are most definitely the man of my dreams." Whatever else happened tonight, she wanted this moment.

Jack pushed his mask on top of his head. He picked up the ends of the shimmery ribbons and rubbed the satiny strings between his fingers. "How long do you suppose it would take to undo that tiny silver bow and unlace this?"

"Remind me to time you later." Her teasing turned serious.

"Oh, there *will* be a later." Praying he could keep that promise, he draped Abby's cape around her shoulders, and they headed for the car.

The evening was cool and crisp with just a hint of chimney smoke in the air. "It's a wonderful night for Halloween," Abby said.

He pulled her closer as they walked. "Absolutely perfect."

The drive to the ball brought back familiar childhood memories for Abby. To distract herself, she concentrated on the scenery. Jack-O-Lanterns glowed in the dark and guarded nearly every porch against the ghosts and goblins that slipped in and out of the shadows. Screams and giggles echoed throughout the neighborhoods.

"I'd almost forgotten how much fun trick-or-treating was," she sighed.

"Not to worry," Jack assured her. "I have the adult version of the game at home."

Under the circumstances, his attempt at humor helped. "I'll just bet you do." Abby shook her head, content to ride the rest of the way in silence.

Jack parked the car and Abby's eyes followed the long, winding driveway to the front door of a huge mansion perched at the top of a steep knoll.

"Gallows Hill?" Abby repeated, as they reached a slatted wooden sign that creaked from a nearby gate. Her fingers absently traced the smooth skin of her neck, just above the collarbone.

"Yeah," Jack nodded, sliding his mask into place. "It was named after—"

An owl hooted somewhere overhead. A loud, haunting screech. Abby jumped and yanked her cape tighter against the crisp October breeze. "Let's go."

Surrounded by an ancient iron fence, the stone structure looked as though it had forced its way out of the earth. The last desolate vines of summer clung hopelessly to its face and jagged towers and peaked turrets appeared to pierce the full moon at its back. Dead trees dotted the mansion's grounds, leaving only barren limbs to hold the outside world at arm's length…until tonight.

Chapter Thirty-Four

Skyclad beneath the full moon, Bridget anointed each chakra point—the crown of her head, her third eye, her throat, over her heart, her solar plexus, just above her navel, and the base of her spine—with frankincense oil. Athame in her right hand, she began casting the circle. Walking the candlelit circumference, she sprinkled salt around the edge until she had come full circle.

"I cast you as my sacred boundary. You will keep me safe as you divide the Earthly world from the realm of never-ending planes. Blessed and bound so mote this circle be.

Athame held high, she called forth the Guardians of the four quarters. As each was addressed, she traced the invoking pentagram.

She turned to face south.

"Enter this circle, Guardians of the South, home of Fire and Salamander. Guard my circle and assist my rite."

Turning west, she commanded, "Home of water and Undine, Guardian of the West appear. Guard my circle and assist my rite."

Facing north, she called, "Enter my circle North Guardians of Earth and Gnome. "Guard my circle and assist my rite."

She faced east. "Home of air and sylph enter my circle," she decreed. "Guard my circle and assist my rite."

She inscribed a black candle and dabbed a spot of patchouli oil on the first finger of her right hand and anointed the wax with it. Her enemy's name was written on parchment and placed under the candle.

"By the power of fire, by the power of earth, by the power of air, by the power of water, by the life in the blood. Abigail Corey take they leave. On this blessed All Hallows' Eve, send her back lest she deceive. As I speak, so mote it be."

•••

Hairs prickled at the nape of Abby's neck, stopping her dead in her tracks. She yanked Jack's arm, pulling him down to whisper, "What was that?"

Respecting, if nothing else, the degree to which her nails were digging into his bicep, he stopped, then shrugged. "I didn't hear anything."

"Shhh," she insisted.

Trusting Abby's instincts, he listened…their eyes met.

"You sense it, don't you?"

Jack scanned the perimeter but found no one in sight. He cocked his head to listen. "What the hell is that?"

Abby turned to face the darkness. Was someone out there? A shiver skittered through her soul. She had heard someone. Abby concentrated on the vague voice playing in her head. What were they saying? *Sent back? Must return?* Phrases she couldn't quite make out, but knew to be haunting, if not dangerous. Something besides Halloween was in the air tonight. There was no mistake about that.

"I don't know." She held his dark gaze. "We'd better get inside." Her hand automatically searched her neck for the amulet that wasn't there. That and that alone, gave her the courage to take the last few steps. But as the huge door creaked open, Abby stood, unable to cross the threshold.

When Abby hesitated, Jack entered the mansion first.

She took the hand he offered and reluctantly followed him inside. In the moment it took for her eyes to adjust to the dim gaslights mounted on the foyer walls, Abby heard the soft sound of tinkling bells that echoed through the air. The eerie melody prickled the hair at the base of her neck.

"Shall we?" Jack linked his fingers through hers.

Somewhat comforted by his familiar touch, Abby took a deep breath and nodded.

Jack yanked the heavy ballroom door until it scraped open and the spirit of Halloween materialized before their eyes. Creatures of the night milled around the dark, cavernous room. The mystic sound of exotic chimes haunted the air. Candlelight flickered from mindless skulls. Cobwebs cocooned every corner and doorway. Dust authenticated each tabletop and sheets covered all the furniture. Slashed and carved into horror-frozen faces, dozens of pumpkins illuminated the darkness at every turn.

When a huge man rushed forward, Abby instinctively stepped behind Jack. Bare chested, the stranger was covered with green body paint and clothed only in tattered cutoffs. It wasn't until he flashed a sexy smile and enthusiastically pumped Jack's hand that Abby relaxed.

Jack pried Abby's fingers from the back of his arm and clapped his hand on the big man's shoulder. "Venucci." Flipping up his mask, Jack turned to his friend. "You remember Abby."

Abby felt her hand sandwiched between the detective's large palms.

"Great costume," Lucky said.

"Yours, too." Abby cut to the chase. "So what's our plan?"

"My strategy is," Lucky leaned closer, "to party 'til we drop," he joked with a straight face. Lucky glanced at Jack then cleared his throat. "All kidding aside, I'm here as your personal bodyguard, Miss Corey."

"Abby," she corrected.

"All right, Abby. Just know that I'll monitor your every move and, trust me, you'll be safe."

Abby studied his face and realized she'd only seen that granite-hard look in the eyes of one other man—Jack Hawthorne. Seeing them side-by-side, Jack a bit taller, Lucky a tad bulkier, she breathed a little easier. "Thanks, Lucky. Sorry if I seemed a bit abrupt, but I've never had anyone try to kill me before."

"Don't worry," he assured her. "Just pretend I'm not here and keep your eyes peeled for the clown with the necklace—no pun intended."

"Let's do it." Jack grabbed her by the hand and headed through the crowd to the buffet.

He ducked the white sheets that had been suspended and shaped as though they were in full flight and ignored the gleaming crimson eyes of the gargoyles that perched around the ceiling and guarded the table. Looking over the assorted delicacies, he asked, "Care for some grape eyeballs?"

Abby's already jittery stomach rolled. "No thanks."

"A rat burger? Spider pretzels? Entrails on a stick?"

Abby shook her head as he rattled off the disgusting menu. "Clever, but I think I'll pass."

"Well, if you're not hungry, how about a drink?"

"That," she sighed, "sounds great."

He pointed to the punch bowls filled to the brim with tomato juice. Jack read the sign, "Type A or O Positive?"

Once again he'd managed to ease her nervousness and in return Abby gave him a grateful smile. "I'm almost afraid to ask, but what's the difference?"

"O Positive is for the designated drivers and Type A is for the party animals. Under the circumstances, I'm sticking with O tonight, but what's your pleasure?"

"I'll have the big 'O'," she teased out of nervous frustration.

"Later," Jack promised and kissed her cheek.

Virgin Mary's in hand, they made their way through the crowd once more and sat down at a table for two. Even with Jack at her side and Lucky nearby, Abby remained tense. When would all this madness end? About mid-thought, someone banged into her from behind so hard it knocked her witch's hat sideways.

Abby saw Jack's eyes blaze as his long arm snaked toward her, then past the side of her head. When he jumped to his feet, their table tipped and his drink overturned. A blood-red stain seeped across the crisp white cloth toward her. She watched as Jack shoved a clown up against the wall, the man's feet dangled in the air.

"Ease up, Jack," Lucky yelled, grabbing his friend by the shoulder. "He tripped."

Breathing hard, Jack looked around. "Tripped?"

"I saw the whole thing," Lucky assured him.

Jack suddenly recognized Leon Wazinski, a timid, little man from the law firm Platt, Sellars, and Wazinski, and he released his grip. "Sorry, Leon," Jack assured the stunned man. "I thought you were someone else," he explained while smoothing the man's ridiculously ruffled clown collar.

"Glad I wasn't," Leon wheezed.

"The show's over," Lucky assured the small gathering of onlookers. "Party on."

Abby took off her witch's hat and placed it deliberately on the table. "Now I know why you hired Lucky," she explained dryly. At his blank look, she continued, "To protect the innocent bystanders."

Jack shrugged and sat down. "Hey, the guy was a clown for Christ's sake," he snorted. "How was I supposed to know he tripped?"

"He caught his over-sized clown shoe on the leg of my chair," she explained.

Jack planted both elbows on the table and clasped his hands together. "Don't you get it? This is your life we're talking about." He steadied his whisper. "I won't take even one chance."

Abby swallowed hard.

When Jack's cell phone rang, he headed for the door. "Can't hear. I'll be right back."

Lucky sat down and gave Abby's hand a sympathetic pat. "Don't worry, he'll settle down."

Abby watched Jack disappear into the crowd. "He's really keyed up."

"Love will do that to a guy."

"Really?" She arched one brow.

He leaned back in his chair. "So I've heard."

"You know Jack pretty well." It wasn't a question.

Lucky perused the room, never meeting Abby's gaze. "He saved my career—big time."

Abby took a deep breath. "Hawthorne's quite a guy."

"I can tell you one thing." He shifted in his chair and leaned toward her. "I've never loved any woman enough to camp out all night in a hotel hallway because she might be in trouble."

There was that 'L' word again. Abby smiled. "Thanks."

Jack burst through the tangle of people on the dance floor, pulled a stray chair up and straddled it. "Wrong number."

Remembering her prank call at the hotel, she opened her mouth to speak then shut it. "Maybe we should mingle."

"Go ahead," Lucky instructed. "I'll stay close.

Leaving their table, Jack and Abby wound their way through the partying throng. Amidst the Draculas and Frankensteins, they ran into Bozos and Emmett Kellys at every turn. "There can't be a clown costume left in Boston," Abby pointed out in frustration. "But not one has approached us."

An hour later, Jack squeezed Abby's hand and inclined his head Lucky's way. They wound their way into a far corner of the room. "What do you think, Venucci. The note said eight."

Lucky checked his watch and shrugged. "It's your call. I know you want your necklace back, but there should have been contact by now. It's after nine."

Abby and Jack exchanged glances. Lucky certainly didn't know the real reason they were desperate to get back the amulet. Hell, even they were hard pressed to believe it much less expect someone else to.

"Let's call it," Jack decided.

Abby nodded. They must have missed something. This place was too noisy to think, so they needed to find somewhere quiet and talk things out.

"Looks like you won't need me anymore." Lucky clapped his large palm on Jack's back and started to stand.

"Not so fast." Jack grabbed Lucky by the arm. "Since it's now officially party time, you might be interested to know a certain lady cornered me on my way back from trying to answer my phone. She asked to meet you."

"I don't think so," Lucky hedged.

"Who knows, maybe this is the one you could sit in a hallway for," Abby coaxed.

Lucky sat back down. "Ya think?"

Jack looked at Lucky.

Abby smiled. "There's one way to find out."

Jack looked at Abby.

Lucky grinned. "That would be nice."

"It would," she told him.

Jack scratched his head and cleared his throat. "Excuse me."

Before Abby could comment, a sexy blonde in a harem girl costume, jeweled naval and all, strutted past the table and smiled at Lucky.

Lucky inclined his head in her direction. "Who was that?"

"You don't want to know," Jack stated matter-of-factly.

"Oh, yes I do," Lucky insisted, craning his neck.

Jack shrugged. "You aren't interested, remember?"

Lucky grinned. "*That* was the woman?"

Jack nodded. "Her name is Connie."

Lucky grabbed the front of Jack's shirt with both hands. "Get her back here."

Now he's interested." Jack winked at Abby. "We'll be right back." He grabbed Lucky by the shoulders and squared him toward Abby. "Say good night."

Lucky grinned and repeated, "Good night, Abby. It's been my pleasure."

Abby glanced toward the blonde then winked at Lucky. "I hope you find what you're looking for."

She stood back and watched as her handsome phantom performed some much needed Halloween magic. Judging from the look on Lucky and Connie's faces, Abby thought those two might just weave a spell all their own tonight.

As tired as she was tense from milling around, Abby arched her back and studied Jack's face when he returned. Much to her approval, his frown lines had momentarily been replaced by a relaxed smile.

"And they lived happily ever after," she assured him.

"I hope so." Jack took her hand. "Let's go somewhere quiet and talk this through."

As they stepped back out into the night and started toward the parking area, the sense of urgency hit Abby like a ton of bricks. "Did you feel that?"

"Yes."

"We have to go faster, Jack."

Without question he followed her lead.

She stepped up her pace, desperately trying to see in the dark. *Not enough*, something told her. *Not nearly enough*.

"Hurry." Letting go of Jack's hand, she jogged. *Still not fast enough*.

Frustrated, she tossed her hat and mask and hiked her skirt up around her knees. "Run!"

Mirroring Abby, Jack tore off his cape and rushed toward the Jeep.

Sprinting as hard as she could down the winding path, she heard Jack's long strides closing the distance between them.

Somewhere mid stride a feeling struck Abby like a bolt of lightning. Before she could process it, she heard a loud sickening thud from behind that stopped her cold.

Spinning around, it took her a second to figure out what had happened. The passenger door of the parked van she'd just passed had opened. Jack had apparently run, full speed, right into it. Now he lay sprawled on the ground.

As Abby hurried back to Jack, someone jumped out of the van. She sensed, more than heard, the driver's approach. At a glance, still cloaked in darkness, the advancing figure appeared burly, standing well over six feet. She knelt over Jack. Felt the pulse in his neck. A strong, steady beat told her he was alive but unconscious. Relieved, but worried, she said, without looking up, "Please help him."

When there was no reply, it was her blood's turn to run cold. Time seemed to stand still. Her breath ceased. She prayed this was all a bad dream. The kind that left you screaming soundlessly. Running for your life in slow motion. Falling off a cliff.

As desperate to know as she was not to know, when Abby felt Jack's fingers twitch, she forced herself to look up and face the man dressed in the clown suit.

"You," she hissed.

Zeke jerked Abby to her feet and handcuffed both wrists behind her back before she could blink. Rounding the van, he slammed her into the front seat so hard it jarred her teeth. He slipped a noose over her head and shoved it down around her throat, pinning her neck to the headrest. Her nightmare reared its ugly head once more and she could hear the angry voices crying, *"Hang her by the neck!"*

The moment he slammed the door shut, Abby fought and strained against the rope until it dug into her skin and she choked.

When that didn't work, she tried frantically to release the door handle with her feet.

"Damn!" Abby realized she'd never be able to work her way free in time, so she screamed at the top of her lungs. "Help! Somebody help me!"

Zeke slid behind the wheel and clamped a large hand over her mouth. "Shut up, Bitch," he ordered, "or I'll splatter your boyfriend all over the street."

Abby ached to sink her teeth into the fleshy palm he had slapped hard across her face, but when she looked into his cold, emotionless eyes, she knew this man would carry out his threat.

Jack was groggy, but when Abby's cry sliced through his consciousness he struggled to his feet. The van made a U-turn in the driveway, and he saw her pale face through the passenger window. Jack bolted. He had to catch up while the driver was still maneuvering through parked cars. Had to get to Abby before the van could reach the street.

On a dead run, Jack grabbed the ladder leading to luggage carrier and hopped on the back with a thud loud enough to alert the driver. He grabbed the metal rack on the roof and struggled to maintain his balance as the van accelerated. Hanging on with his right hand, he yanked the back door handle with his left. He shoved and pulled frantically, but it would not open. The driver swerved right and hit a curb—hard. Jack's feet slipped off the ladder and left him hanging by one arm.

The driver zigzagged recklessly into traffic, still trying to shake him off. Jack swiped at the luggage carrier with his free hand and missed. Sweat beaded on his forehead as he tried again. The van veered. Jack missed. His right arm strained to hold on as his feet flailed. *Where the hell was that step?*

Unable to regain his footing, his fingers burned like fire. Both shoulders cramped. The added momentum of his moving body made maintaining his one-handed grip almost impossible. The cords in his neck and back stretched to the max. He fought to keep his legs out of the opposite lane. Headlights blinded Jack as oncoming drivers turned sharply to keep from hitting him. Still dangling like a human pendulum, he yanked furiously and finally felt the handle click and the door flew open.

Abby's heart nearly stopped when she heard someone land hard in the back of the van. She strained to turn her head, but couldn't. Even without looking, she knew it had to be Jack. When she saw the driver start to reach beneath the seat, she struggled violently to shift her weight and kick one leg sideways. She ground her high heel down hard and pinned his hand to the floor.

"Dammit!" Zeke howled as the vehicle swerved out of control. Horns blared. Jack grabbed the back of Abby's seat and braced himself just before the van jumped a curb and slammed full speed into a tree.

Upon impact, Abby was thrown forward and the rope around her neck nearly strangled her. Gasping for air, she fought to remain conscious. Stunned but unhurt, Jack dove into the front seat as Zeke forced open the door and fell out. Quick to follow, Jack landed squarely on him. In one huge shove, Zeke heaved Jack aside and both men scrambled to their feet.

Squared off beneath the streetlight, they faced one another for the first time. Jack took a split second to size up the guy. He was big. Looked strong. And his Neanderthal reach had to be ridiculous.

Jack was used to fighting in a courtroom battle but never literally for his life. And Abby's. When the man held up his hand in a traditional boxer's stance, Jack knew he'd never been this far out of his element. Like the hypnotic motion of a Cobra ready to strike, the man rocked slightly from foot to foot. Jack raised his fists, mimicking his opponent.

The first blow was lightning fast and hard as hell. Jack felt the big man's right fist connect with his chin, snapping his teeth together. He bit his tongue and tasted blood. A split second later Jack caught a left hook that flipped his head to the right. Jack countered with a punch that glanced off the guy's cheek. Jack spit blood on the sidewalk and, without thinking, took a step forward. The circle that separated them grew smaller.

"Come on, Asshole," Zeke taunted, dropping his arms, showing no fear. "The sooner I finish you off; the sooner I get back to your girlfriend." The streetlight illuminated the man's sadistic grin.

Before Jack could blink the man closed the gap between them, leaping forward, left foot first, and throwing a straight left jab. The punch landed squarely on Jack's chin, snapping his head like whiplash. He staggered backwards several steps, fighting to regain his footing and comeback with something…anything. He swung hard, but his assailant had already retreated out of Jack's reach. Out-matched in skill, speed and brute strength, Jack knew he was in deep trouble.

Still grinning, the man lunged forward again. Going into pure survival mode, Jack aimed a kick at the one spot guaranteed to drop any man. To Jack's surprise, the man actually stepped into the kick and caught his ankle. Holding Jack's foot the man yanked him forward. He struggled to hop on one foot rather than go down, but the man, held his ankle and kicked Jack's other leg out from under him. Jack's ass hit the sidewalk hard. His head bounced on the concrete as he landed hard on his back. The air whooshed out of his lungs.

The man slammed Jack's free leg down and rushed on top of him. Straddling him just above the waist, the man anchored Jack to the ground. In one swift movement he had taken away Jack's ability to scramble to his feet. In this position his legs were useless. Panic ripped through him.

The man's weight bore down on Jack's diaphragm, causing him to pant to breathe. Flailing, but unable to land a punch, he could see his frosty, staccato breaths in the cold night air. Jack arched his back to try to shake off the bastard, but this obviously wasn't his first rodeo. The man rode out Jack's attempts then threw down an elbow landing solidly on Jacks forehead, grinding the back of Jack's head into the pavement.

Pain ricocheted through Jack's head. His vision blurred. Keeping his left hand on the cement for balance, the man threw another elbow. Caught hard above his left eyebrow, Jack felt the skin split. A hot stream of blood ran down his cheek and trickled into his ear. Unable to push him off, Jack grappled for the man's face and tried to claw his eyes. Pulling up with all his strength, he grabbed the back of the man's neck and tried to swing him to one side—even a fraction.

The assailant batted away his attempts and threw down another elbow to the same spot, opening the cut deeper and banging Jack's head on the pavement again. Pain exploded in his skull. His lungs burned. The blood that had run in Jack's left eye now blinded the man's assault from that side. With every ounce of strength he could muster, Jack bucked his hips again and again. Desperate, he struggled to turn beneath the man's dead weight to roll him over and off of him, but with both the assailant's knees grounded firmly on either side of him, it didn't work.

Groping for any kind of leverage, Jack's discovered what felt like might be the only chance to save his life and Abby's. Discarded next to the curb lay a beer bottle. As he flailed for it, the man threw down another elbow, completely closing Jack's left eye. Excruciating pain stopped his attempt short. Just…out. . .of…reach. Clawing he stretched his fingers, the nails raking the concrete. The tips touched the lip of the glass neck. Slipped off. He strained with everything in him until one finger found the opening.

In one last attempt Jack forced his hips up momentarily upsetting the man's balance just a fraction. Using the tiniest bit of leverage he had, Jack threw every ounce of strength left in his body in the direction of the bottle. Infuriated by the momentary shift, the man pummeled Jack with punches. Right, left, right, left. With one eye swollen shut and blood in the other, Jack couldn't see. Both ears rang like a church bell on a cold winter's night. Somehow through the pain and the exhaustion of his struggle, Jack flicked his finger just enough to flick it closer to his thumb, enabling him to grab the bottle's neck. Another shot to his head landed so hard it caused a reflex that sent his hand, bottle and all, slamming into the temple of the man so fast Jack didn't even realize he had done it. He did, however, feel the man's weight shift off him.

Reacting with primal instincts, Jack sat up and rolled over before he could be pinned down again. When he realized his Hail Mary punch hadn't even broken the bottle, Jack's rage exploded. He picked it up and busted it on the man's head then grabbed the front of the unconscious man's shirt. He slammed his fist into the man's face, then hauled him up and did it again. And again. Jack never even heard the sirens when the police cars pull up beside them, never saw the red and blue flashing lights.

"It's over," Lucky yelled as he pulled Jack off the other man.

Panting, Jack jerked his arm away from Lucky and bent over, bracing both hands on his knees. He'd never wanted to hurt anyone before. But he had wanted to hurt this man. Apparently it's not easy to turn off the survival switch once it has been flipped. He staggered to his feet and decisively rolled his shoulders. He could live with that.

Abby watched Jack turn his back on Lucky and make his way toward the van on unsteady feet. No one should ever be pushed that far beyond his limits. She knew he had crossed the line for her and only hoped the price hadn't been too high.

Jack opened the door. He uncurled his fists and gently untied the noose. Lucky was right behind him with a key for the handcuffs. Once she was free, Jack took hold of her trembling hands and helped her from the van. He started to touch the ugly rope burn around her neck, but his hands hesitated. "Your throat," he whispered.

Abby shook her head. "Your eye," she whispered, pressing his badly scraped knuckles to her lips. She had cast the circle and asked for protection, so what had gone wrong? And that's when it dawned on her. When asking for protection, she had specified *at the Halloween Ball*. Had not paying close attention to her words nearly cost both their lives? God, there was so much she didn't know.

Abby's warm tears stung as they splashed onto the tender flesh of Jack's hand, but he did move.

"You're still bleeding," Abby murmured, gently lifting her shirtsleeve to dab some of the blood.

"Jack," Lucky called from the van. "Looks like you still have a horseshoe up your ass." He pulled a gun from beneath the front seat and brought it over for them to see.

"Luck had nothing to do with it," Jack said. "Abby just told me when he reached for it she nailed his hand to the floor with her high heel."

Lucky raised one eyebrow and looked at Abby.

Concern filling her eyes, she managed a wink.

"By the way, Venucci," Jack said, "thanks for the back up."

"Forget it. One of the party goers saw the whole thing go down and called it in on his cell phone," Lucky shrugged. "Besides, that's just what I do."

"Kinda like the cavalry?" Abby offered a shaky smile.

"Yeah," Lucky nodded. He put one arm around Abby's shoulder and the other over Jack's. "Come on. I'll drive you to E.R."

Jack shook his head, immediately paying the price. "We don't have time."

"Like hell you don't."

Abby put her hand on Lucky's sleeve.

"I'm not going." Jack clenched his jaw to manage the pain. "Later, not now."

Feeling Lucky's forearm tense, she caught his gaze and asked quietly, "Is there any other way—for now?"

"This is nuts." Lucky shook his head, then scrubbed a hand across his mouth. "Okay, okay. I know a guy."

"A guy," she repeated. The question in Abby's voice was obvious.

"For Christ's sake, he's an E.R. doc not a veterinarian. Although taking this dumb ass to a vet would serve him right."

"Please," she said.

"For you," Lucky told her, checking his watch. "Let's go. Maybe we can catch him at home."

Chapter Thirty-Five

After the ordeal they'd just been through and their quick stop at Lucky's racquetball buddy's for stitches and pain killer, nothing had ever looked quite as good to Abby as Jack's house. Grateful to be safe, she headed straight for the kitchen.

"How about some coffee?" she offered.

"Sounds great."

"You sit. I'll make," she ordered. And for once Jack didn't argue. A few minutes later with steaming mugs in hand, Abby stopped and leaned against the doorjamb. She smiled. It looked like Jack had not only started a fire, but he had also helped himself to the remainder of her candles. Shadows danced on every wall. Music, soft and mystical, filled the air. The spicy scent of warm wax smelled of autumn. Her heart broke just a little at the sight of his swollen black eye, stitched forehead, bruised jaw and bloodstained shirt. Tonight, he had risked his life for her. Right now, they had to talk.

Abby sat down beside Jack and placed the coffee in front of them. She handed him a mug and watched closely as he took a drink. "Are you sure you're all right?"

"I should ask you the same question." He ran a finger down her cheek. When her eyes closed at his touch, he swallowed hard. *My God, he'd come so close to losing her again.*

"I'm okay," she assured him. You, not so much." Abby looked away from his battered face. "I guess we'll just have to wait to find out how that man figures into all this." She shuddered and Jack pulled her closer.

Before asking, Abby searched Jack's expression. As desperate as she was to hear him say the bald man was the end of the line, she needed an honest answer. "Do you think he's the only one we have to worry about?"

"I don't know," he said honestly. "Lucky is working hard to get to the bottom of this."

"I'm sure he is." Abby debated its relevance, but decided to tell Jack about the conversation she and Maxine had at Starbucks. "Did you know Maxine asked me out for coffee?"

"Maxine doesn't do coffee. And what's that got to do with any of this?"

"Maybe something. Maybe nothing," Abby told him. "And by the way, she does do coffee. She wanted to talk to me. To tell me to watch out for Bridget."

"She what?"

"Maxine warned me about Bridget."

Jack thought a moment. "Well, she's never made her dislike of Bridget any secret. But why would she involve a total stranger? No offense."

"None taken," Abby assured him. "She apparently did feel a need to discuss her concerns with me. But as far as the rest goes, she didn't admit to anything else like the dreams we've been experiencing. Or past lives."

"I don't know what to say," he admitted.

"Okay, Jack," she said matter-of-factly. "Whether or not Maxine is in or out, I really need to know what the hell's going on here. Is this some kind of reincarnation-thing we're experiencing? Do you even believe in that?"

"Last week, I would have said *unequivocally no*." Thoughtful, he bent both elbows and steepled his badly scraped fingers. "Today, I guess I would have to say…*yes*."

She watched the admission settle across his face but said nothing.

"As a lawyer I deal in logic and facts. Yet, somehow the illogical and fictional have morphed into something that appears to be, at least on some level, believable."

"Believable and a whole lot creepy," she added.

"You've got that right." He took a breath and his ribs reminded him of the fight all over again. He exhaled slowly. "And for what it's worth, I don't know where this is headed, but I think we need to stay the course."

"I agree." Abby nodded. "For whatever reason we're in this together, and we have to see it through—whatever that means."

He held her gaze. "So we're good to go?"

"Yes, I guess we are." Abby sipped her coffee. "What about Maxine and Bridget? Do you think they're involved—" she fumbled for the right words "—you know, like we are?"

"Well, if we believe the journal, they are definitely in this with us."

"And do you believe the journal?" she asked.

"What I can't believe is that I'm saying this. But, I swear I remember writing in one." He began ticking off points on his fingers. "One: we actually found it. Two: it referenced a chain of events we've both been dreaming about. And three: it named me, you, Maxine, and Bridget." He shrugged. "What's your take?"

Trying not to focus on his raw knuckles, Abby chewed the inside of her cheek. "Okay. Let's say you're right. So, do you think Maxine and Bridget remember? Or even know about it?"

Jack shook his head and again paid the price for the quick movement. "Beats the hell out of me."

"Too many coincidences." Abby sighed.

"I don't—"

"I know. You don't believe in coincidences."

"No, I don't." He finished his coffee and leaned back in the chair.

"Well then, what about the amulet?" she asked. "We have to get it back, right?"

"That goes without saying," Jack insisted. "Until then, I can tell you one thing for sure."

Abby waited.

"You're safe here with me."

After tonight, she knew exactly how far he would go to protect her. "I know," she whispered, touching his jaw. She turned her head and quickly wiped away the tears that spilled down her cheeks.

"I wouldn't be too sure about that," Bridget purred, materializing from the shadows. Clucking her tongue, she observed, "My, my, Jack. I see you met Zeke."

"What the hell?" Jack started to stand, but felt Abby lay a hand on his shoulder. "How did you get in here?"

Bridget smiled. "Oh, I have my ways, don't I, Abigail?"

Images of Abby's seventeenth century life flashed through her mind like a biographical montage. Growing up in Salem. Falling in love with Jackson Hathorne. Secretly learning her craft. And her existence, with one common denominator, Bridget Bishop. "You're the one behind all this, aren't you?" Abby accused.

"The bulb might be dim, but the light finally came on, didn't it, Darling?" Bridget mocked.

This time Jack stood.

Abby grabbed his arm. "I can take care of Bridget," she insisted. Blue eyes clashed with green in the firelight as the two women inched closer and faced off. Both wore long black dresses with flowing sleeves. One of Abby's, however, was splotched with Jack's blood. Their eerie shadows loomed on the walls behind them, dancing grotesquely in the candlelight as they confronted one another.

"So, the mousy, Midwestern shopkeeper finally got a clue," Bridget hissed. "A little slow these days, aren't you, Abigail?"

Abby gritted her teeth at Bridget's insistent use of her given name. "What's that old saying about revenge? It may have taken over three hundred years, but it tastes pretty sweet to me."

Jack felt like a damn burst as memories flooded his mind. However inconceivable, they had been memories just like Abby had suggested. He turned toward Bridget. "I remember you now. You were the one on Gallows Hill who pointed a finger at Abby. You caused her death."

"Save your closing arguments, Counselor," Bridget ordered. "By the time I'm done with the two of you, she'll be back where she belongs and you—well, I haven't really decided about you yet. If you're anything like that idiot I hired that botched things up tonight, well, My Dear, your chances don't look too good either. I should have known not to send a man to do a woman's job."

"Like hell," he spat.

While Bridget was momentarily preoccupied with Jack, Abby studied her eyes. Abby's throat went dry as the pieces of the puzzle started falling into place. "Sasha." It wasn't a question.

Abby and Jack exchanged looks.

"And the maid?" he asked.

Abby nodded. Two strangers with one thing in common. A violent reaction to her amulet. Not to mention the fact that they were both Bridget Bishop. Abby's hand went to her throat.

"What's the matter, Abigail, did you lose your precious amulet?" Bridget laughed. "My, my. What will you do for protection?"

Abby didn't flinch. She racked her brain and scoured the recesses of her mind, searching for memories of *The Craft*. Concentrating, she stilled her senses and called on every ounce of strength to focus all her energy. The air around her stirred. Even though there were no windows open in the house, an unseen breeze billowed the curtains and teased the hem of her long, dark skirt.

Jack's gut knotted. Prodded by the need to do something— anything—he took a step forward and grabbed Bridget by the arm. "Get the hell out of here."

Bridget raised her hand and literally stopped him cold. "Poor Jackson," she cooed, to his deathly still form. "You never did understand *The Power*, did you?"

Jack's feet were rooted to the floor. He couldn't move a muscle. Arms helpless at his side, he struggled and strained but couldn't as much as twitch.

"Jack!" Abby ran to him but knew she was too late. She touched his arm—grateful, at least, to feel the warmth. "Leave him out of this," she demanded, unwilling to filter the hatred from her voice. "This is between you and me."

"I don't think so," Bridget said matter-of-factly. "You see, Jackson, is most definitely part of the equation. He started out as our bone of contention, or have you forgotten?"

Abby's eyes darted from Bridget's evil gaze to Jack's frozen figure. Memories of his proposal flashed through her mind like a pre-wedding album filled with color and joy. "We were to be married." The words slipped from her lips like a prayer.

"Kind of hard to do with a corpse for a bride though, wasn't it?" Bridget's laugh was shrill.

"That's why you accused me of witchcraft?" Abby charged. "To have Jackson?" Her voice sharpened with every detail that surfaced. She remembered Bridget's obvious jealousy, but never suspected its depth.

Recalling that glorious night on Gallows Hill, the crowd's frenzy, Abigail's lifeless body, Bridget's mouth curled into a satisfying smile.

"You set me up, but the one thing you didn't count on was my last words," Abby pointed out. When Bridget's grin turned to a hate-filled hiss, Abby knew she'd hit her mark. "You didn't, did you?" Remembering the words, she recited, "Protect my beloved 'til I return. Brand the hand of the one he spurned. Neither touch the stone nor cancel the spell, or the wicked one will burn in hell."

Bridget glanced down at her scorched palm.

"I was not praying for my sacred soul like some frightened school girl," Abby spat, pointing a finger in Bridget's direction. The distance between them crackled as lightening split the sky.

"I can't believe with all your unholy powers that you didn't know that I truly was a witch. So, before that noose took my life, I not only saved Jackson from you, I saved him for myself."

The air around them undulated like an unsettled graveyard mist. The candlelight swayed gently to some mystical, rhythmic beat. The night wind howled, scratching and clawing at the windows like something evil that is desperate to get in.

"You'll not save him tonight," Bridget warned. She raised both arms and thunder rolled, rattling the windows. "You'll never put the bits and pieces together in time to save yourself again. More importantly, this time all your power will be mine—"

"This will stop your negative behavior; replace the wicked with a positive favor. Let my magic open this gate, and release him now. This be his fate. As I will so mote it be."

Jack blinked. He bent both knees and rolled his shoulders. "What the hell happened?"

Bridget was only slightly amused. "Looks like your little princess is turning back into a real witch after all." With a flick of her hand, fire flew across the room and exploded into the hearth. "Don't get caught in this crossfire, Jackson. I am warning you."

Abby planted both feet. "Don't you threaten him."

At the tone of Abby's voice, Shadow jumped from an end table onto Bridget's back—exactly the distraction Abby needed. "Bridget Bishop, as the moon's light fades to black, from my spell you cannot turn back, feel your life force drain and leave, to this man no more you'll cleave. As I will so mote it be."

Bridget let out an eerie scream that dwindled into mad laughter. Fading from the room, she warned, "You underestimate me, Fool. Little do you know how I've turned the tables on you again." Her ghostly apparition warned, "I'll return before the morrow. Your life, your fate is one of sorrow. Sent back in time you will depart. And I will have your soul, your heart."

"Never!" Abby raised her arms and every candle around the room flared like a torch. The fire in the hearth flashed, rocketing sparks up the chimney. Outside, thunder rolled and lightening lit the sky.

"Beware the witching hour," Bridget hissed as she disappeared completely.

All faded back to normal. The fire crackled warmly. The candles cast a romantic glow around the room. And Abby sat right where she had stood—in the middle of the floor.

Chapter Thirty-Six

Jack helped Abby to her feet and for a long while they just looked at one another.

"First of all, I don't even know what to say," he admitted. "And secondly, trust me when I say I'm not in any way, shape or form trying to be funny. But I would guess that little production answers more than a few of our questions."

It was all Abby could do to nod her agreement.

"Where in the hell did all that come from?" he asked.

She gestured in frustration—elbows bent and palms up. "I honestly don't know, and it's really freaking me out. It's like the words were coming out of my mouth, in my voice, but I have no idea why I said them. How would I know about spells? Where on earth did those fireworks come from?"

"Well, don't look at me," Jack said. "Apparently Bridget was playing freeze tag, and I was it!"

"This can't be happening," Abby insisted.

"Well, it is."

She thought a moment. "Okay, then. Enough of Bridget. If it's a yes for Bridget, I'm guessing it's also a yes for Maxine, don't you think?"

He nodded. "Apparently Max helped me before. At least that's what the journal indicated."

"My God, Jack, whatever's going on, I've got to remember—"

"You will." He pulled her close. "We both will." Holding her for a moment, he checked the mantel clock—ten-oh-five. "The witching hour is midnight, right?" He felt her nod.

Abby tilted her head back and looked at his handsome face in the firelight. "We were really...do you recall—"

"That other lifetime?" Jack met her gaze. "I do."

Understanding their unspoken vow, Abby replied, "I do, too."

"Everything happens for a reason." Jack took her hand. "I became a lawyer in this lifetime to retrieve the amulet. To meet you *again*."

Abby nodded.

"Do you believe the necklace means more? More than just our link?"

"Yes," Abby answered quickly. "I feel very strongly that I need it tonight, Jack. What are we going to do? We have to get it back."

He grabbed the phone, pounded out the familiar number and asked for Detective Venucci. "We need Abby's necklace. Now."

"I'd love to help, but—"

"No buts," he ordered through gritted teeth. "Listen carefully. I can't explain, but trust me. This is a matter of life and death."

"Sounds like something the police should—"

"Dammit, Lucky, don't play cop with me. I know the damned law."

"You're serious, aren't you?"

"Dead serious," Jack barked. "Pull strings or call in a favor. Hell, break the law if you have to, but get the damned necklace from that bastard."

"Pick it up in twenty minutes."

Jack glanced at the clock—ten-fifteen.

"Make it fifteen." Jack knew he and Abby still needed to sort this through. "Can you bring it to us?"

"Look, I'll get this guy to hand it over. One way or another. But I'm tied up on a homicide."

"Never mind," Jack insisted. A flash of Max snagging the necklace on Gallows' Hill was instantaneous. "Just have it there, and I'll send Maxine Spencer to pick it up. She's my secretary."

Abby met his gaze and nodded. She felt certain Maxine would help him again.

Without waiting for a response from Lucky, he cut the connection and hit speed dial. "Max, I need a favor."

Without hesitation she asked, "What?"

"Go to the police station and pick up Abby's amulet. We need it as soon as possible," he instructed.

"I'm on my way."

As his awareness grew, Jack added, "I'm not sure where we'll be, so make sure you have your cell phone. I'll keep you posted."

"Will do."

Jack hung up and faced Abby.

"She's in," Abby said. It wasn't question. "Do you think Maxine understands she was and is a part of this?"

"Maybe. I don't know, but what I told her was right, wasn't it? About the location. We may not be here."

She thought a moment then nodded. "I think we need to go to the cemetery. To Abigail's grave."

He took her hand. "I think you're right."

As they parked at the cemetery entrance, Jack checked the Jeep's clock—11:15. Flashlights in hand, they entered the graveyard, then stopped. The night was deadly still except for an occasional breeze that rustled through dried leaves. The sky was pitch black except for sprinkling of stars and the full moon.

"Which way?" she asked. "Do you have any idea where she—I—was buried? Oh, God, Jack, this sounds ridiculous."

"I know." He squeezed her hand. "But it's either that, or we're all suffering some kind of mass hysteria, which we're not," he added quickly as they walked. "Look, I have a logical mind that borders on anally retentive. I have been stringently trained in coherent, rational analysis. I deal in facts and concrete evidence. No one should be more skeptical than I."

"But you're not," she concluded.

His tone softened. "No, I'm not."

Reassured, she asked, "Do you remember where Abigail Corey's grave is?" However certain Jack seemed, she still refused to say *my grave*.

Jack fanned his flashlight across the road and back again as they continued. "I'm not sure," he began. "I do know this section of the cemetery is the oldest, so it stands to reason, you—she—is here."

Abby used her light to illuminate the row after row of ancient tombstones. "Oh," escaped her lips.

The mental flash Jack saw was fast. Kind of like a View-Master slide. "There was a tree close by," he told her.

"Would it still be there? Do trees even live that long?"

Another snapshot developed in Jack's mind. "Maybe not, but there was a huge rock. Big enough to resemble a stone bench."

"Like in the journal." Her pulse quickened. Something about what Jack said felt right. She searched the nearby markers with her flashlight. No tree. No bench. Surely she, too, would feel some sense of location once they got close.

"Yes."

Frustrated, she asked, "What time is it?"

He glanced at the luminescent dial of his watch. "Eleven twenty-five."

"Thirty-five minutes." The beam of light she held trembled.

"We can do this," he insisted. "That's plenty of—" The shrill ring of his cell phone echoed in the lonely graveyard. "Maxine?" he answered.

Abby took hold of his sleeve.

"Meet me at the north entrance to the cemetery." He flipped the phone shut. "She's got it," he told her.

Within ten minutes, Maxine arrived and folded the necklace into Abby's hand. "Hurry," she urged. Turning to Jack she added, "Save her this time." Without another word, she got back in her car.

Not knowing what to say, Jack once again took Abby by the hand and looked around. "Let's go." Instinct again told him to veer left. He guided her quickly, but carefully through the rows of head stones.

"These are all around the right time period," she noted, verifying the dates and using them as reference points. Abby hurried alongside him as best she could. As the minutes ticked by, her panic grew and frustration only clouded her senses.

Jack clenched his jaw, not daring to check his watch again. They were running out of time. He knew it. Abby knew it. And he believed somewhere close by Bridget knew it. Her words burned in his mind, warning that even if they remembered, she had somehow turned the tables on them.

That's when he saw it. The silhouette of a gnarly, petrified tree loomed in the distance. He picked up his pace, practically dragging Abby behind him. "Hurry," he urged.

Adrenaline pumping, Abby stumbled yet kept her footing. Barely matching his long strides in the dark, her breathing changed to gulps as she struggled to keep up. Once there, she saw the boulder Jack had described. Its flat top could have resembled a stone bench.

"That's it," he huffed. "We've found it."

Abby felt the amulet warm in her hand. She opened her palm and turned her flashlight away, leaving the necklace in the dark. "Jack," she whispered.

He didn't need to look to see the pulsing glow, but he did. Mesmerized, it resembled liquid gold. "Now what?"

"I'm not sure," she answered. Dreading, but knowing she had to see the name, her name, Abby shined her flashlight on the small, plain headstone. "Nooo," she wailed.

Understanding, Jack comforted her. "I know it must be a shock, to see your name, but—"

"No," she cried. "It's not my stone."

"Look, this is a lot to—"

"It's not mine, Jack."

Jack instinctively brought up his light. "What the hell?" He read the tombstone, "Sarah Spencer, Cherished Daughter, 1686–1692.

Abby's flashlight dropped from her hand. "Oh, my God."

Jack redirected his beam to the tree, then the huge boulder and back to the marker. "I don't care what this says—"

Another flash. He saw Jackson seated on the bench-like boulder, a spray of burgundy mums in hand. The stone he looked at read: Abigail Corey, My One and Only True Love, 1674–1692.

"This *is* the right grave, Abby."

She snatched up her flashlight. "No, it isn't," she cried. Turning her beam on the surrounding markers. "It's nearly midnight, and this is not Abigail's grave."

"Forget the damn marker. It is," he swore, more certain than ever.

"It's not!" Abby started to run, zigzagging through the cemetery. "How will we find it now?" Her flashlight darted and beamed like a laser, spotlighting every marker within its reach. "Please, God, life can't be this cruel again."

By the time Jack caught up with Abby, she was sobbing. Frantic, she clung to him. "Help me find it, Jack."

Maxine's words echoed in his head—*Save her this time*.

Jack eased her away. "You have to trust me, Abby."

She felt the amulet warm noticeably as he spoke.

"Do you?" he asked quietly. "Do you trust me?

Again the stone warmed. "Yes."

He walked her back to the boulder beneath the tree. "I don't care what the marker says. This is Abigail Corey's grave. I ought to know. I buried her there."

Abby's sobs hitched, and she let him continue.

He checked the illuminated dial on his watch—eleven forty-five. "Do you trust that what I'm telling you is the truth?"

"Yes." She took a deep breath and cleared her mind. "Maybe switching headstones is how Bridget tried to turn the tables on us."

"I think you're right." He took the necklace from Abby's hand and slipped it over her head. "We're running out of time, so try to channel what you remember from that All Hallows Eve in 1692."

Abby stood deathly still. She took another deep breath, turned her face skyward and focused on the full moon.

"I think," she began, exhaling slowly, "I think Abigail and I need to come together as one." Her words were soft, spoken more to herself than to Jack.

Jack snuck another look at his watch—eleven fifty. His mouth went dry. Feeling nearly as powerless as he had over three hundred years ago, all he could do was pray Abby could save herself. That's all he really wanted.

As she cast a circle around the grave, she said quietly, "Beloved by the Universe, I, Abigail Corey, both past and present, am loved and protected by all that is divine and pure." She lay down on the earth and closed both eyes, with her head touching the inscribed front of the marker.

Jack watched in fascination as the amulet at Abby's throat pulsed with her every heartbeat…and his? Stunned, but not frightened, he felt the power surge through his body and warm his blood. The age-old rhythm kicked up a warm breeze that, within seconds, surrounded the two of them. As Jack stood cocooned by the darkness, and mesmerized by the comforting, steady throb coursing through his veins, the world around them, above them, and below them absorbed the synchronicity like a parched desert floor soaks up rainwater.

Suddenly, electricity exploded all around them. Instead of the soothing drone, it sounded like hundreds of light bulbs simultaneously dropped onto concrete. Light fragments sparked and splintered. Fireworks erupted within the circle. The pitch intensified. The louder the whine, the faster the wind. The stronger the wind, the colder the air. Jack's ears itched from the reverberation. Like a carnival ride, centrifugal force plastered his clothing against him. Frosty puffs of breath slipped through his chattering teeth.

Unable to move a muscle, Jack strained to keep his eyes open and locate Abby. He blinked in disbelief and blinked again. He was nailed to the spot surrounded by some kind of conjured up, supernatural whirlwind. How could she lay unaffected in its midst? Her dress remained unruffled. Her auburn hair fanned over the grass, every strand in place. Her breath did not form a frigid cloud above her lips. Instead, she remained untouched as if in the eye of a storm.

As suddenly as the wind had gusted, the temperature had dropped and the buzz had intensified to the point of head-splitting, everything returned to normal. The air around them grew deathly still. Warm. Silent. To Jack, it felt like being dropped down a well. One moment he'd been soaring, the next he hit rock bottom like a bag of wet cement. Jack staggered but somehow managed to keep his footing as he looked for Abby.

She stood up, eyes still closed, but Jack saw it. A smoky tendril, barely discernible at first, was inching its way out of the earth behind her. Hesitating as if to decide, do I stay or do I go, it undulated and strained like a baby wriggling from a mother's womb. With each twist and stretch the filmy wisp elongated and broadened. Jack held his breath and watched the misty form writhe and strain. One at a time, legs protruded. Dark shoes with brass buckles dangled. Arms extended and fingers wiggled. White petticoats appeared beneath a long, black dress. And then he saw the face start to emerge. At first the features looked like they were pressing against Saran Wrap. Then, like focusing a camera lens, the image materialized. Green eyes. Auburn hair. Full lips. When the mist around her cleared, Abigail Corey hovered just above the ground.

When Abby's lashes fluttered open, she saw Jack, but he wasn't looking at her. Hairs prickling at the nape of her neck, as she pivoted to follow his gaze. It was like looking into a fogged up mirror in the dark with only moonlight to illuminate your image. Transparent features. Blurred boundaries. Eerie familiarity.

Abby blinked. Looked again. Blinked. She lowered her head, then forced a calming breath. As she raised her gaze, one final glance at the now-clear image of herself was all she needed. Abby closed her eyes again to focus all her energy. "Join our lives, Abigail and me. Make us whole for all to see. Fuse two lost souls and make them one. Nevermore to be undone. As I will so mote it be."

Unafraid, she relaxed and allowed the unification to begin. As she and Abigail united, Abby felt the *whoosh* sensation. Tingly. Breathtaking. Like the scene from a movie when the ghost walks right through someone, and the person feels it but doesn't know what *it* is. Kinda like that. Only better. So much better. Because Abby knew exactly what *it* was. This melding had purpose. This joining of spirits was her destiny. This incarnation was exactly what she has been missing all her life. Finally, Abigail Corey would make Abby whole, and, in turn, she would do the same for Abigail.

Abby's eyes fluttered open. "It's done," she said softly.

Jack marked the time—eleven fifty-five. They had made it in time.

Chapter Thirty-Seven

"Not quite in time, Jack!" Bridget swore, appearing from behind the tree.

The flash Abby got was every bit as defining as it was fast. She saw Bridget as a young girl of about twelve with long dark curls playing by the pond with a much younger girl. Her laughter had turned to cruel teasing, and then she pushed the small, blonde girl into the water.

"Sarah." The name escaped Abby's lips like a prayer. "Sarah was your stepsister." She met Bridget's icy stare. "Oh…my…God. The name on the headstone—Sarah Spencer was Maxine's daughter, and she was only six years old when you let her drown."

Bong! Peeling through the cold October night like a funeral dirge, the first chime marked the countdown to the witching hour.

"Not my fault that brat couldn't swim." Bridget saw Jack check his watch. "That's right, Jack—or should I say Jackson? The witching hour is nearly upon us. So, say goodbye to your beloved Abigail *again*."

Bong!

When Jack lunged at Bridget, she thrust one arm straight out in front of her, its flat palm facing him. The staccato gesture stopped him cold, and the air around him stood still. Bridget exhaled a ragged breath.

Bong!

Abby recognized the same force Bridget had used on Jack earlier. When she rushed to his defense, Bridget turned on her. Abby splayed her fingers, casting sparks.

Bong!

Abby and Bridget squared off. The hum of electricity crackled between them, rekindling an age-old power. Face to face, only twenty feet separated them. Linked by time through space, for the second time in history on All Hallows Eve blue eyes challenged green as the standoff began. With arms raised in confrontation, a palpable, albeit invisible, force connected the two.

Painfully aware of his surroundings, Jack struggled to be free of his invisible shackles. Like over three hundred years earlier when he had been tied to the tree, tonight he fought with every ounce of his being to break Bridget's spell. Like before, he watched the battle for power begin, praying Abby could somehow remember all she needed to hold her own. Sweat dampened his forehead… and he could feel it. This spell was not as strong as the last one Bridget had cast on him. So, he labored harder to free himself. He strained every muscle. Pulled like a sled dog. And that's when he felt it. Something gave—just a little.

With everything at stake, how in God's name could Abby be forced to fly by the seat of her pants? Witchcraft was new to her, at least in this lifetime. Tonight, she had to try and draw on knowledge from her past life. As she and Bridget stood, locked in a macabre checkmate, they stared each other down. Abby knew just checking Bridget's power was not an option; she had to defeat her.

Like two men arm wrestling, the hold was locked. No one moved. No one gave an inch. Electricity splintered the air between them. Sparks flew. The surrounding atmosphere quivered with visible but silent sound waves. No one took a breath.

Bong!

The silence was deafening. The sky grew blacker. The moon beamed brighter. A golden glow bridged the gap separating the two women. With it a discernible hum broke the night's silence. Not a comforting, soothing sound. This was a disconcerting buzz. Like angry bees. Bees with an agenda. Bees that were so pissed off they would be happy to sting you over and over again until you died.

Bridget gritted her teeth. Abby locked her jaw. Energy warmed the distance between them. A force, strong enough to hold them fast, raged between the two, holding them together, keeping them apart.

Bong!

As the pressure around Bridget and Abby escalated, the animals residing in the cemetery scattered. Paying little or no attention to one another, squirrels and rabbits skittered away. Deer and raccoons zigzagged behind them. Birds and bats took flight, nearly blocking out the moon. Owls screeched as even the trees pulled back.

Against the laws of nature, the evergreens, maples and oaks leaned away from the energy field. Creaking, their giant limbs bent and strained almost to the breaking point, as the pure voltage that had been created in that small circle released skyward, searing their branches and scorching their leaves. The smell of smoldering pine and charred bark tainted the breeze. The night sky exploded into a million sparks, breaking the standoff.

Abby watched Bridget's smugness melt—ever so slightly— like warm candle wax. Abby blinked. That wasn't just Bridget's expression that had changed. It was her skin. Literally. A chink in her armor?

Bridget jabbed her front finger in Abby's direction.

Abby hit the ground hard.

Bong!

Rattled, she jumped to her feet and mirrored Bridget's motion. Sparks flew as the force that swooshed between them knocked Bridget backwards ten feet and slammed her into a tree. Her slow recovery gave Abby time to glance at Jack. In the moonlight Abby could make out his breathing and saw his fingers twitch.

Bong!

Singed by the smoldering bark, Bridget pushed away from the blackened trunk—but slowly. She raised both arms above her head in a dramatic, wing-like motion. With the full moon at her back and her long, black sleeves billowing in the cold night breeze, she resembled a giant bat.

Bong!

Able to writhe in slow motion now, Jack watched Bridget bring down both arms in unison. Unable to believe his eyes, he would swear she had aged. Her back was bent. Her face was chalk-white. Her hair was gray.

The force propelled Abby over twenty feet, sending her backwards over a tombstone and knocking the wind out of her. Gasping, she struggled to her feet.

Abby prayed Bridget's powers were weakening at the same rate her body appeared to be, but after witnessing her strength, she knew time was running out. Still trying to catch her breath, Abby yanked off one of the silver laces from her dress as the clock chimed. How many times did this make? Eight? More than that? She wasn't sure.

Bong!

"I was only twelve back then." Abby spoke fast as her shaky fingers tied a knot in both ends. "Too scared of you to tell anyone what I had seen you do." She saw Jack's arm and one leg break free. "But I'm not afraid anymore."

Bong!

As Bridget charged forward, Abby dangled the silver cord in midair. She pulled the amulet from the pocket of her dress and tossed it. The instant Bridget instinctively caught it, Abby spoke, "A weight, a ban, a stop I place, never again to see your face. As I will so mote it be."

Bong!

Even in her weakened state, Bridget writhed and fought like a wild animal. Agonizing, she struggled to escape but stood rooted to the spot. Arms raised to the night sky, she let out a blood-curdling scream. Her neck snapped back and she howled at the moon. Cursing and swearing, she twisted and thrashed. Clawing the air with her crone-like hands, she snapped and snarled like a rabid dog and rushed toward Abby.

Jack broke free and fell to his knees. Shoving off the damp earth with both hands, he heard Bridget begin the spell. Jack raced between them and threw himself in front of Abby.

"Go back in time. Your fate I take. This wish, this vow is mine to make!" When Bridget's arms came down together, it was Jack who was caught the crossfire, not Abby.

Abby saw Jack coming and heard Bridget's words, but everything seemed to happen in slow motion. Jack ran. Bridget began her spell. Jack dove. Bridget extended her arms. Sparks flew. Fog billowed and swirled. Surrounded Jack. Pulled him away.

Horrified, Abby reached out. "Take my hand, Jack!" she screamed. For an instant their eyes locked and his fingertips brushed hers…and then all she saw was smoke.

Chapter Thirty-Eight

"Jack! No, Jack! Nooo!" Fire flew from Abby's fingers. In a white-hot rage, she turned on Bridget and, without thinking, snapped the cord in two. She never saw Maxine running toward her. Never heard her screams. Never processed her warning.

The full moon turned blood red. Lightening split the sky. Abby's eyes glowed like fiery embers as she roared, "For this horrific crime you'll pay. You killed my love. It ends today. You will go back in time tonight. Right now. Be off and take your flight. As I will so mote it be."

Thunder rolled. Lightning flashed. A mist slithered up slowly from the bowls of the earth, circling Bridget and shackling her feet. The silver fog undulated, coiling and wrapping around her body like a snake. Inch by agonizing inch it swallowed her like a python downs its prey. Her screams for mercy fell on deaf ears.

As the sparks settled and the smoke dissipated into the cold night breeze, the amulet fell from its core and landed on the ground. Abby frantically searched for Jack.

"Not possible," she whispered, turning completely around, first one way and then the other. And that's when Abby realized what Bridget had done. She had not killed Jack. Bridget had sent him back. Back to the past? Back to the same place Abby had just sent her?

She fell to her knees. "No, no, no," she sobbed.

Maxine knelt beside Abby and put both arms around her.

"My, God, I didn't think…it's just that one minute Jack was here and the next he was gone. He dove between Bridget and me. To save me."

Patting Abby on the back and holding her close, Maxine listened without speaking.

"I've never felt fury like that before. It just took over. I couldn't think. I couldn't see. I don't even know what spell I used. It all happened so fast. All I knew was that I thought Bridget had killed him right before my eyes." Weeping, she rocked back and forth in Maxine's arms.

"Hush now," the older woman soothed.

"What have I done, Maxine? What in God's name have I done?"

"You protected innocent people from Bridget Bishop's wrath. The Lord only knows what she would have done if you hadn't stopped her." Maxine leaned back and held Abby at arms' length. In a staccato tone laced with sorrow and venom, she spoke each emphatic word with clarity and distinction. "And you banished the monster who drowned my daughter. That's what you did."

Even in the moonlight, Abby saw the anguish and loss in Maxine's eyes as the normally staid and staunch woman let go for just an instant, and the tears began to flow. "I'm so sorry about Sarah, Maxine." And she was.

"You will never know how much what you did tonight means to me, and I thank you for that."

They sat that way for a moment. Both reflecting. Both grieving. Finally, it was Maxine who loosened her grip and cleared her throat. "That was such a long time ago. And life goes on." She swiped both cheeks with her palms and sat up a little straighter. "I loved Jack like a son, but do not blame yourself for tonight."

"But—"

"No buts," Maxine ordered. "I had such a bad feeling when I came here that I couldn't force myself to leave." Shaking her head, she reached over and picked up the amulet. "If you want to cast blame, what about me? Why didn't I speak up about everything? Why didn't I try to find you sooner?" Her voice, like her questions, was deliberate as she placed the necklace over Abby's head and helped her to her feet.

"It's not your fault," Abby insisted.

Maxine looked her squarely in the eye. "And it is not yours."

"So, no one's to blame, but Jack's just gone forever?" Abby asked. "Is that the way it is?"

"I honestly don't know." Unaware of the skitter of animals making their way back into the cemetery, Maxine linked arms with Abby as they made their way back toward the iron gated entrance.

"What about the amulet?" Abby stopped and faced her in the moonlight. She grabbed the necklace at her throat and held it tight. She waited a beat…but it only felt like a cool, smooth stone. No pulse. No heat. "Is the power gone?"

Maxine shook her head in sorrow. "I'm sorry, Abby, I don't know that either."

A single tear trickled down Abby's cheek and pooled on the amulet as the two women walked away arm-in-arm. The full moon illuminated their grief stricken faces. The breeze stopped. Not a leaf rustled nor a night creature stirred. Eerie quiet screamed all around them.

And that's when Abby felt it. The hint of warmth on her chest. The slight electrical pulse in her veins. The undeniable echo of a distant heartbeat against her skin.

"Stop." She jerked Maxine's arm. Eyes wide Abby faced her. Afraid to speak another word, breathe another breath.

Eyes fixed on Abby's necklace, Maxine stood speechless as well. Enveloped in the blackness of the night and what felt like some ethereal void, she pointed to the amulet that had begun to shimmer in the darkness. That solitary gesture answered Abby's unspoken question.

"Oh, my God," Abby whispered. "It's Jack."

Maxine's eyes widened. "What?"

"He's not gone yet." Hoarse with hope, she gave Maxine's hand a squeeze. She felt the older woman return the gesture and saw her tears reflected in the moonlight.

"Try, Child," was all Maxine said. "It's all you can do."

• • •

Pulled and twirled, spun and twisted, Jack's eyes opened as he was ripped from the cemetery grounds and yanked through a gaping, black hole. Sulfur assaulted his nostrils, blurring his vision. Not recognizable time. Nor identifiable space. But some obscure netherworld. The past? No matter. His only thought was to thank God that Abby was safe. This time he had saved Abby.

Lost in a swirling, ebony void, Jack's instinct to fight or die trying kicked in. He fought against the downward pull with all his strength, punching the air, kicking and cursing. After finding Abby again. After saving her this time. He would be damned if they would end like this. He had to find his way back to the woman he loved more than life itself.

• • •

With a quick nod to Maxine, Abby planted her feet shoulder's width apart. Was she responding to ancient memories or acting on instinct? It didn't matter. She held the amulet in one hand and raised her other palm to the sky. The breeze began to stir again, and her skirt billowed around both ankles—softly at first. As the stone warmed in her grasp, the wind ebbed and flowed with each rhythmic pulse. Nearby pine trees began to sway ever-so-slightly. Giant oaks groaned and creaked, their branches reaching skyward like searching, wooden fingers.

Abby stretched and extended and opened herself to absorb every ounce of energy the night had to offer. Beseeching the full moon, she breathed in the crisp, cold wind. As lightening flashed across the cloudless sky, thunder rumbled from nowhere, mimicking the pulse of the stone in her hand.

She took one deep breath, then closed her eyes. October 31 was Samhain—the night when the veils separating the worlds were at their thinnest. On this date the souls of those departed could peer through and permeate the screen to commune with those still on this earth. So, why couldn't someone caught in between—like Jack—be reached as well?

Calling on the very essence of her existence, Abby turned inward to the core of her being. She had to find the thread that connected her to Jack. The undeniable tie that bound them in the past. The connectivity that had survived for over three hundred years only to join them again in the present.

"I dedicate this night to Hecate, Goddess of the Underworld. Witch Queen of the Night, bless the soul of my beloved departed one as well as my own." Her voice intoned with an ancient melodic rhythm.

"Keeper of the secrets of life and death, open the gate to this shadowy realm. Turn my failure and my fear into knowledge and inspiration in the Caldron of your Eternal Fire."

Once again, Abby centered herself.

"To cast away evil was my intent, yet my beloved paid the price To keep away evil I repent, my blood has turned to ice. Bring back Jackson, let him pass. Do not make him pay. A working lasso is all I ask. I demand to have my way. As I speak, so mote it be."

The words were barely spoken when Abby's arms extended overhead and circled above her in the darkness. She realized her fingers now gripped a rope—of sorts. The line that had materialized seemingly out of thin air, felt like heavy, prickly twine or cable. Prayers answered, she called on every ounce of strength in her body, mind and spirit. Arms outspread, she twirled it once then heaved the mysterious cable with all her mite toward the still smoldering circle where moments ago Jack had stood. As the lariat crossed the misty threshold and disappeared into the abyss, the weight shifted so hard in her hands that she fell to her knees. Holding tight, she prayed her strength would last.

• • •

In a feral fight for his life, Jack brawled like a mad man. Lashing. Thrashing. Cursing. As he plunged through time, punching and wrestling, something that felt like a stiff, rope snapped past him and smashed into one wrist. Flesh stung as the skin on the back of his hand split. Warm blood trickled into the cuff of his shirt.

"What the hell?"

Through gritted teeth he writhed and flailed until he caught hold of—whatever it was—the only tactile surface he had been able to find. Not giving a damn what *it* was, he snagged the would-be lifeline. And, thank God, the contact felt solid. The moment his grip took hold his downward spiral screeched to a halt with a jolt so hard it jarred his teeth and snapped his head backwards.

Sweat stinging both eyes, Jack didn't miss a beat but swung his other arm around hard to grab the tether with his free hand. He hung there, but only for a second, to catch his breath. Biceps burning, he focused all his attention on climbing, hand over fist, to pull himself up as far as the line would take him. If he had to, he would battle the demons of Hell to reach Abby again.

• • •

The instant Abby felt the rope snap taut, she struggled to her feet. She would tether the rope to the trunk of a nearby tree in case she did not have enough strength to hold Jack, much less pull him to safety.

Maxine joined her and side-by-side they heaved backward with all their might. Together they edged away from the abyss and toward the tree.

...

Inch by inch Jack worked his way up the rope. Never stopping. Never questioning. Never doubting. And that's when he saw... something...overhead. Was it the night sky? A sprinkle of stars? The full moon?

Panting now, Jack used his last ounce of strength to claw his way out of the bottomless pit. His hand felt a gust of fresh air... *Abby*...above ground air that meant he had almost made it back to the surface. *Abby.* Relief coupled with exhaustion washed over him.

Hand over hand.

Up. Up.

Until something shackled his leg.

"Son of a bitch!"

Desperate hands snagged his left ankle nearly causing him to lose his grip. Sharp fingernails clawed through his sock and dug into his flesh. Blood red nails...he was certain of it.

"Jack!!!"

He heard Bridget's shrill cry echo through the darkness.

"Help me!"

Jack kicked and flailed, but her fingers only held on tighter.

"Jack, don't leave me!"

Jack's grip slipped a notch as the rope started to swing. His palms flamed. He was losing his hold. Along with life as he knew it. And most of all—Abby. Without hesitation he took one last ragged breath and stomped the iron clad grasp with his right foot.

...

Bridget's voice sliced through Abby's head like a knife. This could not be happening. Not again. Maintaining her hold on the lasso.

Abby spoke quickly, the incantation rising from the deepest well of her heart.

"Rescue Jack. May Bridget be spurned. My love comes back. Let Bridget burn. As I speak, so mote it be."

The rope went slack. She and Maxine tumbled backward onto the ground, the flaccid cord still in their hands. Dear God, she'd failed. She'd failed Jack. Her heart screamed as her voice could not.

Mechanically, Abby sat up then pulled Maxine to a sitting position. The cool breeze settled around them as the witching hour drew to an end. Somewhere in the distance an owl hooted. And darkness regained control of the night.

She felt Maxine's arms embrace her.

"So close," Abby murmured against Maxine's shoulder. "How could I get that close and fail again?"

"You did not fail." Maxine extended her arms, leaning Abby back to face her. "If you couldn't save Jack, no one else could have." She pulled the younger woman close again.

"Bridget won." Abby's voice was little more than a whisper. "My God, have I lost him forever this time?"

Abby felt Maxine stiffen. And why wouldn't she? Bridget had drowned Maxine's only daughter and after more than three hundred years, she was still taking Maxine's loved ones from her.

"Abby." Maxine's voice quivered.

"I'm so sorry—"

"No."

"Yes. I let you down—"

Maxine cut Abby off by shaking her hard.

Confused and hurt, Abby blinked. "I said I'm sorry…" Then she followed Maxine's zombie-like gaze to the misty abyss through which Jack had disappeared.

"Oh, my God," Abby stammered.

There, only a few yards away, a hand groped the grass. Followed by another.

Scrambling first to her knees and then to her feet, Abby yelled, "Jack!"

Both women rushed to pull Jack free. Straining and tugging they inched him out of the abyss and onto the ground. Piled in a heap, barely able to breathe, the three clung to one another.

"Bridget?" Abby's voice trembled.

"No worries." Still panting, Jack managed a weak grin. "She's gone."

Taking a second for his meaning to soak in, Abby still had to echo, "She's finally gone?"

"Yes," he managed. "And this time *I* saved you."

"And *I* saved you." Abby kissed his forehead. Pulling Maxine close, she added, "And we could never have done it without you."

Staggering to their feet, they watched as the gaping hole swirled and churned into nothingness until only earth remained. Solid and grass covered. An ordinary cemetery plot shadowed by moonlight.

"Ashes to ashes." Maxine's tone was as dry as the leaves under foot…until she spit on the ground where the abyss had occurred. "And let the Devil have her."

. . .

Later, entwined in Jack's arms, Abby listened to the gentle waves of his breathing as he slept, letting the rhythm wash over her joy-filled heart. With wonder, she cradled the amulet in her hands. She gasped. There, in the center of the stone, two tears had joined together to form one perfect heart. Tears bound together forever. In the morning she would tell Jack. Together, forever, she whispered to the fading night.

About the Author

Chardy Walker Lieb has worked as a nonfiction writer for a Midwest publications firm. Some of her most memorable assignments include an interview with a Russian trade delegation that toured the United States on a technological exchange mission; a "contract killer" feature story; and a commemorative writing project, distributed worldwide, which recognized Garth Brooks as the fastest-selling recording artist in history.

Despite working in the nonfiction field, she has always been an avid reader and was never able to shake her true love of fiction. Yearning to challenge her creativity and unleash her imagination, she switched to writing what she's always loved to read and published *Yesterday's Bride* for Silhouette Intimate Moments.

Chardy lives in Illinois with her husband, a fourteen-year veteran detective, who serves as her "personal expert" on police-related research. Her son also serves as a "daily reminder" of the ever-changing, constantly developing human psyche.

A Sneak Peek from Crimson Romance
(From *The Jade Dragon*
by Rowena May O'Sullivan)

Greenwood Gallery, Raven's Creek, ten years later

"Witches' Warts! I can't see a thing!" Alanna Greenwood's exasperation was obvious. It was her own damn fault she'd lost her magic. Although there was no way she would be admitting that little fact out loud to anyone anytime soon. How the hell could she contact Marylebone, the Supreme Ruling Coven of all witches, to report that cracks were beginning to appear on Gregori every day?

They were barely visible but Alanna had looked at him often enough over the past two years to see even the smallest of changes. She leaned over the water of the ornamental pond to inspect the jade dragon more closely. "Yes," she declared, even though there was no one there to hear her. "There's another one."

Sworn to secrecy by Marylebone not to reveal to a single soul about the life imprisoned within the stone, she debated what she could do but came up with nothing. Zilch.

She rocked back on her heels and stared at the stone fence surrounding the courtyard as the first car of the day roared its way down the street. It was five thirty in the morning, daylight a mere suggestion on the horizon. She yawned and rubbed at her eyes. She hadn't slept well since Marylebone had bound her magic for breaking witch law a few weeks ago.

After making a coffee she'd wandered down from the studio in which she lived, above the Greenwood Gallery, into the courtyard for some fresh air and to check on Gregori. It was a daily ritual, rain or shine and one she generally looked forward to. That quiet time, when the world was made fresh. Where the air was crisp, untainted by the fumes and hum of traffic and the streets mostly empty of people.

She thought of her elder sister Rosa, who nagged her constantly about moving into the small cottage Alanna had purchased a couple of years ago. Lavender Cottage. A beautiful little picture postcard cottage with Wedgwood blue windows on either side of the front door and located right next door to her sister Beth and across the road from Rosa.

It had been her intention to move in immediately after buying it, but life didn't always go as planned. The day after she bought the cottage, Anton, Grand Dragon of Marylebone, the chief bigwig in the world of witches and warlocks had arrived unannounced in Alanna's studio, frightening the living daylights out of her—she would never admit to a single soul she had been scared witless—and assigned her the task of crafting a jade dragon and could she do it as soon as possible, please? So she had done so, thinking she'd move into the cottage afterward. Anton had taken the finished dragon off with him, only to return with it the very next day. He'd instructed her to put him in the courtyard and extracted a promise from her that she would remain living in the studio for the duration the dragon remained with them.

How long will that be? Alanna had asked, knowing she couldn't refuse the Grand Dragon anything.

Anton had merely shrugged. *Who knows,* he'd said. *He's been ensorcelled in several different types of stone over the past few years. No doubt, he'll break his way out of this one, too.* The final charge from Anton, and the hardest to keep, was not to reveal to a single soul that Anton had commissioned the dragon or that there was a soul ensorcelled inside the stone.

So stay in the studio, she did. She found herself strangely drawn to Gregori, as she'd termed him, within twenty-four hours of Anton's departure. The name had sprung fully formed into her mind as she placed him on the stone lily pad in the pond in the courtyard. He'd seemed so lifelike. His ruby eyes had glowed eerily, and she had thought for a second he'd spoken to her. *Gregori.* So that's what she'd named him. The name stuck and now everyone knew him by that name.

Why Marylebone had chosen her was a complete mystery. She was nowhere near to achieving Mastership. There was no way she was as responsible as Rosa, her elder sister. Weeks ago, Rosa had bound her magic with one of the most powerful Dragons to walk the earth and had been Called to Marylebone and made immortal.

"How am I going to advise Marylebone of the cracks?" Frustrated didn't go halfway to how she felt. And it was all her damn fault. "I suppose I'm going to have to 'fess up to Goran. Surely that won't be breaking any laws?" She scowled and kicked a stone with her slipper. It hopped across the courtyard to settle next to a hydrangea.

Goran's presence in Raven's Creek was why the wrath of Marylebone had descended upon her and Beth. They'd both Called down Goran Thoreaux—accidentally—and made him Earthbound. A magical misadventure resulting in a royal slap on the hand by Marylebone.

Calling down an immortal was forbidden in the world of Witchdom.

"They should explain the laws in finer detail," she muttered, knowing full well all laws were taught before being allowed to perform a single spell and those laws had been drummed into her years ago. "Who knew thought was as important as action!" Where was the detailed explanation alongside such a rule? Something along the lines of *Calling down a magical being can cause mayhem. Calling down a magical being can result in having your magic bound by Marylebone until further notice.*

Magic was her life's blood. She was born with great magical potential, and excelled as a young neophyte in training at Kowhai Coven, the governing body for witches and warlocks in New

Zealand. She used her magic as a focus when sculpting. She'd crafted Gregori at night and managed to keep Anton's secret, even though it had cost her. She was now guardian of a jade dragon with the soul trapped inside. Why Anton put Gregori in there she didn't know, but she figured he must have done something really bad to be stuffed into the beautifully crafted stone casing. Something far worse than a case of magical mayhem.

She inspected Gregori one last time. His eyes flashed red fire and she wasn't certain if the sun creeping over the fence caused it or whether the soul trapped inside had heard her thoughts and was attempting to communicate.

"Damn it!" she uttered for the second time that morning, not an uncommon phrase from her. "Witches' Warts with knobs on," she muttered another curse and rubbed her hands down over her silky red PJs as she stood. "When the hell am I getting my magic back?"

Alanna trudged through the courtyard in her big fluffy slippers. It was going to be a hot day, but right now it was still early and the warmth was yet to reach the inner courtyard. The sky was turning a delightful blue. The bottlebrush tree in the corner of the courtyard was looking hopeful. She picked up the hose and turned the tap on at the wall. "I can no longer hear you, my friend," she said to the tree, "but I know it's going to be a scorcher today, so here's a little liquid to keep you happy until tonight. Don't drink it all at once."

Alanna wandered about, chattering inanely, as she watered the rest of the plants. She would have to disappear upstairs soon. She didn't want Rosa or Beth to find her mooching about in the courtyard talking to the plants.

She'd lied to her sisters enough. Living in the studio above the Gallery was one of them. She'd told them over and over about how much she loved living there, preferring it to Lavender Cottage. Privately, she longed to move into her home. Teasing Rosa about not wanting to live there had got her through the first two years of guardianship of Gregori, but that was wearing thin, even for her.

She wished she'd never clapped eyes on him. She was as much prisoner as he was. "Bastard," she muttered, her temper flaring. Grabbing an old cloth, she tossed it over the offending dragon. She then emptied the remains of her coffee onto a rose bush and marched inside, heading upstairs to the confines of her studio flat.

Strange, but she thought she heard the dragon laugh.

• • •

Gregori could taste freedom. He knew the woman, Alanna, who came to check on him every morning was his soul mate. He'd known it when entrapped against his will. But right now all he cared about was freedom. When he finally managed to escape, he would be out of this tiny courtyard that had been his world for the past two years and he wouldn't look back.

He'd been imprisoned in all forms of stone over the past ten years, but this jade one had been the most difficult thus far in his attempts to break free. Still so damned angry with Anton, Eleisha, and Zelda, he spent a lot of his time imagining how he could make them pay. He only hoped that freedom wouldn't see him doing something stupid. They were wrong. All of them. He had nothing to do with the Greenwoods' deaths and before they hunted him down, he would spend what time he had left finding out just who had done the despicable act of heartlessly killing Alanna's parents, and not facing up to their crime.

Gregori looked around the courtyard through magically enhanced ruby eyes. An intentional kindness by Anton, but it turned out it was a cruel joke. Not only could he see, he could hear; he could sense emotions but wasn't able to communicate with anyone. Except once, when he'd cried out his name to Alanna. She had heard him. She must have, as she'd started calling

275

him Gregori the day after Marylebone placed him here. Frozen in this object, with only his will and the time to work out the spells surrounding him, he was in a living hell.

But not for much longer. He'd known how to dismantle the protection spells for some time. They were not strong enough to stand against his magic. It was the Maori blessing surrounding the entire Gallery that was causing problems. It was an earth spell, stronger and more complicated than anything he'd ever encountered. The blessing's connection with spirit and the land were intertwined with the sister's spells, and every time it sensed he had found a way out it rewove itself, repairing the links. But they were weakening. It would be a matter of days before he was free once again.

In the mood for more Crimson Romance?
Check out *The Other Side of Heaven*
by Morgan O'Neill
at *CrimsonRomance.com*.